THE Gospel

According to ...

A Fictional Story of the People Who
Encountered Jesus

Martha Carver Harris

ARCHWAY
PUBLISHING

Archway Publishing books may be ordered through booksellers or by contacting:

Archway Publishing
1663 Liberty Drive
Bloomington, IN 47403
www.archwaypublishing.com
1-(888)-242-5904

Because of the dynamic nature of the Internet, any web addresses or links contained in this book may have changed since publication and may no longer be valid. The views expressed in this work are solely those of the author and do not necessarily reflect the views of the publisher, and the publisher hereby disclaims any responsibility for them.

Any people depicted in stock imagery provided by Thinkstock are models, and such images are being used for illustrative purposes only.
Certain stock imagery © Thinkstock.

ISBN: 978-1-4808-0993-2 (sc)
ISBN: 978-1-4808-0991-8 (hc)
ISBN: 978-1-4808-0992-5 (e)

Library of Congress Control Number: 2014914714

Printed in the United States of America.

Archway Publishing rev. date: 11/21/2014

The Gospel According to . . .

A fictional story of the people who encountered Jesus

—by Martha Carver Harris

"Jesus was not killed by the worst in mankind, but by the best in mankind: Jewish religion and Roman law. Because even the best in mankind could not tolerate the perfect goodness of God."

—◄●●►— Charles Fitzsimons Allison

"And they watched him, and sent forth spies, which should feign themselves just men, that they might take hold of his words, that so they might deliver him unto the power and authority of the governor."

—◄●●►— Luke, Chapter 20, verse 20

Dedication

To Father Randolph M. Bragg, whose teaching shaped my understanding of God. To both Father Bragg and Father John Roddy, whose helpful editing and guidance propelled me along the road to publication. And to Mrs. Gwen Bragg whose artistic eye gave me needed direction.

—⬦— Martha Carver Harris

Contents

PART I

THE Gospel
According to …

1 Darmud, Temple Spy

I was starting to be obsessed with him. It wasn't normal. My Temple superiors (I'll get to them in a moment) told me to hound his footsteps wherever he went. Galilee, Judaea, Samaria, the coastline—it didn't matter. I was to remember and report what he said, but I was not to be seen. That was why, one day as I was listening to one of Jesus's enigmatic, allegorical teachings, which I'm sure left half the peasants around me in the dark, someone asked a direct question and I moved in closer to hear his answer.

I need to add that it wasn't his words I found intriguing (I rarely had the patience!), or his position in life. He dressed like a laborer, lucky to have the sandals on his feet. He had no physical beauty either—not what people from my native Egypt would have called desirable. He was too rugged for that, too careless of his appearance. I couldn't put my finger on it—why he drew those crowds—but I felt it too. His authority. He opened his mouth and people got quiet. They listened. Naturally, some scoffed, but most faces lit up, even shone, while he was speaking. All these things of course are merely atmospherics. Not appropriate for my report to the Temple authorities. I try to keep it brief, factual, detached. No sense in letting them think I'm going soft on the target.

"And who is my neighbor?" some fairly well dressed member of the crowd had asked Jesus in response to his constant harping on the topic of doing right by your neighbor. This was an idea that actually originated with our beloved rabbi Hillel's teaching. Rabbi Hillel had said, "Anything you hate to be done to yourself, refrain from doing that to your neighbor." Or something like that. Jesus had given it a more positive slant: "What you would like to be done to yourself, do also to your neighbor." It was clever of him, but it wasn't original.

Anyway, the questioner in my opinion did not appear hostile. But Jesus's companions, who had placed themselves as usual in a casual but protective ring around Jesus, shifted their positions and tensed as they faced the crowd. Jesus in contrast looked directly at his interlocutor, smiled, and without a hint of wariness began to tell a story.

The story, I am sorry to say, was about me.

"A man was on his way to Jericho," he began, "and was overtaken by robbers, beaten, robbed, and left naked on the side of the highway."

A week ago, I confess, I was on my way from Jerusalem to Jericho. I saw up ahead of me a man lying by the side of the road. He was middle-aged, bearded, covered with wounds, and unable to get up. As I approached, he called for water and said something hoarse, which sounded like "Robbed! Help me!" I looked around behind me and saw a cluster of people not too far back. They appeared to have more time than I did because they were laughing, talking, and strolling at a slow pace. Anyway, I mumbled as kindly as I could, "Ask them, the people behind me. I'm sure they will help you." And I scurried on.

In Jesus's story, both a priest and a Levite passed by but failed to stop or help the man. He was finally helped, bandaged up, and taken to an inn by a dirty Samaritan.

"Now who do you think acted as neighbor to the wounded man?" was Jesus's question at the end of the story. His eyes scanned the crowd and settled for a few long, uncomfortable seconds on *me* before returning to the man who had asked the question.

The answer was obvious: the Samaritan. But Jesus's unspoken question was, "And who did *not* act like a neighbor to the wounded man?" That's why I think his eyes lingered on me.

You see, I was on my way to deliver a report to my Temple superior, Eleizer. Anxious to prove my worth, I had traveled all the way to Jerusalem only to learn Eleizer had scooted up to Jericho for a few days. I had busted my ass collecting facts on my new target and finally had something to show for it. I did have qualms about ignoring the wounded man because when I turned around, I noticed that the other group of travelers had not stopped either. But by that time, I was getting frantic about missing Eleizer in Jericho, wasting more time, and failing to get one of his rare nods of approval. Anyway, I had no illusions about my own uprightness or morality. I knew I was a worm.

A larger concern was Jesus's allusion in the story to a priest and a Levite—persons connected to the religious establishment. This was too close for comfort. Did he recognize my face? Did he know that I was working for the Temple?

I was only a few weeks into the game. But in the months to come, I would keep myself more discreetly hidden among the people listening to Jesus—obscured by a rock, concealed in a tree clump, or camouflaged in the crowd behind taller men. Close enough to hear but not close enough to be noticed, or so I thought. As a measure of discretion, I had already taken to questioning members of the group as people dispersed. I had met many alluring women this way.

For I was first and foremost a womanizer. I make no excuses. Women are the one thing that makes life worth living, and dangerous. My native home of Alexandria, a prosperous seaport on the *Mare Nostrum* shores of Egypt, had the finest assortment of exotic, voluptuous, fire-filled women I could ever desire. But this is precisely what got me exiled and why I am in Palestine today.

Beautiful, wicked Alexandria. Built by Alexander more than three centuries ago, it had not suffered terribly under the decades of Roman rule. True, we were no longer self-governing. The Romans didn't trust us that much. But our royal palaces still lined the water-front, our exceptional library—now moved to the Serapeum—still accommodated hundreds of scholars annually, and our magnificent lighthouse still stood on the island of Pharos as a beacon to foreign ships. Most importantly, we Jews—numbering about one million persons—still retained a special status in the city, still worshipped in our synagogues, and still held on to our prosperous quarter in the northeastern section, awarded to us by Alexander. The remainder of the population included Greeks and Macedonians (the most privileged class), then Syrians, native Egyptians, and slaves from the Upper Nile.

Alexandria was a sizeable metropolis and the second most important city after Rome. As with other Roman cities, we were quite Hellenized. Young Jewish boys vied to enter the Greek gymnasia. The Romans may have ruled, but our architecture, our literature, our philosophy, our sports, our entire outlook was Greek. Even our sexual mores. Serious Jewish study did occur, and there was a certain strait-laced quality to the Jewish community I grew up in, but outside of that, laxity and frolic.

Thus, it was hard for me to believe that the license I took with women there would have offended anybody. But when I started the prostitution ring . . . well, my adoptive uncle Alexander Lysimachus threw up his hands. God knows he had made his share of dirty money in Alexandria, being a tax administrator for the Romans.

"—but human flesh is something you don't traffic in!" he shouted.

"Why not?" I asked. "There are slaves bought and sold every day in this city!"

"Yes, Darmud, but you are forgetting the religion of your fathers. You are forgetting the Law."

"But women are a commodity just like everything else! Wheat, grain, olives, oils, and perfumes."

"God did not intend it that way. Your uncle Philo would throw you out of the house!"

"I never see my uncle Philo. He's always at the Serapeum. Or discoursing with his students at the synagogue."

"That's enough. You have conveyed to me in a number of ways

that you are ready for adventure, yearning for travel. Now's your chance. You will go away for several years to Jerusalem."

"*Jerusalem?*"

"And you will work."

"Wait a minute. I am working *here*. Why, this ring of girls will produce more money than I have ever—"

"No, I mean real work. With your brain. You have demonstrated a certain intellect and powers of observation here in Alexandria that I consider uncanny for a young man. Although you have never applied yourself and spend more time in strange women's beds than you do at the Serapeum, I think you would benefit from being under a much stricter eye than my own."

"But what are you proposing? You are known to some of the Temple elite in Jerusalem because of your donations there. *You're not going to have me study the Law?*"

"No, both you and I know that would be a failure. That's much too tame for you. I am writing my close friend Eleizer, a Pharisee and a member of the Sanhedrin. I am describing your talents *and* your inclinations in the clearest light possible. I am asking him to find you a job to match."

"It could be anything! He could have me cleaning out the rooms where animals are sacrificed!"

"Not if the Temple wants to continue receiving my excessive donations. No, they will find you something good. Something that will suit you. Have faith—"

"I can't . . . I well, I . . ."

"And don't let me hear about any more fucking predicaments. I mean that literally. Your allowance by the way is curtailed until we get an answer from Eleizer."

And that was the end of the story. I was stuck. Raised in a poor Jewish family just south of Alexandria on the shores of Lake Mareotis, my real father had little money except what he could eke out of his work in the lakeside vineyards. As a sideline, he used his small boat to transport amphorae filled with wine from various ports along Mareotis up to the market in Alexandria. He often took me along when he made special deliveries of wine to the Jewish

Quarter and other wealthy customers, because I was big for my age and strong. Though an utter coward on the lake (I could not swim) I manifested a quick wit and entertaining sense of humor while delivering the amphorae on dry land. In this fashion I caught the attention of a servant of Alexander Lysimachus—a Jew and the richest man in Alexandria—who was a regular client of my father's. Lysimachus was looking for a bright young man to assist him as secretary, and it was acknowledged that I certainly had the intellect, if not the persistence of application. So after negotiation and the standard payment to my natural father, Lysimachus and his brother Philo adopted me. I was sent to one of the Greek gymnasia and after hours set about the task of studying Torah. Both endeavors were an absolute failure, but by the time my adoptive uncles realized it I had charmed my way into their affections, and knew they would not send me back home. My real father, though fond of me, was happy with the arrangement because it gave him one less mouth to feed. Also, he salved his conscience with the notion that I would one day become a great doctor of the Law.

Instead, I became the biggest hell raiser north of Lake Mareotis. I never knew how easy it was, because I was well-dressed and suddenly had money to burn, to fuck everything in sight. But courtesy of Uncle Alexander, who had the dough, and Uncle Philo, whose mind was so in the clouds that he couldn't keep track of actual physical persons like me, I had total freedom. So I would put in an earnest and attentive morning at the gymnasium, an afternoon with Uncle Philo and his disciples discussing the Law, while my evenings were spent exploring pussy. It was heaven.

My downfall came, however, when my greed took over. Given the legacy of my uncle Lysimachus, who had a good eye for money, I began to invest part of my allowance in small, profit-making enterprises. The seamier side of life which I inhabited, i.e. the labyrinthine streets of Alexandria far away from the Jewish section, turned out to offer a number of opportunities. Greeks, Syrians, Egyptians in this Hellenized world did not observe the same scruples as we Jews. Literally anything was allowable. So I started out investing in stolen commodities—hot pearls, horses kidnapped from some caravan train, fine gossamer clothing pilfered from some rich household. None of these came to much. The purveyors were eventually caught or killed, and I myself barely escaped the clutches of a wronged party on one occasion. Finally I blundered upon the buying and selling of women. It seemed like an intelligent choice. Who better than I knew the type of girl who could look desirable and demure with her clothes on, but would turn into a tiger cat when undressed? I was like a livestock trader. I knew good woman flesh when I saw it.

I was already two months into what was proving to be my first successful business venture when Uncle Lysimachus called me to his study. Two weeks later, I was on the boat to Jerusalem.

Jerusalem turned out to be a magnificent city, and so in retrospect I was not disappointed I had come. It was just as Hellenized as Alexandria, with grandiose palaces, luxurious baths, a theater, amphitheater, and hippodrome. Monumental white marble arcades were everywhere. It was neither quaint, nor Jewish. And of course there was the Temple. A shining, startling, magnificent jewel of tribute to the history, culture, and Hellenized tastes of the Jewish people. Built by Herod the Great, and regarded as one of the wonders of the world. People who served on the temple staff numbered in the thousands. This included musicians, singers, weavers, treasury personnel, Temple police, Temple guards, and people who cleaned up. Most of these elite staff were Levites, subordinate cultic figures responsible for the care of the courts and sanctuaries—and everything else. They were born into the position. But there were various gradations of "holiness." Levites merely assisted in sacrifices performed by the priests, and were allowed no further than the Altar of Incense. The Holy of Holies—that innermost, most sacred place in the Temple—was restricted to the High Priest, and even he could enter only one day a year, on the Day of Atonement.

The Temple was governed by the Sanhedrin, a body of seventy-one members torn by rivalry and centering around two schools of thought. One school, the Pharisees, believed in both the Written Law

(Torah) and the Oral Law, or legal commentary on how to carry out the Torah. They spent most of their days sitting inside one of the nine porticoes of the Temple arguing about legal fine points with their counterparts. Some of the Pharisees were surrounded by a flock of students, hanging on every word. The other school, the Sadducees, totally dismissed the legal commentary and clung only to the Torah. They didn't believe in the afterlife. They devoted themselves to the priestly functions of the Temple, and seemed to monopolize this job more than the Pharisees. They were also more upper class.

Many of the Temple staff were politically sophisticated. They understood that the Roman occupier kept them on top, and allowed the Temple "enterprise" to continue only as long as Jewish leaders could control the outcroppings of rebellion which kept popping up all over Judea and Galilee. This was not easy to do unless you established a network of individuals whose job it was to fan outward to the countryside, and report on what was happening. I don't know how long the Temple's spy network had been in operation before I arrived, but it appeared fairly well established. This was to be my job as well.

Eleizer looked up from writing something and watched me enter the doorway. His office was just inside the southernmost portico of the Jerusalem Temple. He motioned with his head that I should come closer and stand in front of him.

"Your Uncle tells me you have talents. A keen eye, a cocky demeanor, manipulative intellect, facile with words, and able to charm your way into and out of almost any situation. He also says you're lazy as shit. Does that about size it up?"

I shifted my weight from one foot to the other, smiled, and was about to formulate some glib response when he added, "I may have a job for you."

"We have a smallish staff; I won't tell you how many," he said, "of Temple observers or reporters. It is their job to travel about the country—Judea and Galilee—independently, keeping a low profile, and to report on disturbances or what may be developing into a disturbance."

"As your Uncle Lysimachus may have told you, we in the Temple are serving—even existing—at the sufferance of the Romans. The slightest threat to Roman authority results in the crucifixion of any number of our people. A greater threat could get Temple activities suspended or worse yet occupied by foreign forces. We all remember history, the destruction of the Temple, the exile to Babylon. We don't need that again. And we don't need our livelihoods plundered or our people crushed. My job is to see that doesn't happen. One way I do that is to keep track of events as they occur. That's why I need you. You will be one of our observers."

"What kind of disturbances are you talking about?"

"Well the most prevalent kind is some upstart Jewish teacher who thinks he's a prophet, and corrals hundreds of people to listen to him out in the desert. Sometimes it's the Essenes, a small religious sect that lives in some caves nearby, but mostly it's the traveling preachers."

"What kind of harm do they do? I mean politically."

"They stir people up. Get them angry. Sometimes they inspire ill-timed assassinations, or attempts to slaughter members of the Roman contingents about the countryside. The perpetrators are not very clever about it. It usually results in their death, and the crucifixion of numbers of other persons who weren't even remotely involved."

"What's the worst that could happen?"

"Oh the Romans could march in, shut down the Temple, make us worship Caesar and, if we refuse, slaughter us all."

"So a lot is at stake. But what do you do with the information once you get it?"

"It depends. But in general, we simply try to plant stories and undermine the ringleader's validity with the people. Usually that solves the problem. Sometimes we send in people overtly connected with the Temple to engage them in discussions and trip them up. It's surprising how well that can work, especially if the preacher is not too smart. But it can be dangerous. The people can be fiercely protective of them."

"What if neither of those two methods solves the problem? And the people get more and more rebellious, and—"

"Well in that case, we have to take more extreme measures. But we always attempt to exercise justice and discretion."

Not totally satisfied I asked, "So, how would I communicate with you? I mean, safely."

"You will have to work on your own story for traveling around the countryside. You could be a trader. A man with family scattered about the country. But any information you collect would be conveyed directly to me, in person, or to one of the four contacts I designate. You may want to take notes on your journeys, so you won't forget things. But make them discreet. Don't get caught with them."

"Who are these, ah, 'designated contacts'?"

"They're handpicked by me. All of them. Simply put, they're loyal Levites in outlying districts—Sepphoris of Galilee, Tiberius, Caesarea Maritima and Scythopolis. My assistant will give you a list of names. Memorize it. These are prominent and respectable men of substance who can assist you in numerous ways and get messages back to me. Only these four will know the precise nature of your duties. Outside of me, everyone else in the Temple will believe you are a student of the Law."

"Will there be financial support?"

"Well of course. You will get living expenses and regular pay as Temple staff. In addition, you will have as much money as you need to carry out your duties. Funds can be replenished, upon request, by any of your designated contacts. But don't get lavish. I recall that you have that tendency."

"But—"

"Your job will be to attract no attention whatsoever. Blend into the populace. You may utilize sub-sources, but be clever in the way you go about it. Elicitation from sub-sources is usually effective enough, and it doesn't involve an exchange of money. Everything you do, even the way you dress and the way you spend money, should be calculated in such a way as not to attract unwanted attention. You lose your utility that way. Remember, you are to be a silent, unobserved observer, and report back to me. You are not to engage directly with the Subject you are following."

"And what if I decide the job is not for me?"

"I don't think that's an option. And of course, there are penalties for failure. Your Uncle does not want your ass back in Alexandria for three more years. You have no money, no other contacts. I suppose you could return to whoring. Are you picky? The Romans often like solid fellows like you."

So of course I accepted the job. What the hell. It was a way to live until I got back to Alexandria. It would involve travel in a country I had never seen, and maybe a stray encounter or two. I always heard upcountry women were eager and lusty. But I already despised (and feared) Eleizer. I wondered if all the Sanhedrin were as insulting and insinuating.

Only a few weeks into the job, I got my first major assignment. The Subject was a man named Jesus, a Galilean from Nazareth, who had healed somebody's withered hand. It didn't seem like a major offense to me, but they pulled me off another job I was doing in Qumran and told me to get my balls up to Galilee. I could not for the life of me see why the Pharisees and Herod's people were worried. But this event—which occurred on the Sabbath at a synagogue in Capernaum—caused a major stir among them. They accused him, Jesus, of defying them, or claiming authority which he didn't possess. There were other minor offenses prior to this, like eating with a tax collector who invited a number of his shoddy acquaintances over, and like plucking ears of corn on the Sabbath. But they amounted to nothing really. What really galled them was that Jesus was managing to undermine the established religious structure. He acted like he knew more than the scribes and the Pharisees!

That, and the fact that absolute hordes followed him wherever he went. There were not only the local, uneducated 'Am ha' arets from the countryside in Galilee (one would expect that), but after the withered hand incident, people also from Judea and Idumea in the south, from beyond the Jordan in the east, and from Tyre and Sidon on the western coastline all began to flock to him. Sometimes it resembled a vast moving army in the desert. And at the head of it, a tall, singular, quiet fellow who spoke with force and authority, but who was casual and unassuming about his popularity, as if he wanted his followers not to focus on him at all. This absolutely baffled the Pharisees, who had spent their whole lives craving the center of attention, and who demanded respect from the simple folk. And the Herodians, who enjoyed power and privilege and riches as part of the court. I mean, what else was there? Both parties felt Jesus had hidden motives as depraved or power-hungry as theirs, and was simply biding his time.

But why *did* the simple people follow him? Knowing the trashier side of life, I think a lot of people flocked to him simply to be healed. Leading up to the withered hand incident, Jesus was already purported to have healed a number of people, including the mother of one of his followers, a man with palsy, and a leper with oozing sores. He was supposed to have cast out unclean spirits—including one in the Capernaum synagogue—in the presence of everybody on the Sabbath. It was right after this event that the word got around and people started seeking him out. They would bring their sick on pallets and march miles to get next to him, even to touch the hem of his garment. Many, many simple folk believed he had magical healing powers.

I entered my role with the usual amount of skepticism. Eleizer had provided me a list of known persons allegedly healed by Jesus, or allegedly rid of unclean spirits. He wanted me to find them and interview them, as time allowed. But principally I was to shadow Jesus, concealing myself among the multitudes that followed him. I was to provide a day by day estimate of the numbers who walked with him, and in which sections of Galilee. I was to note any significant increase or decrease in these numbers, and what might have provoked it. Above all I was to listen carefully to Jesus's words to these crowds, and try to nail him on specific statements—namely, anything smacking of rebellion or instigation of rebellion against the Romans, or anything amounting to blasphemy against our God. These would be punishable offenses, and my standing would be greatly enhanced if I could deliver them.

"So far, he has shown a great deal of insolence towards our leaders. He refuses to adhere to the laws of purity. He and his disciples are far too jovial. His answers to our questioners—and these are Pharisees and elders of good standing, with a sincere intent to learn the truth and to keep our people in the right path—are seemingly straightforward, but there is an undercurrent of sauciness, of impudence. His interpretations of the Law, and the way he twists our noses when we challenge him, have all started to undermine our standing with the people," said Eleizer, wrapping up the briefing. "Any questions?"

"What is it that you most fear about this man?"

"Well that's a hell of a question. We fear nothing from him, per se. He's a laborer, an artisan, a former *carpenter* for pity's sake, who thinks he got a call from God. What we're fearful of is the Romans' reaction to us, the Jewish state, if they believe Jesus is fomenting rebellion."

"Then his insolence, or sauciness as you put it, is beside the point. What you are really worried about is losing control of the situation, losing your power of persuasion over the people."

"Yes, because ultimately that could lead to rebellion against the occupier, and we wouldn't be able to stop it."

"I see. And if Jesus never utters the provocative words you anticipate, then I drop him and move on to another case?"

He looked at me coldly. "It is not for you to know or anticipate your next assignment. Do this one well, and we'll see what else you are worthy of. If anything."

"Yes, sir. Well then I will take my leave."

As I walked out Eleizer's door, gathered my things, and headed for Galilee, I realized I could trust no one in my new setting. Eleizer was concealing many things from me, I was sure. But most apparent was the rank jealousy and competition that he and other Temple officials felt towards this man Jesus. He was outdoing them at their own game. I quickly understood that if I could *not* get incriminating evidence on him, I was screwed.

2 Mariamme of Sepphoris

He had a lean angular face, a large arching nose under a regal brow ridge and cantilevered eyebrows. Intelligent eyes. Manly ears. Powerful chin. His head was large, and abounded with dark curly hair. He cut an imposing figure, a masculine figure, and he had huge calloused hands. Women's eyes followed him, and turned to look at him when he entered a room. Men watched him too, somewhat warily, but they couldn't ignore him. Despite this, he was strangely shy in people's presence, even reticent. He would look at the person addressing him and hear him out without interruption, no matter how stupid or challenging the statement. When he did talk, he mostly talked about God. He took an original viewpoint. His God was like a brave and persistent soldier fighting the war all alone. Not the prissy taskmaster the Pharisees seemed to promote.

I first saw him when he and several of his followers entered Magdala, just on the outskirts where a small boy watched his master's donkeys and women carried their water jars to the well. He was laughing and clowning with his companions, not at all the dignified figure people later claimed.

I didn't have time for him then. I noticed him of course, it was hard not to, and because of the rambunctious quality of his companions I made a mental note to ask someone later who he was. But I was in a hurry. I had business to do in another village, potential clients to contact. So Jesus (as his name turned out to be) was the least of my worries.

Later before departing Magdala I noticed a crowd outside the synagogue. Usually I don't get near the place. But this time, I pulled my robes around me, modestly covered my hair, and drew near enough to overhear the conversations of some onlookers. It seems that a new rabbi, named Jesus, was teaching in the synagogue.

"Get a load of this guy! Did you hear how he responded to the Rabbi?"

"Yes and I liked it. Served him right. Did you see how he twisted the Rabbi's argument against him?"

"What d'ya mean? All he did was quote the Scriptures."

"Exactly, but he knew the meaning of them better than the Rabbi."

"Oh so you're an expert too? How do you know the meaning of the scriptures except for what the Rabbi tells us?"

"Shhh. This guy is intelligent. He speaks with authority. I'm going to move in closer."

"But where does he come from? Who is he?"

Nobody knew.

Since it seemed as if Jesus's speaking would go on for several hours, and I was fearful of getting close enough to hear him—it would have meant entering the synagogue—I turned away and proceeded to my next stop, returning home to Sepphoris just before sundown. My elderly husband, though disinterested, would be expecting me.

After Magdala, rumors of Jesus and his so-called miracles started to play like wildfire about the countryside, but it was months before I saw him again. Crowds of people left Sepphoris to hear him out in the desert, sometimes only ten stadia away, but I never took the time. People also came from Samaria, Judea, even Jerusalem, and amazingly even from the Decapolis across the Jordan. Crowds followed him wherever he went. Though a believer, I was ashamed to reveal my own interest in a so-called prophet to anyone I knew, especially my family. The importance of God in my life was a closely kept secret. On top of that I was too proud to walk out there alone, unaccompanied, in my fashionable dress and daring lifestyle. I was already the subject of speculation. What respectable woman travels about the countryside as a tradeswoman, without her husband? What more might they say if I strolled out there to hear a holy man? Lastly, I was ashamed. I knew the life I led. I didn't make excuses for it, but I knew its implications. I didn't want to hear the Truth, if that's what was being preached in the desert. I didn't want to look at myself in the light of day.

The light of day eventually shone very brightly on me, and that was how I met Jesus face to face. It occurred maybe five months after my original glimpse of him in Magdala, during my trip to Jerusalem. It was an important trip, my first attempt to interest any of Grandfather's influential friends in the balsam products our family produced.

One of these friends was a well-connected, middle-aged gold merchant. He name-dropped to the point of nausea. He was thin, beak-nosed, immaculate in dress, and given to sexual innuendos to showcase his prowess. Bored by his marriage but scared of his wife, he lacked the courage or passion to indulge his priapic fantasies.

Or so I thought. The day I arrived Samuel received me in his vast library. He was alone.

"Well, Mariamme, how lovely to see you!"

"Where is your wife? I was hoping she would be here."

"Oh she and the servants are out doing the marketing. There are some important holy days coming up."

"Yes of course I know. But I thought she would be especially interested in trying out some of our products."

"Products? What products. Please sit down. Make yourself comfortable."

"You remember, don't you, that Grandfather had always

threatened to develop his own balsam groves, south of Sepphoris? He hated paying the outrageous prices Herod demanded."

"Yes, I am aware. Herod developed a veritable monopoly, using his royal lands around Jericho and elsewhere. I encouraged your grandfather to compete many times. But I surmise he never got around to it before he died?"

"No, he didn't. But since his death, our family has made a concerted effort to develop these groves. We've come up with a line of perfumes that are better quality than Herod's, and at a cheaper price," I said as I opened my pouch and started laying samples out on the table. "I thought your wife Sarah would like to try some of them."

"Well of course she will be interested! She loves that sort of thing. Are you comfortable? Would you like a cup of wine?"

"Only a small one, thank you, and I—"

"Tell me," he said, getting the wine. "Is perfume the only product you will develop from your balsam groves?"

"Oh of course not. The perfumes will only be of interest to the ladies. As you know, balsam has a number of medicinal uses—"

"Yes I know. It's supposed to be a cure for dimness of sight, headaches, and other things. Cataracts, healing wounds. Too bad it's so damned expensive. There," he said as he handed me a cup of wine and smoothly sat down next to me so that his thigh was brushing against mine. I moved precipitously to the right and in the process spilled wine down my front.

I should have seen it coming. He was there in a flash trying to blot my dress with a cloth and practically smothering me.

"What are you doing?" I yelled and stood up, careless that the wine had now splashed on both of us and all over my balsam samples.

"Ummm. You smell almost . . . sweet!" This presumptuous goat had stood up with me and moved closer with his feet astride either of mine. I tried to get away from him by backing up and this caused me to lose my balance. I fell back on the divan. In a second he was on top of me, unraveling my hair with one hand and fingering his way down my bodice with the other.

At this point his sister walked in.

"Samuel!"

His oversized nose looked up, and there I was twisting and struggling under him. Then she started screaming.

I managed to roll off on the floor, get to my knees, and scramble to an erect position. I was trying to spot my missing sandal and straightening my robes as I edged towards the door, leaving Samuel to face the music. What I didn't count on were nosey neighbors who heard the commotion and began to look in. The irony of the situation was that the Jewish satyr and I had gotten up to absolutely nothing, but standing there with my hair in disarray and my dress akimbo I felt strangely guilty anyway. So when the neighbors pounced and held me by the hair with my neck bared to the sun, I could say nothing. I thought they were going to slit my throat. Instead, with the sister yelling invective, and Samuel still cowering in his library, the neighbors started dragging me, pulling me towards the Temple. This spectacle—with me at the center, torn dress, scratched face, hair flying—attracted more people, so by the time we entered the Temple courtyard, it was a mob. But a crowd was already gathered there. It was focused on a large-headed, kingly-looking man in a whitish robe, seated at the base of a column. It looked as if he were delivering a lecture, or addressing a group of students. When he saw us approaching, he looked up. At that moment I recognized him as the man I had seen in Magdala months before—Jesus.

They threw me towards him. I managed to remain standing. Jesus didn't look at me but waited politely for them to speak. He focused intently on their faces and by this time some religious leaders I recognized as Pharisees moved in.

Someone, an older guy who leered and licked his lips, spoke up first. "This woman was caught red-handed in adultery."

Another man yelled out (this one sort of priggish-looking), "By our law she should be stoned!"

People all around started picking up big rocks and bricks left over from one of the many construction sites in the Temple. They were sweating with anticipation and had hungry carnal smiles on their faces.

Finally, one of the Pharisees spoke up with mock respect and deference, "Teacher, what should be done with this woman?"

Jesus looked directly and intently at this man until the Pharisee's eyes shifted downward, and looked away. Then Jesus stooped over as if he hadn't heard him and began writing with his finger in the dirt. Many people would have liked to cite this instance as proof of Jesus's unstable mind. But only I, standing nearby, saw what he was writing. His words in the dust were addressed not to them, but to me:

"Mariamme, why?"

The other odd thing was that in stooping down to write in the dirt, Jesus had placed himself between me and the most hostile part of the crowd.

When the grumbling of the men holding rocks got louder than I could bear, and I (shrinking farther backwards behind Jesus) was afraid even to look beyond people's sandals, Jesus stood up and said calmly and clearly, loud enough to be heard by everyone there, but not shouting:

"He who is without sin among you, let him cast the first stone."

He watched them. A few seconds passed in silence and I ventured to look up. The crowd was just standing there, frozen in silence. Then Jesus very nonchalantly stooped down again, this time squatting, and began writing in the sand. Again, his message was addressed to me.

"Mariamme, where is this leading you?"

It occurred to me that if the crowd had started stoning me, Jesus would have taken the brunt of it, since he had placed his own body, low to the ground, as a shield between them and me. A few minutes passed then I started to hear stones drop on the dirt. One by one starting with the old boffer who had licked his lips, then the prissy Pharisees, down to the youngest who came for the spectacle, each man dropped his brick or his clod of earth, stepped over it, turned and walked away. Their faces were sour. Jesus stood up.

"Woman, where are your accusers?" he asked.

I looked around and saw that everyone had departed. A lot of stones were lying round about on the sand.

"There are none, Lord," I answered.

"Neither do I condemn you. Go, and sin no more."

I gathered myself up and my scarf which had fallen off in the melee, ducked my head, and with my knees shaking managed to stumble then scurry away. I didn't even look back. I didn't even thank him. I went to my rented quarters, packed up my things, gathered my servants, and with tears streaming down my face, started the trek home to Sepphoris.

What complicated the event for me was the fact that I was as guilty as hell. The crowd had merely mistaken my accomplice. How Jesus knew my name or anything about me was unclear. But his question, "Why?" hit me straight in the gut.

Why, indeed?

3 Darmud, Temple Spy

Moving up through Galilee, stopping in various towns along the way, I started to notice the stark cultural divide between Jewish people in the countryside and the Temple elite. The country people were less Hellenized and regarded the Jewish Temple as the center of their faith. The Temple elite were open to foreign culture and mostly seemed to regard the Temple as their livelihood and source of power. I wasn't sure how many leaders in the Temple actually believed in God more than they believed in the Ritual. I knew there were a few Pharisees—like Gamaliel, and his late grandfather Hillel—who were quite devout. But I thought many others might be in the same category as Eleizer, cynically protective of the status quo. Anyway, it wasn't my problem. Since I had never been really religious, I didn't care. But I had a tendency to observe and analyze whatever I saw, and that's what I saw.

I arrived in Capernaum (Jesus's de facto headquarters) not long after Jesus had apparently "chosen" from among his followers twelve special ones who would be his closest adherents, or disciples. To

these, presumably, he would explain the oblique parables with which
he puzzled the multitudes.

> *Secret note to myself: why does Jesus speak in parables?*
> *Why doesn't he just belt it out? Would plain words get him*
> *arrested?*
>
> *Secret note to myself: Jesus's twelve include Simon*
> *Peter; James and John, the sons of Zebedee; Andrew; Philip;*
> *Bartholemew; Matthew; Thomas; James son of Alpheus;*
> *Judas Iscariot; Thaddeus; Simon the Canaanite. Chosen*
> *briefly before my arrival on scene.*

As I arrived in Capernaum, people were departing the village
in a steady stampede, some even running, but not in a panic. They
were headed toward the shoreline of Gennesaret. They had excited,
expectant looks on their faces. Some were lame, blind, and being led
or carried by others. But most were healthy normal people in a big
hurry. Some shouted, "This way! He's here! Come on!" I turned and
ran along with them, anticipating something newsworthy.

The mass of people was already gathering along the shoreline of
Lake Gennesaret in front of a ship, cast slightly out from the shore.
In the ship sat a large-looking man, poorly dressed, in his early
thirties. About my age in fact. He was muscular, strong. Dark hair.
Big hands. Intelligent face. I guessed this was Jesus himself but I
didn't want to ask anyone directly, for fear of identifying myself as
a stranger.

I turned to someone near me. "Have you heard him before?"

"Oh yes, every time he stays in Capernaum, we hound his dwelling. But the crowds are getting so big, I'm glad he's moved to a boat
on the shoreline. More room to hear him."

I decided to sit quietly, and see what else I could pick up by
simply listening. I was almost totally convinced this was Jesus. Sure
enough, I caught several people nearby mentioning his name, and
indicating with their heads that they meant the speaker in front of us.

I didn't get much content from Jesus's talk, but made note of his
technique, which was to employ allegory. Simple things. For instance

he spoke about vineyards and tenant farmers, sheep and sheepherders, small shopkeepers and stern judges to illustrate his point (which generally escaped me). Some people whom I questioned said he spoke in this obscure fashion because he wanted to hide the truth of what he meant from everyone but true seekers. He was giving us God, but his words were calculated to hide God from anyone with only a frivolous intent.

I thought this was an interesting theory, but it didn't convince me. I was out to find a sinister motive in Jesus and by damn I was going to find one.

As Jesus's talk ended, he sent the crowds away to their homes. He and his twelve adherents cast off in the ship. There were a number of little boats about, and some naïve enthusiasts boarded them and set sail to keep up. Seeing an empty space in one of the smaller craft, I dashed through the lake tide and jumped in. No one raised an eyebrow.

Evening had already fallen, I forgot to mention, and by the time we had all gotten about an hour from shore, the lake started to kick up and a strong wind started to blow, splashing huge waves over our bow. I was more than a little anxious since back in Alexandria I had seen people drown in the Great Sea, and I did not know how to swim. Moreover we were in a very small boat. We looked over to the ship Jesus was in, and it was being tossed about more than we were. As the wind increased, men on deck were yelling and trying to get the sails down before the ship high-sided and took on too much water. A big wave hit me in the face and soaked my garment. I started to shake uncontrollably. I cursed the day Eleizer and Lysimachus and the prostitute ring had gotten me into this situation.

I looked over again to the big ship. A tall figure, which I identified as Jesus when the lightning flashed, stood at his full height at the stern of the boat. He wasn't cringing as the waves washed over him, and he wasn't holding on to any rope or railing. From what I could tell he was completely calm. This was in contrast to the helter-skelter panic of everyone else on that boat, running around shouting like madmen. Jesus spoke something. I couldn't hear it, but I knew he had spoken.

At that very moment the wind ceased. The waves quieted down. And we were in a soft, breezy spring night with the loveliness of a clear moon above us.

Jesus then spoke something else to his disciples on the ship, which I could not hear, but knew he had spoken. The disciples in response seemed to hang their heads. Several hours later, with the sea still calm, we all arrived safely on the other side, somewhere near Gadara, the country of the Gadarenes.

To flesh out my report of the incident I set about questioning people in the other little boats which accompanied Jesus's ship, to see if anyone else had caught Jesus's words just before the wind ceased. No one had, but they knew he had spoken. Later, piecing together various accounts which filtered back second and third-hand to me from someone who had a close relationship with one of the disciples, I learned that Jesus's initial words were "Peace, be still." These words preceded the cessation of wind and wave. His follow-up statement was to berate the disciples for their lack of faith. But most tellingly, the disciples' conversation among themselves after the incident in-cluded the question, "What manner of man is this, that even the wind and the sea obey him?"

I thought this tended to sensationalize the event, and would probably be selective in what I reported to Eleizer. I did not want to get him riled up.

So I concentrated more on what happened next, when we got to the country of the Gadarenes. And that was strange. A mad man living in the tombs along the seashore confronted us as soon as we disembarked. He was naked and raving, bloody all over as if he had been cutting himself with rocks. He ran straight up to Jesus as he and his disciples were alighting from the boat, got down on his knees and screeched,

"What have I to do with you, Jesus, you Son of the most high God? I adjure you by God, that you torment me not." He was wild-eyed, and swaying slightly left to right.

Jesus immediately barked a command: "Unclean spirit, come out of the man!" then asked (as if to the spirit), "What is your name?"

There was some sort of growl from the mad man in response,

which I could not understand, and there ensued what seemed like a short exchange, or negotiation, between the mad man and Jesus in reference to a herd of pigs grazing near the mountainside about a half a stade off. They both looked in the direction of the pigs as the mad man made a series of hoarse grunt-like noises.

Finally Jesus nodded what seemed like an assent and forthwith the herd of pigs, about two thousand of them, started squealing and mounting each other in terror, running in circles, and ultimately moving at breakneck speed down a steep hillside which led to the sea. They were literally falling and tumbling over each other to get down that incline only to end up at the bottom, in the deep water of the sea. The entire herd went down in the water and disappeared, and the squealing stopped.

The swineherds, who had been yelling at the top of their lungs to keep the pigs from stampeding, stared down the cliff into the bubbling water then ran panic-stricken in the opposite direction. Meanwhile I turned around and the "mad man" was sitting quietly with Jesus on the ground, conversing in a normal voice. Someone had placed a cloak about his naked body. Jesus was addressing the "mad man" as if he were an old friend, and as if it were the most normal thing in the world to have encountered each other here near the tombs, along the shores of Gennesaret.

A short while later the swineherds were noisily making their way back towards Jesus and his group of followers leading a band of locals from Gadara who were obviously whipped up into a state of excitement. It looked slightly like a dangerous mob in the distance, but when they got up close they stopped short in wonder, and stared at the "mad man" who was sitting calmly next to Jesus, clothed, and in his right mind. The locals all seemed to recognize the former "mad man," probably because he had been a terror to everybody, including fishermen and little children who wandered too near the seaside tombs. When they learned what had happened, and saw evidence of the missing pigs, their anger-turned-wonder became wide-eyed fear, just like the swineherds. They begged Jesus to depart from their shores.

Jesus quietly stood up, gave the former "mad man" a friendly pat on the shoulder, and moved towards his ship. Immediately the "mad man" ran after him.

"May I come with you?" he asked urgently but politely.

Jesus responded no, but told him to "Go home to your friends and tell them how great things the Lord has done for you, and has had compassion on you."

And with that Jesus and his disciples got in the ship, and we smaller boats filled up with our passengers, and we all passed to the other side of the lake.

As we sailed I made mental notes about the meaning of these two incidents—the quieting of the waves and wind, and the casting out of a demon from the Gadarene mad man. Neither event constituted a criminal act. Jesus had not claimed supernatural powers in so many words. But taken together, the two incidents pointed to something not human, and were likely to stir people up. I decided to suppress everything but the barest facts, which I could confirm with my own eyes. These would include the calming of the mad man, but would totally exclude the calming of the storm. Eleizer would laugh at any implication that Jesus could control the natural world (I did not believe it myself), and it would only undermine my credibility. I would edit out such details until I had a better grip on Jesus's activities and his claims about himself. After all, I was scratching for sedition, blasphemy, and rebellion against the state. These were the items that would nail him.

4 Mariamme of Sepphoris

When I got back to Sepphoris, exhausted from my near-death experience in Jerusalem, I went to my chambers and shut the door. A servant girl silently delivered a note that had arrived for me several days before, shielding a dried-out yellow daisy. The handwriting I recognized. The scent of the paper I knew well. It said "Ave" and had clearly traveled many miles to get here. I asked the girl if anyone else in the household saw it delivered, or knew about it. She (her name was Sophia) said no. She had proven trustworthy up until now, so I had to believe her.

I knew the charges of adultery against me in Jerusalem—though false—would have terrible repercussions as soon as they filtered back to Galilee, and with no mercy expected from my husband. So I clung to the note, placed the daisy between the pages of a book, and waited for the other shoe to drop. It wasn't long. In the meantime I managed to stay confined to my room and think a great deal. What had brought me to this point? In answer to Jesus's question, "Why, Mariamme?" it might have started with

Sepphoris—that secular, Romanized, Hellenistic corruption of a city where I was born.

Sepphoris of Galilee was an ideal marketplace for any kind of education you wanted—sports, theater, literature, sex, what have you. It was a sophisticated town. My mother was a strong, determined woman with a severe work ethic, a strict morality, and a weak husband (my father) who left her high and dry when I was nine. I had a brother and a sister, and wealthy, worldly grandparents.

Though most of the residents of Sepphoris were Jewish, we were not the type that took it too seriously. Most families had made an "accommodation" with the Roman occupier. We liked the greater variety of produce and commercial goods their presence in our city brought. And though Herod Antipas (whom the Romans had placed in charge of Galilee) was hated elsewhere, our merchants and tradesmen were rather happy that he had decided to rebuild our city. Everyone regarded its destruction by the Romans after the death of Herod the Great as a huge tragedy. We were eager to make amends. Eager to have the Romans back. And when Herod Antipas decided to make Sepphoris his new "showpiece," with an amphitheater, two marketplaces, temples, colonnades and baths to rival the greatest Greek cities, we were delighted. This meant lots of employment, lots of trade, lots of money for everyone.

My grandfather Judah was an administrative officer in Herod's government in charge of procurement for major building projects in Sepphoris. He had a good amount of power over his compatriots. For that reason, he was honored, wined, dined, and deferred to by the Jewish residents of Sepphoris, and held a prominent place in the Synagogue—even though he wasn't a man of firm faith. Being an educated Jew who spoke Latin and Greek as well as Aramaic, he conversed well with the Romans and received favors from them for settling minor conflicts involving the Jewish population. His granddaughters (my sister Elizabeth and I) were considered a significant catch. A parade of suitors presented gifts every week, and asked for his blessing.

"But you've got to know your Herodotus!" he said to me one day, when he noticed my borrowing a salacious Greek bodice-ripper from his library. "You've got to memorize Homer!"

"I thought you were just interested in marrying us off. What good is an education?"

"Don't be stupid. Men are unreliable. You could end up like your mother. You need an education."

"Grandfather, we're Jewish. Shouldn't we be studying Moses, the Psalms, and the Prophets instead?" I was bored and felt like arguing.

"That too. But this is a bigger world than little Judea and Galilee. The Romans control us. The Greeks have subverted our architecture, our sense of beauty, our entire culture. If you want to get along in this world you've got to know Greek literature! You've got to know Roman writers! You've got to speak their language!"

And so it was that my older sister Elizabeth and I began to receive our Greek lessons and secular training from an expensive Greek tutor. My older brother was sent off to Athens for a "real" education. But Elizabeth and I had to listen to a smart-assed Hellenized slave purchased by my grandfather. His name was Dionysos.

He was about twenty-eight years old, short of stature, slight, mustachioed, but bounding with mental energy which usually came out in the form of wise cracks at someone else's expense. He walked at a forty-five degree angle, as if battling strong winds, and his legs were slightly bent like a spider's. But he made us laugh, and he made us read.

"Whatever else you do, for God's sake read!" he used to say.

Dionysos didn't believe in any gods but himself.

When I turned sixteen Dionysos took a fancy to me. He knew I delighted in his wit, and that did his ego good. But by my sixteenth birthday he was beginning to look at me in a different way.

My father had not been a bad man, and when he left Mother it wasn't to hurt her. It was just that she crushed him. Her constant criticism, her nagging about his unfulfilled potential, her aggressive desire for him to succeed—it just overwhelmed him. He had a gentle, poetic spirit, and was very comical in a humble, self-deprecating way. He had studied various languages but wasn't any good at them. He had this yearning to see the world, to travel. He used to watch the caravans come in and out of Sepphoris—I would sit with him—and he always had the most wistful look on his face. He had been the adored centerpiece of his mother's life, handsome, graceful, urbane, intelligent and never had to try very hard to make a success as a young man. But now as a married man, with a hard-driving wife and an equally aggressive father-in-law, he just shriveled inside himself. One day he was up, and off, with a kiss on my cheek and a pat on my sister's shoulder. And he never came back.

This departure made my mother even more determined to whip the rest of us in shape. She worked morning to night keeping up the property, helping my grandfather manage his estate, and tending to us. She looked at life as a duty.

In contrast our tutor Dionysos scoffed at everything. He would have been sold immediately if my mother had heard some of the jokes he made about her and my grandfather. He was careful not to do it in front of my sister Elizabeth, who took things so seriously. But in front of me, he got away with murder, and his comments kept me merrier than I ever thought could happen. It wasn't all fun and sarcasm. Dionysos dragged me through Aristophanes, Aeschylus and Thucydides and strangled me through Protagorus, Anaxagoras, Virgil, Horace and Livy. I was already fluent in Latin and Greek when Dionysos arrived on the scene, but he made it come alive. For instance, I hated Aristophanes's wit, but when the same mocking sarcasm came out of Dionysos's mouth, I collapsed in laughter. There was something so enjoyable about tearing down every idol in front of us.

Dionysos used to lead me and my sister Elizabeth about the lower market place in Sepphoris, to acquaint us with our Hellenistic heritage and various rude forms of expression. He would sneak us into the great amphitheater to watch the gladiator fights and the Roman sports competitions. My sister died of embarrassment each time she viewed a naked athlete, but Dionysos and I chuckled and made jokes about the good-looking ones. I was in over my head, but I pretended well. In the presence of Dionysos my mind expanded in a very lewd direction.

And so we came to our moment of truth.

"Let's take a walk down Terpsichore towards the baths."

"Can't. Elizabeth's not feeling well."

"I didn't suggest taking your sister."

"You know I'm not allowed out of the house alone."

Dionysos just smiled. He had seen me the night before when I had scaled the wall around our compound and sat on its height. He had also observed my escaping over the wall. We lived high on the summit of the city and my favorite view was from a nearby cliff in the moonlight.

"Well maybe for a little while. Let me grab my shawl."

We walked down into Sepphoris, down into the maze of streets named after the nine muses, and ended up at the final approach to the baths, where Dionysos turned into a side street I had never seen before.

"A friend of mine lives here. I promised to drop by for a second, do you mind?"

"No, guess not."

We entered a red wooden door set slightly askew in its frame, and needing a paint job.

Inside it was red, rosy, warm with soft light. The oil lamps placed strategically about the room featured the typical Greek erotica: outsized phalluses; naked smiling women on their hands and knees. The silken purple pillows scattered everywhere gave the room a quality of oriental languor. A pitcher of wine and two skyphoi sat discreetly to the side.

Dionysos turned to me and said, "Guess he's not here yet. Let's wait a minute." He carefully removed my shawl and as he did so he bent down and kissed me on the back of the neck. I jumped and pretended to be alarmed.

Dionysos ignored this reaction, led me to one of the silken lounging places, and sat down beside me. He was sitting too close. He reached for the pitcher and served us both a skyphos of wine. I sipped mine and noticed the bottom of my cup was decorated with a woman's pubis.

"I've been waiting for three years to be alone with you," he said in that straight-faced way he always had when you know he's joking.

"Yes, Dionysos. I'm quivering with anticipation myself."

We continued in deadpan exaggeration for the next fifteen minutes while we both consumed several cups of wine. I was beginning
to feel hot in the ears, and I heard this drumming noise in my head.
At this point Dionysos put his arm around me, stroked my cheek,
blew slightly in my ear, and hummed babalooo. I giggled while he
kissed me on the neck and leaned on me slightly. I toppled willingly
towards the purple pillows while balancing the wine in my right
hand. He started nibbling at the top of my bosom. Simultaneously
he slipped his left hand under my robes and started working his way
up my leg, conquering inch by inch of territory until he arrived at
the critical command post. By this time the warmth, the wine, the
surrounding purple glow of the room had me melting, liquid, desirous. It all happened so quickly after that: he was inside me riding
like a bull, up and down, up and down, rhythmically, steadily, and
watching my face. His sweat was dripping in my eyes so I closed
them and tried to enjoy the moment. Hard to do. Dionysos's friend
walked in three minutes later and though I was obscured somewhere
among the purple pillows, there was Dionysos bare-assed and pumping away above me. As if on cue, he climaxed. I on the other hand
experienced abject terror.

I quickly pulled myself together, still dripping and smelling of
sex, and hurried towards the door. Dionysos made his apologies to
the friend (whose name I never knew), the lounging pillows were
a mess, and our wine had long ago spilled on the floor. Dionysos
avoided introducing us, threw my scarf over me, and hurried me
out. We walked silently back through the nine muses and I wasn't
sure what to think. I worried if I were pregnant. I wondered what
Dionysos thought. I feared my grandfather, mourned my loss of
virginity, and finally concluded,"ye gods!" In all, about an hour and
fifteen minutes had elapsed.

When we returned to the compound it was only mid-morning,
servants were scurrying around, and Mother was screeching orders
because someone important was coming to dine. I quickly parted
from Dionysos and went to my quarters. I could have been naked
and dancing in olive oil—no one paid any attention to me.

It's hard to recreate what ran through my head the next several days. I wavered between a secret pride about my stealthy advancement into womanhood and a morbid fear of the consequences. I thought the Almighty God would be more understanding about it than my mother. Mother was the real problem. She had a keen sense of smell, too, so I steered clear.

Things went on as before with my family but Dionysos right away grew distant, even cold. He seemed to drag himself to his tutoring lessons with Elizabeth and me, and to want to get away as fast as possible. No more walks to the amphitheater to see naked athletes. No more excursions to the marketplace. My mother remarked that Dionysos might be sick. My grandfather raised his eyebrows and said nothing. As for me, I took Dionysos's reticence as discretion. I kept waiting for him to suggest another walk down Terpsichore. He never did. He stopped joking during our lessons, and his comments about my grandfather and our family were increasingly barbed.

"What the hell is bothering you?" I finally asked him one morning as he walked towards the gate. He smelled sweetish, strange.

"I'm on an errand for your mother. I'll see you later."

"Can't I go with you?"

"No."

He hurried out and I had too much pride to grab his arm or spin him around. After all I, one of the glorious princesses of the house, had already come down to the level of a slave once. I wouldn't do it again.

I bided my time and watched Dionysos go on several quiet "errands" for my mother over the next several weeks. I never heard any reference to these errands by my mother, nor did I ask. I had no reason to doubt them. Finally, though, when Dionysos's aloofness was cutting a sharp-edged gash into my self-respect, when my pride was aching, and when I had still not, *still not*, had my monthly menses, I slipped out on my own twenty minutes after I saw him depart. I thought of looking for him at the lower marketplace or the amphitheater, but the crowds would be enormous. Instead I found myself wandering down the streets of the nine muses, down Terpsichore, back to that side street and the little red door that needed paint. I tried it and it wasn't latched so I pushed it slightly, peeking into a soft rosy light and a kind of slapping noise. When my eyes focused better I saw the big hairy bottom of a man pounding up and down, scrotum bobbing about, and the slap, slap, slap of sweaty flesh against flesh. On the underneath side unfortunately was Dionysos. Face down, butt in the air, eyes scrunched together, and a complacent even triumphant grin on his face.

That was the end of my first love affair.

I started my menses three days later. And a week later, because of an insidious little doubt I had placed in my grandfather's mind, Dionysos was sold to a traveling merchant.

Because I was almost seventeen years old my grandfather declared my education was finished, and it was time for me to be married. My sister Elizabeth was already betrothed. Grandfather started to parade a line of crinkly old men in front of me—all of them rich, fortyish, well-bred, but wretched to contemplate in bed. So I yawned in their faces, acted disinterested, and did everything I could to make myself unattractive. A year passed in this manner.

I was now considered old enough (almost an old maid!) to go outside the compound with only a servant to escort me. Elizabeth was at home with her first child, and had no desire to keep me company. I would choose old Amos, our kindly mute servant, because I knew he wouldn't squeal about where we had been. I still liked to stop by the amphitheater and sneak a look at the athletic games, the naked men striving and sweating and vying against each other. I liked to imagine one of them as my husband, not the slack-skinned gentlemen Grandfather kept marching through our household.

It was on the second Thursday after the Feast of the Tabernacles in my eighteenth year that a group of Roman auxiliaries rode through Sepphoris and stayed for more than a month. We all wondered about the meaning of it because our quiet city was in the process of renovation, very prosperous, awash with construction jobs, and a peaceful beehive of activity. A jewel of good behavior compared with the rest of our rebellious country.

I had my old servant Amos with me, a shopping basket on my arm, and was lingering thoughtfully while watching the Greek-style games at our amphitheater. I was very pretty in those days, I forgot to mention. Dark long curly hair that kept sneaking out from under my headcover, a fine well-developed bosom, a graceful carriage, and a small waist. I dressed well, in the finest linen fabric, and I had a rather saucy gait, long dark eyelashes and what I'm told was a suggestive smile.

"We'll stop here for awhile," the commanding officer said to his soldiers.

I turned and saw about twenty ironclad, uniformed men with beautiful thighs marching towards me and Amos. Behind them were two rather important-looking men on horseback.

One of the men on horseback dismounted, handed the reins to a soldier and approached the gate of the amphitheater. He was maybe thirty years old but his face was hard and handsome. His body was like a tree trunk, massive with muscle but compact, and his legs were like the marbled appendages of the gods studding our amphitheater.

"Good morning, Madame," he actually said as he passed by me, his helmet under his arm, and looked me up and down, very deliberately and with an amused smile.

He must have seen me doing essentially the same thing to him, as my eyes scanned over his body when he approached the gate. So I blushed mightily, and turned away. Amos saw the pleased smile on my face, but fortunately he could say nothing to anyone about it. I made him hurry on with me towards the marketplace.

In the days that followed this encounter I found myself meandering every several days, with Amos, past the amphitheater gate. I never ran into the same man again face to face, but through gossip at the marketplace I learned more about the group of Roman soldiers visiting our city. It was led by a man named Pilate. He was prefect of Judea and Samaria for the great Tiberius Caesar. He was reputed to be a fair judge of disputes, brutal in his punishments, but not corrupt. He was supposed to represent one of the better examples of Roman rule in our conquered country.

The following week our house was garlanded for an important visitor from the Roman administration. Servants were rushing around with pots of food, amphorae of wine, and live animals to be slaughtered. My mother was unapproachable, but I was able to elicit vague details about the head of a Roman contingent coming to discuss some Roman-Jewish squabble involving our city's baths. Under Roman and Greek culture, any alteration of the human body was considered a repulsive deformity. Jewish circumcision, which revealed the head of the penis, was viewed as lewd and unsightly in the Roman baths. Therefore wealthier Jewish citizens who wanted to enjoy the municipal baths and attain equal social footing with the Romans had gone through the delicate and painful procedure of a reverse-circumcision, an epispasm. It depended on how it was done, but the result was not always perfect—or pretty. Consequently, Jewish visitors to the baths in Sepphoris had at first been laughed at, then openly mocked by the Romans. Several fistfights had broken out and one prominent Jewish businessman had been killed. A Roman had his arm slashed down to the bone. There were rumblings about further disturbances, and fear that trouble could spread and ignite the unrest that existed elsewhere in Galilee. So, not knowing any details, I guessed that the Roman administrative visitor would be coming to command or solicit my grandfather's help in heading off any flare-up. There might be other business as well. The conversation in any case would not be for women's ears, so I knew my mother, sister, and I would be banished from sight.

On the other hand, being the brassy personality that I was, I stood on the balcony overlooking the inner courtyard of our compound, and watched the Roman officer and a small band of soldiers approach. To my surprise, accompanying the short solid soldier who appeared to be the leader of the contingent was *the same man I had seen a week before.* At the amphitheater gate with Amos! As he came into our gate with a five-soldier escort he looked up and around our rooftops—I suppose all soldiers do this—as if to get a grasp of the terrain of battle, know the escape routes, fend off any points of attack. In his circular glance he took me in—with my hair uncovered, my face fresh in the twilight. I smiled at him. His eyes returned to me with a quick recognition, and he smiled back and tipped his head. That was all.

From that day forward and for the next several days my heart was soaring with the expectation that I would meet this man again, somewhere in Sepphoris. I discreetly collected the following details: Pontius Pilate was the short solid man who had business with my grandfather. His jurisdiction did not extend to our city, but he quartered his auxiliary troops not far from us in Caesarea Maritima. It was in answer to a call for help from Herod Antipas that Pilate had paid a call to Sepphoris and spoken with my grandfather. The man who accompanied him that night was his temporary adjunct, on business from Rome. I had not yet learned his name.

"Mother, what was the business of the Roman soldiers' visit to Grandfather two nights ago?"

"Oh Mariamme, don't be so nosey."

"I'm just curious. It was a rarity, wasn't it?"

"Yes, it was."

"Does it mean trouble?"

"No, I don't think so. They needed your grandfather's assistance on a local dispute. There may have been other business as well. I don't know."

"Well who was the man accompanying the lead officer?"

"Daughter!"

"He was rather striking, don't you think? He had the air of power."

"How did you even know about him? You were closeted in your room."

"Ah, I got several details from the servants . . ."

"No, you were on the balcony, weren't you? Watching as usual."

"Well . . . sort of."

"Alright, daughter, but this is it. He was what is known as a *speculatore*. A special member of Tiberius Caesar's Praetorian Guard."

"Well what was he doing all the way out here in Galilee?"

"I have no idea. Ask your grandfather."

It wasn't long until I ran into him again, this time at the upper marketplace buying pomegranates. He was wandering through with a small group of soldiers, laughing, plucking fruit from the venders' stalls. He must have seen me from a distance because he walked straight up to me. My servant was at another stall nearby.

"Madame, I believe we are acquainted. Through your grandfather Judah bin Asher?"

I stood with my hands on my hips, cocked my head, squinted at him and said, "Possibly."

He said, "Allow me to introduce myself formally. My name is Titus Flavius Vitellius. I had the pleasure of dining with your grandfather a week ago today. Do you possibly recall that evening?"

"Possibly."

"Well *possibly* we could continue this conversation over a cup of wine? My quarters are quite near here."

"I'm afraid that's not possible."

"Well perhaps another time." And, reaching for a bright, purple rose of Sharon from the next stall he plucked it, handed it to me, and said, "Please do not be afraid of me. I mean you only well." With this he gave a slight nod, or bow, and allowed me to take my leave.

My cheeks were burning all the way home and I had forgotten my purchases and had to send Amos and another servant back to the market for them.

The temptations of Sepphoris were multitudinous: perfumes, silks, caravans full of tapestries and jewels, libraries, literature, sunlight on the temples, naked gladiators, fields outside town to wander in, and Greek slaves you could purchase for any purpose, or any reason. But I had never felt the pull of a man such as this. After that spider-like figure of Dionysos and his treachery, Flavius Vitellius with his sturdy gait, his manly carriage, his square-jawed face seemed like a god in comparison. I had heard the stories about Caesar's *speculatori*, but this man didn't seem capable of conspiracy, intrigue, creeping around in the shadows. He seemed kindly, honest. His blue eyes sparkled with humor.

One of my habits during the period of Grandfather's parade of eligible bachelors was to escape to the countryside, escorted by a servant or two, and think deeply about what I wanted in life. I had managed to survive the crisis with Dionysos, avoid pregnancy, and keep everybody in the dark about my deflowering. But I was becoming restless, caged, and worried. I calculated that my future husband would expect me to be a virgin. Especially if he were young.

Virginity might be less important to an older man who would feel lucky to have me. But I was unwilling to settle for an old fart so I continued to stall, putting off Grandfather, claiming dissatisfaction with all suitors, and retiring to the nearby fields to gather wildflowers.

It was on one of these occasions when a Roman cavalry unit came riding by and halted. The man at the lead got off his horse and approached me. It was Flavius Vitellius. Amos (who had accompanied me) almost went apoplectic. Vitellius had a slight frown on his face and asked,

"What is the meaning of your being out here all alone in the wild, with only one servant?"

"I do this all the time. Why not?"

"It is not only unseemly, but very dangerous. Especially for a person of your stature. Does your grandfather know about this?"

"I'm not certain."

"There have been reports of brigands and uprisings in these parts. Come, I will accompany you home." He motioned for his horse to be brought to him, and walked beside it. He extended his hand to me.

I did not take Vitellius's hand, but obediently followed alongside. Amos walked several paces behind. We remained silent.

We approached the city gates of Sepphoris in this manner, and walked up the summit to my grandfather's villa: Vitellius leading with me, his horse walking behind, Amos dogging our steps, and a whole line of soldiers on horseback following in lockstep. It was quite a spectacle.

"Well here we are. I will caution you not to be so imprudent in the future," Vitellius said severely. Then he smiled a charming sort of half-smile as he bowed his head slightly and took his leave. Amos literally pushed me inside the house.

There was no flurry about this incident until the following day, when word had gotten back to my grandfather. He demanded an immediate audience. I tried to prepare.

"Mariamme, the time has come," he said as he looked meaningfully at my mother sitting beside him. "You are to choose."

"Choose what, Grandfather?"

"We cannot have more of these scenes with a member of Caesar's Praetorian Guard."

"Scenes?"

"Don't think I lack my spies. I know about the flirtation at the fruit market. I know about the escort home yesterday. You are to remain in the house until you are wed. Tomorrow you will choose your husband."

I put up a resistance, feigned illness for several days, refused to eat, wept, yelled, broke statuary. But it did little good. Grandfather's mind was adamant. Eventually, after reviewing the parade of eligibles, I chose a grey-haired man of forty-five with just a touch of ravenous sparkle in his eyes indicating he might be feisty in bed.

"Are you absolutely sure, Mariamme? This man though gloriously rich is more than twice your age."

"Yes Grandfather," I said threatening another bout of rage, "I am certain."

"Alright, child. I am tired of fighting you."

And so our vows were made, and I had landed a husband so ecstatic to dive into my naked thighs that he didn't stop to notice, or care, that another pioneer had been there first.

What I had not counted on was my new husband Jeremiah's loose flesh, stringy arms, and the soft jelly consistency of his back side. And he couldn't get it up. Not ever. Our conjugal bed involved forcing that shrunken anteater-like appendage into myself and pretending I was enjoying it. I remained barren. And after the first several months my husband Jeremiah spent less and less time at home. As a result—mostly out of revenge—I started engaging in various trysts outside my marriage. My grandfather was not easy to fool, but he was increasingly preoccupied with his health and his scrutiny had relaxed. After all, I was a safely married woman! The secularized culture of Sepphoris and the range of nationalities trading there permitted a certain license among its inhabitants. I found I could conduct discreet affairs with several lovers at once, with no one being the wiser. I would spend hours at a time away from home. My husband never noticed. My mother was too busy, and Grandfather by this time was confined to bed. But sex was the only way I could get control of my life.

5 Mariamme of Sepphoris

On my twentieth birthday, Grandfather died. I had been married more than eighteen months, with nothing to show for it. I was having filth dreams, in which I—barefoot—was expected to mop up a latrine coated with fecal residue, and then to bathe in the same basin. I connected these dreams with Jeremiah—and maybe with my illicit lovers. I hated them all.

The death of my grandfather brought a great many visitors to our house, to pay their respects. On the third evening after the notice went out, and three days after Grandfather was already in the grave, we heard an additional commotion outside our doors. Several servants came running with news that a group of about twenty legionaries was outside. Soon, two soldiers made their way through our courtyard and up the steps to where my mother and her relations were clustered, offering a condolence gift. One of them was Pontius Pilate. The other was—Flavius Vitellius! He looked older, tanner, sadder, and had a deeper crease on his forehead. Other than that he appeared as solid and steely as before. I was seated among all my relations, completely dry-eyed, listlessly contemplating whether Grandfather's death would make any difference at all. At that moment I looked up and saw him. Our eyes met.

He took a step back, didn't make any obvious acknowledgement, but fixed his eyes on me for several seconds. Then he bowed to my mother, mumbled some words of sympathy, and departed with Pilate.

My brain was on fire. I couldn't breathe and felt the veins in my temples pulsating wildly. I got up and excused myself, going in the opposite direction up the stairs. Then I took the back way, the secret way I knew as a child, and inched out on the balcony overlook where I had first seen Vitellius enter our courtyard less than two years before. It was at least ten minutes since the men had left our gathering. But there he was, standing quietly in our courtyard as if waiting for my appearance. I don't know how long he might have waited if I had not appeared. My chest was heaving and I couldn't think of anything intelligent to do so I plucked a yellow spring daisy from one of our roof garden containers and threw it towards him. He stooped down to pick it up, lifted it to his nose and savored it. Then he smiled that lovely secretive smile of his and said, "I will call on you tomorrow"

"But I am married!"

"What does that matter?"

The next day he appeared at our compound in the early afternoon, when most of the household was dozing. Mother (strangely complicit) welcomed Vitellius, sat him in our salon, ordered wine, and breezily mentioned to one of the servants that his visit involved the family's balsam trade. Then she graciously disappeared, leaving us alone. Vitellius and I talked until early evening.

"But I thought I would never see you again!" said Vitellius, standing and grasping both of my hands.

"I too. What are you doing back in Galilee?"

"Business, as usual."

"I don't want to be inquisitive, but I want to know. Will you be here very long?"

"Long enough," he smiled.

"My grandfather made me marry because of you."

"I know, I know, I heard when I got back to Rome. I myself am not allowed to marry. Not until I retire from the Guard. Sejanus's rules. He's my superior. But do not let us talk about that now. I have missed you so. Are you happy? Does your husband treat you well? Come, let us sit down."

We sat, and I told him I was not terribly happy in my marriage. He listened sympathetically, then said, "But at least you are rich."

"That is true."

"And I take it you have a certain amount of freedom?"

I said nothing.

"I see . . . and your husband?"

"My husband has other interests."

"You mean . . . ?"

"Yes, prostitutes probably. He is never at home."

"Hmmm. But what do you do with yourself all day?"

I remained silent.

"You know, I haven't thought of anyone else or anything else since we met two years ago."

"That's impossible. You're part of Caesar's *speculatori!*"

"How did you know that?" He looked startled.

"I thought it was common knowledge. Anyway, in my household. My mother told me."

He thought for a moment and said, "Do you know what the job entails?"

"Not exactly."

"Well for one thing, we do a lot of travel. Often as special messengers for Caesar."

"Is that all?"

"No. That's not all," he said then stopped. He added, "but that's what brings me to Galilee."

"Do you think you might come back often?"

"I have no way of knowing. Things are unstable now. Trouble for the Emperor." Then he asked, "Have you any children?"

"No, no, it never . . . never happened. I . . ."

"Well we will see what we can do about that."

"That would be hard to explain." I was secretly thrilled.

"My dearest Mariamme, I am a practical man. I can't afford to be sanctimonious. My job makes me hover between life and death on a daily basis. If I got you with child, I would expect you to find some way to make your husband—whatever his name is—believe it is *his* child. You would have no choice. And in that manner, we could continue to see each other. At any rate, as long as I am alive."

I was speechless.

"Unfortunately," he continued, "it will not be today. I have to leave for Jerusalem tonight, and be back in Rome shortly afterwards. So for the moment, let me simply get to know you. Let me look at you, delight in your movements, savor the sound of your voice. I promise you, I will be back."

And so we talked. Vitellius demonstrated a wide knowledge of the world and a tolerant, I am told "Roman" attitude regarding differences in culture and religion. He believed in Rome, its system of law, its efficiency, its engineering, its prowess in battle. But he also saw that Rome's way wasn't the only way. He talked of Egypt, where he had spent his earliest years as a soldier, of the vast underground canal system in Alexandria, the immense library containing books from all over the world, and of the Pharos (Alexandria's lighthouse) that was as tall as our hippodrome in Sepphoris was wide, and could be spotted by ships hundreds of stadia out to sea. He talked of the Celts in Britain and the inland reaches of Spain, who were wild, emotional, swaggering nomads with no real system of government beyond the tribe. They fought their wars naked, built circular houses, practiced human sacrifice, and followed a cult of the skull. Their gods were a chaotic herd of figures, animal or human, that bore no resemblance to the majesty and orderliness of the Roman pantheon. He spoke of Greece, with its strange predilection for vice and its worship of the male body.

This reminded me of my Greek tutor Dionysos whose seduction of me was the single compelling reason for which I married an inept and repulsive old man. I recounted the entire story to Vitellius.

"And I have been in utter despair ever since!"

"But how have you survived such horror? And for two years?"

"I became reckless. I took lovers."

"Anyone you are fond of?" he asked with equanimity.

"No. I hate them all."

Vitellius laughed at this, then asked quite seriously, "And have you managed to escape discovery?"

"As far as I know, no one is aware."

"I would like to review your techniques. We may need them."

I loved him for this. He did not condemn me for what had passed. He even seemed to enjoy the notion of my desperate escapades, and my amateurish attempts at subterfuge.

Then he said quite seriously, "Now that you know me, and my intentions, I expect you to end all such engagements—except for your husband of course, when required. Do you understand?"

I looked at him, and nodded yes. I had begun to trust him.

We also talked about Vitellius's work. His role as *speculatore* was actually quite subtle and complicated.

"You see, we are the eyes and ears of Caesar. Also the hands."

"What do you mean?"

"Well, the Praetorian Guard deliver messages for Caesar, report on developments."

"And the hands?"

"Occasionally we capture and transport prisoners back to Rome. Sometimes, we use the simpler version."

"Which is . . . ?"

"Well, assassination. It goes with the job."

I looked at this brutally handsome man and noticed the intense muscularity of his hands. Yes, I could see it.

"How many have you had to kill?" I poked him.

He looked at me solemnly, without smiling back. "I try not to count."

"Is that why they won't let you marry?" I got serious.

"It's not unique to us. The legionaries follow the same rule. Sejanus—that's our commanding officer—wants total allegiance and this is one way to enforce it. No entanglements. It also makes men less reluctant to die."

I didn't know what to say to that. I wanted to change the topic. "Tell me about Sejanus."

"Lucius Aelius Sejanus. The most powerful man in the empire."

"How can that be? He's not Tiberius Caesar."

Vitellius looked into the distance and sighed. "When Caesar retired to the island of Capreae several years ago, he cut himself off. He left things in the hands of Sejanus."

"What is Sejanus's position? I thought he was only head of the Praetorian Guard."

"He's actually the Praetorian prefect. Tiberius ignored Sejanus's equestrian class and had him elected first praetor, then consul— offices legally reserved to senators. The Emperor gets whatever he wants, Roman law and tradition notwithstanding. As a result, Sejanus now controls everything."

"I don't understand."

"Well, it's information he controls. Everything goes through him. All the emperor's correspondence. Sejanus's men—we *speculatori*—transmit all the emperor's messages to and from the colonies and the provinces. It gives Sejanus the opportunity to filter out any opposing view, or negative criticism of himself, before it gets to Tiberius. Very simple really. And with the authority to order arrests and assassination, Sejanus's power almost knows no bounds. He has his fingers on everything that happens in the empire, both militarily and administratively."

"But what kind of man is Sejanus? Can he be trusted to rule Rome?"

Vitellius simply shook his head. "We'll see. Rome is in a very risky situation."

I never asked the question, out of fear I guess, whether Vitellius himself could be in any danger. He probably was, because overarching everything he exhibited an almost madcap sense of the brevity of life and the requirement to delight in it while we could. His vitality and cool practicality permeated everything he did, like a soldier off to war.

When Vitellius left, I didn't despair. I began to receive lovely missives from him, delivered from all over the world. He used his special "network" to get them delivered directly to my hand, without the knowledge of my family, or many times even of Amos. Sometimes just an "ave," sometimes a quote from Homer, and sometimes a long, amusing letter recounting his experiences. They arrived like clockwork about once a month and gave me the hope, no the assurance, of seeing him again. In the meantime, I threw myself into our balsam project.

This was something Mother and I had talked about for a long time. My grandfather owned vast amounts of land outside Sepphoris, some of it adjacent to Herod's royal lands to the south. Nestled in among the date palms was a sizeable grove of balsam trees, or shrubs, which would be enormously valuable if developed. Trades people were generally frowned upon by the elite families of our acquaintance, but grandfather never harbored such sentiments. He always wanted to expand production and market our balsam line all over Galilee, Judaea, and Samaria. So far, we had only produced enough for family consumption. After Grandfather's death, Mother and I hired additional workers who knew the delicate art of extracting the resin without killing the tree. It involved slitting the bark with a stone instrument and capturing the slow seepage over a period of days. Then the resin had to be combined with other materials so it could be marketed. It was a very time-consuming process, but enormously profitable. The gum from balsam was worth its weight in silver. It had curative qualities, served as a painkiller, and made people smell good. It had numerous medicinal uses. And it was rare. Even the caravans bringing spices from Southern Arabia and via the Red Sea all the way from India didn't contain our quality of balsam products. It only grew in Judaea and Galilee.

As we expanded our line of products, Mother and I worked on the books, nailed down the costs, and mapped out a distribution strategy. We began to see we had not been bold enough in our thinking. Sepphoris was positioned on one of the main highways linking vital commercial areas of Galilee with Damascus and Jerusalem. It was also close to Ptolemais for shipments to Rome and beyond. I made a list of wealthy and influential friends of my grandfather, as well as people he had done favors for. I took it upon myself to do the preparatory footwork in contacting these potential customers and distributing samples.

Within a short time I was making the rounds from Sepphoris to

Ptolemais and even down to Jerusalem. Occasionally I would travel over to the villages along Lake Gennesaret where a small group of wealthy Jewish families made my trips worth it.

It was on one of my early trips to Magdala that I had my first glimpse of Jesus. It was five months later that I had the disastrous experience with that predatory Jewish gold merchant and got dragged to the Temple square to be stoned for adultery. It was that same day, just a few days ago now, that Jesus—a complete stranger to me—had stood up to defend me, and asked me those questions written in the sand: "Why, Mariamme? Where is this leading you?"

⸺⸻⸻⦿⸻⸻⸺

It took awhile, but surely enough, as something dead begins to rot, information trickled back to Galilee that a woman from Sepphoris named Mariamme had been caught red-handed in an incident of adultery in Jerusalem. It was all downhill from there. My husband Jeremiah couldn't look at me; would not even give me an audience. I was told by my aging mother, tearfully, that I had to take what money I could along with her jewels and about a hundred balsam samples that we stored at the house and get away as far as I could get. She was fearful of what my husband might do, or have done to me by others because it was well known he didn't have much personal valor. I saw her wisdom and set off without a word in the early morning with my servant Amos. We carried with us as much money as we could find on short notice, Mother's jewels, a large pouch of expensive balsam products, and the trade figures and contacts we had used to develop our perfume, oil and ointment business. These latter items, I hoped, would help me get a start in whatever new living I could forge out of my wits and hard work. Amos had a friend in Magdala he thought would help us, so we headed there.

I tried to send a note to Vitellius in Rome, explaining my circumstances. I expected nothing from him, but I wanted him to understand. I hoped for . . . something. At least a word.

6 Mariamme of Magdala

We arrived in Magdala towards nightfall. Amos's friend in Magdala was a widow with two rooms. She existed on a small pension left by her husband. Short and sturdy, with bowed legs but lovely slender ankles, Nainah was grandmotherly and practical, and in her no-fuss way immediately took us in until I was able to find adequate dwelling for Amos and myself. This was not difficult, and within days we were able to move into rooms nearby. Gradually, within the coziness of Nainah's kitchen, I responded to her warm meals and frank conversation, and was able to compartment and set aside for awhile the devastating events within my own life.

I began to look forward instead of back, and plan how I might support myself and Amos under these new circumstances. Magdala was on one of the trade routes from Damascus to Ptolemais. It was mostly known for its fisheries and dried fish processing, marketed throughout much of the Roman world. I figured it could use a little sweet-smelling perfume. The balsam products I had brought with me would serve as a start. I needed a customer base. If I sold enough, I believed I could convince my grandfather's growers to sell me additional supplies without the knowledge of my family.

It was upon our return from an initial marketing trip that Nainah, Amos, and I passed through a barren stretch far north of Magdala and near the Sea of Gennesaret. Suddenly after rounding a bend we spotted great crowds—probably five to eight thousand people—on a hillside, all seated, and all enjoying some kind of meal. It was such an unusual occurrence that we stopped to see what was happening.

"See the man at the top of the hill?" a man asked in response to our question. He pointed to a large figure in a drab colored garment seated casually on the summit. "It is he who fed us. None of us brought any food for ourselves."

"That's right. Most of us are far from home. We've been here all day!" said another woman nearby.

"He told us not to leave. He asked us to sit down on the grass, and then he fed us!" another woman said.

"But no one knows where he got it," said the man. "Some child here had five loaves and two fishes. It was this small amount of food that fed us all!"

"No it wasn't. Someone must have brought something more," said the first woman.

"Yes it was. His disciples were just as empty-handed as the rest of us when they came out here," said the man.

"No, don't make me laugh! He couldn't have created food out of nothing!" she screeched back.

"But who is he, whom do you refer to?" I interrupted them.

"Jesus of course. Who do you think? Haven't you heard that he's been teaching in these parts and healing the sick?" she responded.

"Most of us heard he had come out here, in the wilderness, and we followed him from all the towns about," said the man.

"Yeah, we tracked him down. It looked like he was trying to be alone, but we wouldn't let him. There are too many sick among us," said the woman, sounding petulant.

"And now he's fed us. I wonder what he'll do next!"

"Poor man, he's got to be tired himself."

"Yes, and discouraged. John Baptist was his friend, and his cousin."

"John Baptist? Who is that?" I asked. "What happened?"

"He was beheaded by Herod," the second woman spoke up, largely silent until now, and looked around furtively. "Probably because he spoke the truth about Herod and his brother Philip's wife."

"I never heard John myself, but if you believe the stories, John Baptist thought Jesus was the One Who should come. The Anointed One."

"John was a prophet."

"And now he's dead."

We looked around and there were several men, a few of whom I recognized as ones that walked with Jesus, moving through the crowd of thousands with large baskets and gathering up the fragments of food left over. We continued talking.

"But what does John Baptist have to do with Jesus?" I asked. "I mean other than being his cousin. Did they join forces and teach together?"

"No they never did, but they both spoke the Truth," said another man nearby who had been listening to our conversation.

"But look up on the hill, there's something happening!"

We all looked and there appeared to be a scuffle. We moved much closer to see what was going on. The followers of Jesus had laid what looked like twelve or so baskets at the feet of Jesus, and each of the baskets appeared to be replete with food, still not consumed. There was a growing rumble, or mumbling from the crowd which turned into a low roar. A surge of movement. Some of the people nearest the top of the hill were trying to rush at Jesus. Jesus's disciples had made a protective ring around him, as if to prevent anyone from manhandling him. It wasn't clear what the crowd's intentions were. Someone had made a leafy crown of some sort, and was lifting it high, as if to put on Jesus's head—but he couldn't get near him because of the disciples. Fists were raised overhead. More yelling. The disciples were yelling back, trying valiantly to hold their cordon around Jesus. Someone punched one of the disciples in the jaw and knocked him to the ground. Another had his nose bloodied. Then a man started shouting, "Let's make him our King!"

Others took up the cry. "Let's make him King!" Fistfights were erupting everywhere as some in the crowd tried to defend the protective ring of disciples, and pull the offenders off, while others tried to penetrate that small inner circle bodily. At the center, the epicenter of the commotion, was Jesus standing serenely and quietly, and without fear. Then he spoke.

"Peter, James, John, take the others and walk down to the boat. *Now.* Get into it and I will join you later."

Jesus's voice was not loud or shrill. It was low and commanding, and it struck out in the late afternoon light like a thunderbolt. We heard it even from where we were standing. With those words, everyone stopped in his tracks. The man with the crown of leaves raised high lowered it. Some others who had been shouting got quiet, looked around, then looked down. Some others who had grabbed the garments of the disciples withdrew their hands and stepped back. The disciples stared in disbelief at Jesus.

One of the heftier disciples said, "But Lord!"

Jesus responded simply, "Go, go."

The crowd around the disciples parted politely and let the disciples file through. They walked, no, trudged unwillingly down the slope, continuing to look back at Jesus standing like a lonely sentinel at the top of the hill. The crowd on the hillside continued to remain quiet, subdued.

Once the disciples were safely into the designated boat—apparently the boat they had used to arrive at this desert place—Jesus addressed the crowd. "You are fed by the grace of God. Keep His nourishment also in your hearts, and feed on his Word every day of your lives. But now, go home to your families. Remember to help the young and the old and sick along the way."

With those words, people on the hillside started gathering up their things, and their children, and their sick ones, and turning homeward. The rambunctious crowd at the top of the hill, which had surrounded Jesus and his disciples, were the last to leave. One or two looked angry, and still had clenched fists, but most of them looked ashamed. One man turned to take one last sheepish look at Jesus's face and figure, and dropped the crown of leaves he'd been clutching.

Jesus continued to stand at the top of the hill, firmly and stalwartly, entirely alone until everyone had left. We turned to go ourselves. It was late, and we had to get back to Magdala before dark. But I wondered in my heart what manner of man this was, totally without fear.

On the way back to our village, Amos, Nainah, and I were approached by a tall, thin-faced man with a long neck, proportionately small head and shoulders, but massively built towards the ground. Like a Cyprus tree. Nevertheless, he was attractive. I thought the sparkling alertness of his eyes conveyed a certain interest in me.

"Were you part of the gathering near Lake Gennesaret just now?" he asked Amos, the only man in our company.

Amos motioned that he was dumb and unable to speak, and pointed to me. I responded.

"Yes we were, but we only saw the last moments of it. The near-fight with Jesus's disciples. What was happening there?"

"I'm afraid I was trying to find out myself."

"Have you ever listened to Jesus's teaching before?" I asked.

"Yes, some of it. It's provocative, but it appeals to the simple people."

"From what I hear, it should appeal to anyone who wants to hear the truth," I said.

"Would you be one of those people?"

"I don't know. I've avoided it for the longest time."

"You mean the truth?"

"Yes."

"Where are you walking to?" he wanted to know.

I told him Magdala. He was traveling through Magdala, but was on his way back to Jerusalem.

"Jerusalem? What do you do in Jerusalem? You've come a long way."

"I'm a student of the Law . . . and, part of the Temple staff."

"That's impressive," I said, and introduced myself by name. He did the same. His name was Darmud.

"Where will you be stopping the night? It's too late to make it all the way back to Jerusalem."

"Well, I have some friends who will take me in for the night. They live on the far side of Magdala. I must say, it would be a pleasure to hear more about your thoughts on Jesus . . . and on 'the truth,' whatever your conception of it is. I'm sure you have plenty to say about both!"

"The next time you pass through Magdala, come dine with us. Ask for the tradeswoman, Mariamme. We are two steps from the market."

"I assume you mean you and your husband?"

"No, I am referring to myself, my business. I, I . . . have no husband."

"How intriguing. Well this is where I turn off, so I will say goodbye. For now."

He looked directly in my eyes, smiled, then threw his kifiya around his head and disappeared towards the south. Both Amos and Nainah stared at me with astonishment. Simple as they were, they knew it was irretrievably brazen for a Jewish woman to speak with an absolute stranger. And the way I had spoken with him! And I had asked him to dinner!

I looked at the both of them and set my face towards Magdala. It was none of their business and whom indeed was I trying to please now? Not my husband, he had thrown me out. Not our stuffy acquaintances back in Sepphoris. They were triumphantly trying to worm their way into my former position. And not my dear sweet Vitellius. It had been three months since I had heard from him and three months since I had sent the letter with news of my exile. Still no reply. I was giving up hope. Anyway, proprieties be damned. Here was an attractive and intelligent man, and he might even be a worthwhile business connection. I would do as I pleased. I would talk with whom I liked.

"Well what brings you all the way from Jerusalem?" I asked, as Darmud appeared at our door about a month later.

"Temple business. Tedious stuff. Seeing you was the only hope that made it palatable."

"How nicely put."

"I believe at one time you extended an invitation to dinner the next time I passed through. If this is inconvenient for you, I . . ."

"No, not at all. Please come in. My servant Amos is preparing the food right now, and my friend Nainah is on her way. We have plenty for a fourth, and will be happy to have you."

"I will return after a short time. I have one person to see at the Synagogue first, and would rather not distract you from your work of preparation. I am most anxious to hear about your life since I saw you last."

I was relieved, and pleased by his thoughtfulness. Our home was a small place, and the kitchen was the smallest, hottest, and steamiest room in the house. It would be awkward enough sharing a meal with a total stranger whom I had met on the road! This short delay would give me the chance to prepare both Nainah and Amos. I didn't want them to be clucking and shaking their heads throughout the meal in disapproval.

Surprisingly, the evening raced by, and we all laughed our heads off at the amusing stories Darmud had to tell of Temple life, and of his trips on the road. We never did understand, not one of us, exactly what it was Darmud did for the Temple—other than to study the Law and sit in discussions under Solomon's Portico. But he brought laughter back into our house, and a kind of friskiness that I hadn't experienced since before my marriage. I felt young again.

At the end of the evening I saw Darmud to the door and lingered with him outside the threshold while Nainah and Amos put away the meal and washed the utensils. It was a warm, moonlit night when the air was so soft it felt like an extension of your skin. Darmud had charmed his way into my affections during that meal and I wasn't anxious to say goodbye for another month or more.

"When is the next time you'll be traveling through?"

"Soon, I assure you. My travels are irregular, and dependent on a number of factors, but I will come find you again."

"It's odd that you are up here again while that man Jesus is in the neighborhood. I hear he is preaching up in Capernaum."

"Oh really? How entertaining. I have to be up that way myself. What have you heard about his current activities?"

"Nothing direct. Just indirectly. I have heard that he cleansed, no, healed ten lepers. A person here in Magdala is the sister of one of them, and her brother—the former leper—came home to his family the other day after his encounter with Jesus. He was totally clean. Not a trace of his former sins. No sores. No anything."

"You don't believe that."

"I don't know what to think. But I would not call Jesus's activities 'entertaining.' I would call them astonishing. I mean if they are true."

"What is the name of this character, this brother who used to be a leper?"

"Jonathan, I think. His sister works down at the fish market. Why?"

"Oh I don't know. It might be interesting to hear his story directly."

"You would do that? You would seek him out and talk to him?"

"Why not? I sought you out after meeting you only once!"

"That you did. But I think for quite different reasons."

"On that you are right, Mariamme. And there are still other good reasons to seek you out again. Goodnight." He bent down and kissed me lightly, sweetly on the lips, and lightly grazed my nipples with one of his hands. I didn't pull back. I was pleased. My old/new self was starting to blossom again.

And so began my friendship with Darmud, student of the Law and member of the Temple "staff" in Jerusalem.

Darmud came through frequently after that. When I pieced the chronology together, long afterwards, I saw that Darmud's trips *always* coincided with the presence of Jesus in the general area. Capernaum, Philippi, it didn't matter. Even during Jesus's trip to Tyre and Sidon along the coast, Darmud was present. I wanted to ask Darmud if this were a coincidence, or somehow part of his job. But it seemed too intrusive, too stark. Time passed and I was increasingly reluctant to crowd Darmud. I could sense he was skittish, nervous about being precise. He couldn't be pinned down about anything—not even the time or date I would see him next! He got very cold when pressed. I didn't want him to take flight. This was especially important after I started sleeping with him.

Other links had already been severed. The note of divorcement from my husband—received before I left Sepphoris—had been final for months. My letter to Vitellius had never gotten a reply. I no longer expected one. I buried this sorrow deep within me and tried to concentrate on the present. On developing a business. On my friends Nainah and Amos. And on the increasingly intense and tortuous episodes of my encounters with Darmud. It was a downward spiral. Darmud was sweet poison for awhile, but his venom ate into my very soul.

7 Darmud, Temple Spy

Memorandum on Mariamme of Magdala: Highly educated, but poor. All the earmarks of a lady. No protector in evidence. Old woman and deaf mute afraid of her. Good material for sub-source.

Unwritten note: A juicy morsel if I ever saw one. Well-rounded figure, lively dark eyes, erect carriage. Likes men. Has some kind of history. Pursue.

My initial meeting with Mariamme occurred just after one of the alleged "mass feedings" of Jesus's followers. I'd missed the event because of my periodic need to leave my target and make reports on his activities. It was too grueling to run back to Jerusalem each time, so I came more and more to rely on my Levite contacts in Galilee. Still, it was hard to run over to Sepphoris or up to Tiberias and still keep up with Jesus's itinerant preaching which covered a wide, wide landscape. So I missed a lot of his events. Fortunately, I got in on the "mass feeding" at the tail end, just as

crowds were breaking up, and seized upon a small three-person cluster to start my non-threatening questions. One member of the group
was a lovely, shapely woman, which made it all the more pleasant.

However, I addressed my question to the man. He turned out to
be mute, and directed me to the lovely woman:

"Were you part of the gathering at Lake Gennesaret just now?"

"Yes we were, but we only saw the last moments of it. The near-
fight with Jesus's disciples. What was happening there?" The lovely
woman assumed I had been there, too.

Not wanting to dispel that notion, I said, "I'm afraid I was trying
to find out myself."

She asked me if I had heard Jesus's teaching before. Here, I could
answer the truth. We bantered back and forth regarding whether
what Jesus engaged in was "truth," whatever "truth" was.

I asked the lovely woman, "Where are you walking to?" She told
me Magdala, which is where I was stopping that evening.

She asked me the same, and I divulged that I was returning to
Jerusalem the following day. We exchanged names and because of
the Jerusalem connection, I quickly added that I was a student of
the Law and part of the Temple staff. She seemed impressed. I made
a foray into learning whether I could see her again. She gracefully
but assertively told me where she could be found, and asked me to
dinner the next time I was in town. She also revealed that she had
no husband.

I tried not to respond with any blatant eagerness, but I gave her
a very direct and cheerful smile, then wrapped my kifiya around me
and headed south.

Mariamme would serve—like many others—as an unsuspecting
secondhand source of information about Jesus's activities in Galilee,
and of people's reaction to him. Important for atmospherics. This
would justify continued contact, should Eliezer or other members
of the Sanhedrin ask. I made it a point to stop by her village rather
more often than necessary.

A month later I was back at her door in Magdala, responding to
that dinner invitation. The positive signals from Mariamme continued all evening. It was clear she wanted to see me again, and again.

It seems I had awakened her from some sort of torpor, or sadness. As if I were a bubbling fountain she had discovered and was drinking from, and couldn't get enough for her thirst. Well I would give her a nice solid appendage to satisfy any desire she had in mind. She could drink from it any way she liked!

The day after dinner at Mariamme's house, I quickly made arrangements for a permanent dwelling in Magdala which would be available to me as long as I required it. By design, I secured a place on the opposite end of the village from the synagogue and inside a labyrinth of streets near the marketplace—a spot where Mariamme might frequent without diverging from her normal routine. I did not want a squalid, sordid hut because that, in any woman's mind, would reflect the sordidness of what she was doing. So I took care that the accommodation did not smell, that it was bright and clean and well kept, and that it had a roof terrace. The property would serve the practical purpose of storing my simple disguises for the mission at hand—that is, following Jesus. But the ulterior motive was clearly Mariamme.

Our next encounter was about three weeks later, at the marketplace. I recognized Mariamme from a distance and boldly walked up from behind to surprise her.

"I didn't know you were here! Why didn't you tell me?"

"I just this minute got into town. How are you? Come, sit here under this tree with me for a second."

"How long will you be here?"

"I really can't say."

"As usual." She smiled.

"But I am here tonight," I smiled broadly. Then added, "Will you be my guest this evening?"

"What do you mean? You have no means of entertaining. You have no home in Magdala, no place to invite me—"

"Now I do. I have rented a small but pleasant dwelling here on the north end of town. It will facilitate my frequent travel through these parts. Will you come with me now, so you will know where it is?"

"Well I guess I could just come and see. I have to get back quickly though. I am expecting one or two potential customers this afternoon, and it wouldn't do to be absent."

"Only one or two?"

"Well I'm just getting started. Things are slower than I thought. But I know if I am persistent . . ." she trailed off almost dejectedly.

"What is your business, by the way? Do you have a space at the market? What do you sell?" I really didn't want to hear the details but I needed to distract her and get her walking. I took her gently by the elbow and smiled sweetly.

"Slow down! It's . . . it's a long story. I don't have much of anything going yet."

"Well in that case a few minutes away won't hurt you. Come."

The street location of my rented chambers was a respectable neighborhood, and Mariamme found the surroundings charming. There is nothing like the appearance of wealth to make women feel secure. And to my surprise Mariamme agreed to come back for a short visit after sundown.

Several hours passed while I laid in grapes, wine, figs, cheese, bread, olives, apricots, made sure I was stocked with candles and lounging cushions, and prepared for a visitor. When Mariamme arrived I led her up the exterior steps to the rooftop. The Galilean night was soft and scented; a breeze skirted around our shoulders and blew Mariamme's curls back from her face. She looked so lovely in the moonlight. She sat erect like a queen. We discoursed on a number of subjects, including Thucydides, Herodotus, Homer, the Greek playwrights. She had read them all.

"You have the education of an aristocrat! How is it you find yourself here in Magdala, selling . . . whatever?"

"When I know you better I will tell you more."

"Were you exiled like me?"

"Exiled? What do you mean? Where were you born? Not in Jerusalem?"

"Nope, I am a proud descendant of the Jewish Diaspora. I come from Alexandria. Egypt."

"No! That's impossible. But you sound like one of us. No I take that back. I've noticed a slight difference in your speech, but only very slight."

"Yes, I came from Alexandria a number of months ago. This is my first time in Palestine."

"You must be a well-connected young man to land a position at the Temple so soon after arrival. Did you have special pull?"

"I have a rich and influential uncle. But let's not talk about that. Tell me more about yourself. Where were you when you studied the Greek playwrights, the historians? Are you also acquainted with the philosophers?"

"Well I can't say I was ever an expert, but yes I studied those too."

"And where was that?"

"In Sepphoris."

"Is your family from Sepphoris?"

"I don't want to talk about my family. Yes it is. But I would like to leave that part of my life in the past."

"Then you were exiled, just like me! Did you get sent away for wild behavior?"

"Darmud!"

"Sorry. That was my crime. Wild behavior. Alexandria is a very sinful city. Even nice Jewish boys can get into trouble there."

"Alexandria sounds like Sepphoris."

"It's the Greek influence. And I certainly do not detest it. In fact, I am fascinated by it."

"It sounds like you and I have certain affinities in common."

"Was Greek culture what got you into trouble?" I asked.

"Let's change the subject."

"I can think of a new topic that would delight us both," I said, as I bent down and kissed her on the lips. At the same moment I ran my fingers lightly over the front of her neck and swirled them down to the swell of her bosom. Her nipples were standing straight out; I could see their shape through her garment.

I blew out both candles and said casually, "Aren't the stars so much brighter in the darkness?"

She looked up to the sky as I slid over to the cushion in front of her. I hoisted her up bodily to sit on the ledge surrounding our roof terrace and leaned my head backward into her lap. We sat like this for a long time gazing at the stars while I toyed with her ankles, removed her sandals, and rubbed her soft feet. Gradually I worked my hand up the insides of her legs until I could feel the warm moisture of her thighs. She gasped, but did not stop me. In the absolute darkness and silence on top of that roof, I then lifted her skirt over my face and went to work on the softest, most silent, and moistest part of her. She was delicious, tasted salty and sweaty all at once. Then I reached up and slid her gently off that ledge onto the pillows lining the terrace floor and made love to her in the moonlight. It was one of the nicest experiences I can recall, except that she cried afterwards.

As is my usual habit, I am anxious to move on after such an experience. I felt a little nervous because of her tears, and was impatient for them to get over with so she could go home. I was somewhat taken aback when it seemed that she expected me to escort her back to her house. Escort her? Most girls I've known wouldn't dare to suggest . . . but then this one had mysterious, perhaps aristocratic origins. Well she certainly hadn't behaved aristocratically on my rooftop. Anyway, I did as she asked, and mumbled a polite if restrained goodbye to her at her door.

"When will I see you again?" she inquired just before she opened it.

"I'm not sure. I never know my schedule. I will contact you when I contact you."

She looked at me for a long second, then bit her lip and gave a small, acquiescent smile. Then she was inside her door.

As a rule I find that treating women with a strong hand is the best way to go. One should never respond to their demands to know your schedule, or when you will see them again. A cold, curt reply is all they deserve. Nine times out of ten they will revert to simple childlike creatures and gratefully accept whatever treatment you dole out. But start giving them details, explanations, and they think they own you. Mariamme had behaved as expected— meek and submissive in the face of my brutal goodbye. I didn't think she would be any trouble for me, and I could see her whenever I wanted, or drop her if she bored me.

It was a couple of months before I saw Mariamme again. I had been in Magdala a few days but hadn't made any effort to pay her a call. I was in the marketplace pleasantly chatting with two nubile young things servicing the fig stand—pretty, curly-headed, and very giggly in response to my inventive statements comparing the rounded figs with mature womanhood. Their mother was some distance away, speaking with another fruit vendor, so I felt free to explore my imagination. Suddenly from behind me I felt a poke in the back. I turned around and it was Mariamme. She was smiling brightly, happy to see me, but looked thinner, older, and there was the hint of a shadow under each eye.

"Hello! I didn't know you were in town!"

"Hey! Watch it! Well hello Mariamme," I said with no smile in response.

She appeared deflated, but kept talking and tried to continue smiling. "Have . . . have you been in town long?"

"Just a couple of days. How's business?" I looked at her then turned to the two young curly-headed girls and winked. They giggled back.

Mariamme noted this, but chose not to see it as the insinuation I had intended it to be.

"Not too good. Not yet, anyway. Still working at developing a market for my products."

"Well, I will talk to you later. I'm in the middle of negotiating a price for these figs, and then I've got some other business to take care of." I dismissed her coldly, and turned back to the two young girls.

Mariamme moved away silently with her head down. I couldn't tell out of the corner of my eye whether she was crestfallen, or just angry. Served her right, for poking me. I hated that. It conveyed a familiarity I didn't want others to see. After all, Mariamme didn't own me, and there were other succulent figs out there to bite into.

As I continued talking to the two little figlets, I noticed Mariamme's old woman companion Nainah, whom I hadn't seen earlier, stomp by the fig stand. She had witnessed the entire scene, absorbed its meaning, and was undoubtedly trying to catch up with Mariamme now to comfort her. Nainah looked at me with daggers in her eyes.

After the meeting in the market place, several months passed. I had no real intention of seeking out Mariamme again, although I kept the abode in Magdala out of convenience, since my travels tailing Jesus sent me through the Lake Gennesaret region so often. But by a strange coincidence I came upon Mariamme and Nainah again in the spring, as part of a crowd up near Chorazin listening to Jesus. They didn't see me at all. They were sitting on the grass listening to the man, Nainah looking stern and serious, but Mariamme with a face almost lit up with rapture. It looked as if no one in the world existed for Mariamme but Jesus, and what he was saying. This pricked my interest. I always felt somewhat aroused when I noted women's interest in some man other than myself. Interest in me, I took for granted, it even bored me. But interest in someone else, well here was vindication waiting to happen. Here was a personal challenge, a battle of wits, a seduction to orchestrate. It always excited me.

This was another one of those occasions that I had not really focused on Jesus's words—which were always either too trite, or too obscure to note down—but I had focused on the crowd following him, singling out the persons I might accost for eyewitness commentaries or incriminating evidence later. I saw Mariamme from a distance based on her signature purple and red head scarf—an old worn piece by now, but clearly it took its origin from the finest bazaars in Persia—and immediately I noticed Nainah severe and drab standing beside her. Though Mariamme's face was even thinner and cheeks more hollowed out than several months earlier, the expression she wore as she listened to Jesus made her look positively beautiful. None of the impish, seductive look she had flashed at me the first time we met. Her expression was all light and adoration, all focused on Jesus. I was perversely inflamed with interest.

When the crowd around Jesus broke up, I raced to her side. Mariamme looked puzzled, surprised, but Nainah shot me an acid look and tried to hurry Mariamme forward.

"Wait, Mariamme, how are you? Where have you been? I looked for you in Magdala." I knew damn well this could not be verified, one way or the other, and it was a nice claim to make—however untrue.

"I, well I . . ." Mariamme looked as if she were coming out of trance.

"I've been so busy with my work for the Temple lately. I apologize for not reaching you sooner. I've so missed talking to you . . ."

Mariamme looked almost as if she were trying to remember who I was. Had Jesus affected her that profoundly? She looked older.

I plowed ahead, ". . . and so if you don't mind, I would love to catch up on what you've been doing lately."

"My mistress is tired. She needs to go home to rest," said Nainah, trying to dismiss me with a severe look and shake of her head.

At this moment Mariamme seemed to come out of her stupor. She looked at me questioningly. "Darmud? Is that you? Where did you come from?"

"It's quite a coincidence, isn't it? Happening to run into you and Nainah at one of the teachings of Jesus? Did you enjoy what was said?"

"Enjoy it?"

"Well, did you learn something? I didn't hear everything from start to finish. I got here late. I must admit I was a little lost in the verbiage."

"I can't begin to describe what He said, except to say it is the Truth. God's Truth."

I started to counter that commentary, but realized I was not dealing with a rational person, so I tried a more mundane approach. "Where are you and Nainah heading now? Home?"

"Yes we are," said Mariamme.

"Well I'm heading to Magdala, too. Perhaps we could share dinner tonight."

Nainah chimed in, "Not possible. Amos already has the Mistress's dinner on the fire."

Mariamme objected gently, "Nainah, there is plenty for a guest at our table. Let's bring Darmud home to dine with us. Darmud, does that sound acceptable?"

"I would be most grateful," I said to both Mariamme and Nainah with all the sincerity and humility I could muster.

Nainah grumbled, but did not say another word as we walked on to Magdala.

Opening the door of Mariamme's house, Amos almost slammed it shut when he saw my tall figure and face peeking out from behind

Nainah and Mariamme. Instead, we were ushered in, and shared a surprisingly tasty if sparse meal together. There was no wine.

I gathered from this, and from looking about the room which had less in it than before, that Mariamme was coming onto hard times. Her business, whatever it was, was not developing the clientele she had hoped for. She was being forced to sell off small, precious items like jewelry, fabrics. She looked careworn. Still, Mariamme was able to summon up small little smiles when I brazenly flirted with her and told her how lovely she looked (Nainah, on the other hand, scowled), and I outdid myself with funny stories about traveling, and politics in the Temple. As usual I kept it light, and totally unverifiable.

After dinner I suggested a short walk to Mariamme while Nainah and Amos cleaned up. Mariamme allowed herself to be led without protest into the moonlight and I promised Nainah and Amos I would take care of her. They both looked worried and glanced furtively at each other.

Mariamme and I strolled to the edge of the village, past the cemetery, and into the olive groves which descended down to Lake Gennesaret. There I started kissing her with the old passion I had mustered that first night on my rooftop. One kiss led to another one lower down, and my hands on her shoulders, her breasts. Before I knew it I was under her skirt and plugging her up against an olive tree. She seemed to give herself to me with a sense of abandonment and anguish I did not recall the first time. There were no tears at the end, just silence, with Mariamme looking at the ground. I helped her get her clothes back on and in order and replaced her scarf. Her back and her buttocks must have been terribly scraped from having been knocked up against the olive tree so vigorously. I escorted her home, and pulled a twig out of her hair just before I scooted her inside—one of my more tender moments.

Mariamme had not asked me this time when we would see each other again. She seemed to be harboring an incredible sadness when we parted, or something I couldn't quite put my finger on. Anyway, I made no attempt to see her again for several months, even though I stopped several times in Magdala and people known to both of us—namely Nainah and Amos—had seen me at the market place.

I needed a break. A slight regret was stirring within me and it was connected to Mariamme. I wanted to crush it.

I might add that during this long hiatus, neither did Mariamme seek me out! She knew where I lived. When she heard I was in town she *could* have stopped by. Most women would be more insistent. After several months and a few (very few) sleepless nights, this fact worried me sufficiently that I again decided to pay her a call. I stopped at her door in early evening, when I knew supper would be on the stove and she would be home from the market. Nainah answered the door.

"She is not here."

"Thank you, Nainah. When will she be back? May I wait?"

At this point, Amos appeared directly behind Nainah, short and stout with his arms folded across his chest. Nainah said, "That would not be convenient. We are not sure when she will be home."

"But where can she be at this hour?" I asked suspiciously.

Nainah did not react to my insinuation, and in fact did not answer my question. "I suggest you come back on another day."

Trying once more, I ventured, "Well when she does return, could you please convey that Darmud stopped by, and would like to invite her for—"

"She will be getting back too late for anything this evening."

"But how can you be sure?"

I was met with stony silence. I made my goodbyes as cordially as possible, and walked off. There was something inherently fishy about Nainah's story, and I was hot around the neck about being turned away so rudely. Didn't they know that Mariamme adored me? I decided quickly, almost haphazardly, that they were hiding something. Mariamme had another man. I ducked about from doorway to doorway, lingering in the neighborhood, pacing the streets, trying to decide what to do. About an hour passed before I heard two people walking and a woman's low voice which I recognized as Mariamme's. I hung back in an alleyway while they passed me by. Her companion was a man! I couldn't tell what age, but he looked in the darkness like a sturdy fellow and his gait was energetic, his voice deep. Mariamme thanked him at her doorway, they held or pressed hands for a second, then she was inside.

I couldn't think straight after this, I couldn't breathe. How dare

Mariamme, whom I had fucked with all the power and brilliance of Serapis on one of his cows, treat me this way? It was unheard of. She may have high-flying pretensions, but she was acting like a steamy overripe Sappho, a cunt of a Cleopatra, a . . . a . . . and then it occurred to me. Mariamme was on hard times. She had sold off her jewels, her things of lesser value. Now she was selling *herself.* Nainah and Amos were in cahoots with her and protecting her.

This situation worked in and out of my imagination for nights on end. It festered within me. It haunted my nightmares. It pricked my doubts. What if Mariamme had launched into prostitution even before she met me? What if she were working me up as one of her customers? I almost choked at the thought. I who was always the commander, the tyrant, the lord pharaoh to the women in my life. Being taken advantage of, being duped! I vowed to revenge myself. I bided my time. In the meantime I started to have wet dreams about Mariamme herself. She had become for me the insidious temptress, the earth mother, the wicked and punishing Aphrodite who tortured love out of her victims, beat them, and made them scream for more. I wanted to fuck her more than ever.

My last encounter with Mariamme came to me suddenly, fortuitously, happily, while I was steaming around in my own element with the wits and wags of the local synagogue in Tiberias. I was visiting my Levite contact Ishmael, who had just replenished my funds and had received my most recent, detailed account of that scoundrel preacher Jesus. Ishmael and I were seated in his office—some distance from the local synagogue—enjoying a cup of wine and celebrating a moment of nasty gossip about some Temple altar boy. At that point a servant announced,

"Sir, a woman to see you. From Magdala. She claims she has an appointment."

"Oh Darmud, I quite forgot. I had promised a merchant to look over her medicinal products and ointments, with the idea of replenishing supplies for my wife, and at the synagogue."

"Who is she? Do you know her name?"

"I quite forgot her name, too. But this won't take long. Please sit there and enjoy your wine."

I sat, and watched silently as Mariamme of Magdala entered the room, blanched when she saw me, and almost dropped her small bag of products. She looked quickly at Ishmael.

"Hello, sir. It is kind of you to . . . ah . . . let me interrupt your busy day, and I—"

"That is quite alright. Indeed we had an appointment, did we not? I've forgotten your name . . . um . . ."

"Mariamme of Magdala, at your service." Her voice was shakey. She did not smile. She looked more like a supplicant than a vendor.

"I am . . . a . . . a purveyor of oils and perfumes," she continued. "I understand you are . . . ah . . . in charge of securing supplies of this sort for the synagogue here?" She was trying not to look at me.

"Yes that is true. I hope these are high quality items because I am responsible, you know."

"Only the finest, sir." She was doing better. By sheer force of will she seemed to be concentrating only on Ishmael. Pretending that I didn't exist. I snorted loudly, crossed my legs and took another sip of wine. She glanced quickly at me, then went on rather hurriedly.

"They are all balsam-based products from the area of Sepphoris, sir. A new line of production which is purer than what you are used to. I have brought samples—oils, perfumes, medicinal ointments, items which might interest you. Would you like to see them?"

Ishmael was extremely cordial, and asked Mariamme to show him what she had. She brought out a small array of very fine high quality perfumes and ointments and laid them carefully on the table, as if they were all she owned. Ishmael ceremoniously sniffed each one, fingered it, turned it over, sniffed again, and daintily wiped his hands between each selection. Out of about 10 available, he selected 5 of the finest. "These will do. Here is your payment. But I would like to purchase fourfold of each product selected. Can you have them delivered to me within the month?"

Mariamme's eyes lit up, and she answered, "Yes, sir. Indeed I can. I will obtain them and deliver them directly to you myself." She gathered up her remaining wares, and made ready to leave. In departing she nodded politely to Ishmael, and made one curt nod and apologetic half-smile in my direction.

I sneered back, and looked as cold and derisive as I possibly could.

Mariamme ducked her head, set her chin, and hurried out.

Ishmael waited until she had departed, then looked at me with astonishment. "What was that about?"

"You don't know who she is?" I asked.

"She is Mariamme of Magdala, seller of fine oils and perfumes."

"Well that may well be, but it is merely a cover story (as we say in my world). Her real business is prostitution."

"Oh, scandalmonger! A small little skinny brown sparrow like that? Dressed the way she was? A *prostitute*?"

"She is notorious in Magdala. I can prove it," I lied. "I have an accommodation there, you know, and some sources, so I know what goes on."

"Wait a minute. As I recall you also had a source named Mary or something, from Magdala. She is mentioned in at least one of your reports on Jesus—the sensational feeding on the hillside. Is she one and the same with this woman?"

"Well, prostitutes make excellent sources. As you know, they get around."

"If that's true, then I shall have to cancel my purchase. I can't possibly take into my home—or into the synagogue!—any item from the hands of a sinful woman."

"My thoughts exactly. That is why I am warning you. And that is why, I might add, that I took the unusual unprofessional tack of identifying a source to you face to face. I would only do so for the highest moral reasons."

"Thank you, Darmud. You have saved me and the synagogue from sacrilege. Heh heh, you diabolical talented Jew."

"Always glad to be of service," I smiled and finished my wine.

Five minutes later, I listened to Ishmael as he gave orders to a trusted synagogue guard. The balsam products purchased today were to be sold to the first interested gentile. The large future purchase from Mariamme of Magdala was to be cancelled without explanation. A note would be sent to Mariamme tomorrow.

8 Nainah, Widow of Magdala

Despite my age and my poverty, I am a practical and commonsense old woman who knows a scoundrel when I see one. This Darmud of Alexandria and Jerusalem, who insinuated himself into my lady's heart months ago, will very soon be the death of her. I am sure of it.

Let me back up. Life brightened beyond measure when Amos brought her to me. Mariamme. A fugitive from Sepphoris. She was young, pretty, determined, and aristocratic. Haughty to the outside world, but kind, generous and valiant towards those whom she loved. And I, a childless widow, by God's grace became one of those people. Amos was the other. He is a friend of mine from our childhood, here in Magdala. A horrible run-in with foreign soldiers when he was a boy—they used him, then cut his tongue out just for fun—left him mute. Eventually his father sold him to a rich household in Sepphoris, where he had a stable position looking after the grandchildren. Our first meeting in twenty-five years was his appearance at my door in the middle of the night with the beautiful Mariamme.

Mariamme's story came out gradually, as she and I became friends. Obviously Amos couldn't divulge it. But his steady presence and his faith in Mariamme let me know that he worshipped the ground she walked upon, and would give his life to protect her. Soon, I began to feel the same.

It wasn't enough that Mariamme's husband had run her out of town, and left her penniless. But now she had this bloodsucker Darmud hanging around, his male appendage at attention and ready to pounce. I wondered how long it would be before she succumbed to his charms and fell into his bed. After all, she was still young, still desirable, and still ready to be desired. Her present circumstances all but eliminated the prospect of marriage with a decent man, and she had very little to look forward to in that domain. So why wouldn't she respond to a handsome, big bastard with a grin on his face and a handy tool in his pocket? But I hated to see it.

There are some women who like to be ill-treated. I didn't think Mariamme was one of those. She had been raised in the lap of luxury, pampered, coddled and indulged by her grandfather during all of her childhood years. She had that feisty, lively intelligence that doesn't take anything—even an insult—lying down. She either gets her own back, or deprives the offender of her intoxicating personal presence—forever! But the knocks in the head she has suffered at the hands of men since her youth seem almost too much to bear. That together with the calumny about being a prostitute. Now this snake oil artist Darmud was trying to make her into the very woman she was not. He saw her as a whore—the way he saw all women—and by Moses he was going to make her into one. Anyway, that's how Amos and I saw it.

I was sure after the supper invitation to Darmud's new dwelling that Mariamme was in trouble. Amos accompanied her there and just for safety's sake lingered behind after Darmud escorted her up to the rooftop. Based on what I could tell from Amos's account of the evening—conveyed in hand gestures and his inventive acting out—he was reassured as long as the rooftop conversation was audible, and the rooftop candles were blaring. But when the lights went out, and the roof got silent, Amos got worried. There was nothing he could do except wait, but he stormed and fretted silently until—about an hour and one-half later—he saw Darmud and Mariamme making their way down the rooftop steps to the street. The couple was mostly silent as they walked home. Amos's sixth sense was that something important had happened, and he and I both guessed what it was.

After that, Mariamme seemed happy and somewhat dreamy in aspect. Neither of us could communicate with her on the topic of Darmud, so I held my tongue (Amos didn't have one!) and waited to see what would develop.

As the days then weeks passed by there was no sign of Darmud. Mariamme did not speak about it, but we knew it hurt her. She began to lose weight and develop circles under her eyes, but I thought that might be related to the difficulties of getting her oil and perfume business going. It was proving to be a struggle. She had only a limited number of balsam products to sell before her supply was depleted. Her grandfather's growers were willing to sell her new supplies—and without the knowledge of her family—but she needed money to pay for them. Her living expenses drastically cut into any profit she had made thus far, and left little to spare. Also her status as an unmarried woman was a difficulty. No one in Magdala knew who she was or where she had come from. This aroused suspicion. Her lack of roots, her aristocratic bearing, her fine speech, and her profession as a tradeswoman just did not correlate.

One day, about two months after the rooftop seduction, Mariamme and I were in the Magdalene marketplace when Mariamme suddenly tensed. She saw a figure very much like Darmud from the back, standing and conversing with two girls at the fig stand. I sidled off to buy some vegetables in order to give Mariamme freedom of maneuver, but watched her from a short distance. She walked up to Darmud from behind and poked him playfully in the back.

He looked instantly around with the kind of cold stare you might give the most despicable stranger, and unsmilingly said,

"Hello, Mariamme. How's business?"

He turned and winked at the two young girls on the other side of the fig stand as if he had just made a dirty insinuation, then looked back at Mariamme.

Mariamme ignored the two girls, tried to keep a pleasant expression on her face, and told him briefly that business was not going too well.

At which point Darmud abruptly and coldly dismissed her, saying, "I will talk to you later," and turned his back. He continued joking with the two young girls.

As I watched Mariamme, she backed away silently, almost as if she had deserved this rebuke. It was awful. Thirty seconds later I passed close to Darmud and gave him a very evil eye.

It was after this incident that Mariamme went almost totally into herself. She rarely spoke and seemed listless and defeated. She could not marshal the energy to call on potential customers. The light was going out of her eyes. Amos and I knew we had to do something.

Around this time we heard that the traveling rabbi Jesus, whom up to now we had only seen at a distance, had sent seventy of his disciples throughout Galilee to preach the story of God's Kingdom. Two of the disciples were staying at the home of a friend and neighbor in Magdala, and we had been invited to come hear them. Amos and I dragged Mariamme with us.

The two young men were seated on the floor, and were already surrounded by twenty or so others. More people were arriving, so we squeezed in while we could still get a seat. Benjamin, son of Josiah, and his brother Yehuda were just a few years older than Mariamme, simply dressed but presentable and well-spoken. They were from Scythopolis, one of the Greek cities of the Decapolis, but they were Jewish.

"He is not like other men," Benjamin was saying as we walked in.

"No, he is something more. He seems to know he has power and authority, but these are manifested in quietness, almost in shyness. He doesn't try to intrude upon you, or overpower you with his intellect."

"They're talking about Jesus," I whispered to Mariamme and Amos.

Benjamin continued, "And when you talk to him, he listens carefully, profoundly, doesn't interrupt. He treats you with respect. And yet, and yet . . ."

"And yet he seems to already understand what you're trying to tell him, to read your heart even before you open your mouth," finished Yehuda.

"And his response is never critical, but it always penetrates to the very truth of the issue."

"Yes," Benjamin added, "he never minces words. He always tells you the truth, even when it's hard to hear. But somehow it's not hard to hear because you know it's the truth. And you feel, somehow, that Jesus is your advocate— not your adversary—and is trying to guard you, save you from some impending tragedy that may befall you down the road."

With this, I noticed (watching out of the corner of my eye) that Mariamme sat up straighter, and seemed to be listening more intently.

"But why—other than his obvious intellect—do you think Jesus is something beyond an ordinary man?" asked our host Nathan.

"Well you've heard of his healings all over Galilee. '*The blind see, the dumb speak, and the poor have the gospel preached to them.*' It is part of the prophecy about the coming of the Christ, for Heaven's sake!"

"Yes, yes, I've heard of the healings," said Nathan. "But how do we know it's not just a trick? I mean there are others who have claimed to heal people—"

"But that's just the thing," said Benjamin. "Jesus doesn't *claim* to heal anyone! He just does it! I've seen it with my own eyes—ten lepers cleansed in a twinkling! A man with a withered hand made whole! A man with palsy carried in by his friends and lowered through a rooftop. After Jesus's words he gets up, picks up his bed, and walks out of the house as if he were vigorous and strong all of his life."

"Yes, and Jesus not only doesn't *claim* to be healing these people. After healing them, he usually asks them *not to tell* anyone," added Yehuda.

"He also has power over demons," said Benjamin.

"How do you mean?" asked Nathan.

"The demons seem to fear him. They cower before him and plead with him to leave them alone."

"How do you know this?" asked Nathan. "That's way too extraordinary to believe."

"Well again, I've seen it with my own eyes. Heard it with my own ears. I have actually heard the demons address Jesus, saying, 'We know who you are! You are the Son of the Most High God! Have nothing to do with us, Jesus of Nazareth!'"

"But that's extraordinary!"

"How does Jesus respond?"

"How does he respond? First he tells them to be silent. Then he commands them to come out of the person."

"And you can tell afterwards that an exorcism has taken place?"

"Well," said Benjamin, "to give you an example, we were there when Jesus cast out the demons from that mad man in Gadara. You heard the story. There were multiple demons inside the man, and they caused him to run about naked among the tombs and in the mountains, and to cut himself with rocks. When Jesus arrived onshore from Lake Gennasaret the mad man (or rather, the demons inside him) rushed at Jesus and acknowledged him as 'Son of the most high God'! *We heard them.* Then they asked Jesus to leave them alone and not torment them. Jesus cast the demons out of the man, but sent them into a herd of swine, about two thousand animals in all, which rushed down the hillside and drowned themselves in the sea."

"Yeah, but how did you know the mad man was freed of demons afterward?"

"Because immediately the man came to his right mind, and sat down and conversed calmly and intelligently with Jesus. It was amazing."

"But how did you know the man wasn't planted there beforehand, by someone who wanted to prove Jesus's credentials as a healer?"

"Well," said Benjamin, "the only proof we have is what our own senses told us. The fellow wasn't pretending. He was real. Oh, and of course that the entire town of Gadara came out to see what had happened, and they acknowledged by their astonishment that the man had been truly mad before. They literally stopped in their tracks when they saw him sitting in his right mind, fully clothed, and having a conversation with Jesus. Then they kicked Jesus out of town!"

"What?" exclaimed Nathan.

"Because they were afraid of him," said Yehuda. "They didn't understand what he had done and it scared them to death. You have to admit that it's unlikely the town folk were in cahoots with Jesus. Not if they booted him out afterwards and asked him to leave their shores."

Benjamin broke in, "Nathan and all here gathered. Believe, or don't believe what we tell you. But don't stop there. Come out and see for yourselves. You will be able to make your decision best by hearing him speak. By watching him, listening to him. Then you can make up your mind."

"Yes, the worst thing you could do would be to ignore Jesus completely, or not have time for him," added Yehuda.

"But tell us what all this can mean? That is, what is the significance of Jesus? His casting out demons, his healing of the sick, his alleged power and authority and teaching?"

"We believe he is the Christ of God. Come to save Israel."

"Yes," added Benjamin. "And for that reason you *must* come to see and hear him yourself."

Mariamme was very still during the story of the mad man from Gadara, and I noticed she was scarcely breathing when they voiced the speculation that he was the Christ. Her eyes locked on both young men as they continued in conversation with our group, led by Nathan, late into the evening. Benjamin and Yehuda repeated some of Jesus's teachings, which were beautiful and full of truth. When we left the assembly my knees were shaking, but I felt peaceful and happy. I especially felt glad when I looked at Mariamme's face and knew the evening had done her some good.

After that evening, Mariamme seemed to come alive again. She told us later that she had had a previous meeting with the man Jesus in Jerusalem less than a year before, and that he had "saved" her (that was the word she used) from an awful fate. She did not provide other details at the time, but we knew her encounter with him had been significant. The two young men, Benjamin and Yehuda, seemed to be alight with some of the same qualities—joy, seriousness, bravery, valor—that Mariamme attributed to Jesus.

Several months passed. No sign of Darmud thank goodness, and Mariamme seemed to be improving. She got busy with her oil and perfume trade again, and actually had some success in selling some of her few remaining products for a neat sum in Tiberias, Bethsaida, and Philippi. Enough of a profit to buy more supplies. She expected to travel back to these cities in the next several months and try to interest leaders of the synagogues. She speculated that the synagogue business would secure her a long-term commercial foothold by establishing her reputation as a reliable supplier. In the meantime she had acquired paying customers in Magdala and Gennesaret. Amos and I were encouraged.

It was in this positive frame of mind that we all traipsed off to Chorazin early one morning. We heard that Jesus was again in the area and we wanted to hear him speak, from beginning to end, not just settle for secondhand accounts. Mariamme herself was quite anxious to go, and for the first time in months she started to manifest that lively, sparkling laughter again.

It was about a two-hour walk. As the black basalt hills rising up to Chorazin became visible, we saw the crowds already gathering between the village and the Sea of Gennasaret to its south. The hillside was warm and already green in the early spring with wild flowers. Plentiful olive groves covered the land in lush clusters of shade. I could see newly sprouting wheat fields in the distance. At the height of the hill we were climbing was a ring of vigorous-looking, thirty-to-forty-year-old men, some of them seated, but all casually facing outwards down the hill, and at their center was a tall, erect, and large-shouldered figure standing quietly. This person, I assumed, was Jesus.

We found a place on the warm black rocks, and waited. I chatted a bit with the group next to us, and there was a low buzz of conversation, wind, crickets, and bird call. Suddenly Jesus began speaking and the day got very still. The sun was still out, the clouds still moved, but it was as if time stood motionless. No undercurrent of noise you usually hear in large crowds. Just the sound of Jesus's calm masculine voice speaking to us. Not yelling, just speaking, and it seemed to be audible even to those farthest away, because no one was straining to hear him.

Mariamme, sitting beside me, was quiet and still, her face fixed on Jesus.

He spoke about the hypocrisy of the Pharisees, which was music to my ears, and said that all secrets—I suppose even the secret conversations of the Pharisees—would one day come out.

Possibly in reference to the Pharisees he said, "Be not afraid of them that kill the body, and after that have no more that they can do. But I will forewarn you whom you shall fear: Fear him, which after he has killed has power to cast into hell; yes, I say to you, fear *him*."

I'm appalled to say I thought of Darmud at this moment.

Jesus spoke about everyday worries like getting enough food, or clothing, or drink, and told us to leave these things to God.

". . . your Father knows that you have need of these things," he said. "But rather seek the kingdom of God; and all these things shall be added unto you. Fear not, little flock; for it is your Father's good pleasure to give you the kingdom."

Jesus did not stand still during his discourse. He started walking and in one stride had blithely breached the protective ring of his disciples. He strolled casually through the crowd, up and down the hillside while talking to us. He looked directly into people's eyes, smiled kindly, patted small children on the head, put a hand on an old woman's paw. He made it personal.

When he circled back up to the summit, still speaking, he looked directly at Mariamme and talked about the division of family members, one from another, as if he knew exactly what had happened to her. His look was not critical, but sympathetic and sad. Mariamme had tears in her eyes.

When Jesus had finished speaking, people started moving down the hillside to the lake, or in the opposite direction up to Chorazin. But we remained stationary, mesmerized. Mariamme looked as if she were in a trance, or in a different dimension. We finally started moving in the direction of the road back to Magdala.

At that point a loud voice boomed in my ear, and I knew we were in for it. A large figure loomed over us saying, "Wait, Mariamme, how are you? Where have you been?" and lied about having looked for her in Magdala. It was that poisonous spider Darmud.

Mariamme was not fully with us yet and did not recognize him, so I jumped in and tried to discourage the encounter. Unfortunately this seemed to jar Mariamme out of her stupor, and not knowing what else to say she fell back on her upbringing and good manners. She invited that insect to dinner.

Darmud fell all over himself being entertaining at the table and was lavish with compliments for our mistress who, in spite of herself, blushed once or twice with a modest, disbelieving smile. If truth be told, Mariamme looked several years older than when she first met Darmud, and had all but lost the bloom and sparkle of her youth.

After dinner Darmud suggested a short walk and Mariamme quietly acquiesced. I know she considered herself detached and no longer vulnerable to Darmud, as if she had given up on him a long time ago. She dismissed my discouraging shake of the head, as if to say she would go out of mere politeness, and be back soon.

Well she wasn't back soon and as the minutes passed by, a cold foreboding lodged in my stomach. Amos and I had finished washing and putting away the dishes long ago. Now Amos was pacing back and forth while I was nervously trying to do some mending. The door opened and Mariamme walked in alone. The skin of her face and neck was red and smudged, her hair was mussed, and her robe was slightly off-center. She walked cautiously, as if she were in pain. The worst sign was the manifest defeat in her face, in her bearing. She could not speak, but gave a small apologetic smile and went straight to her bedroom.

Over the weeks to come, when we again did not hear from Darmud, I watched Mariamme go down. It was no longer (I believe) a desire for Darmud or the pain of missing him. It was the shame of once again having succumbed to his insidious charms, of allowing him to inject her with his toxic attentions, only to be destroyed by him at some future date through debasement, ridicule, or interminable waiting. It was as if Mariamme had ceased to believe she was anything more than Darmud's estimation of her—a whore. She could no longer see a different Truth.

More time passed and Mariamme received the resupplies she had ordered from her grandfather's balsam groves south of Sepphoris.

With very little enthusiasm she made plans to visit the synagogue leaders in Tiberias, Bethsaida and Philippi, and attempt to gain a commercial foothold among that influential group. Amos and I both accompanied Mariamme to one of her first prospective customers in Tiberias—a prominent Levite named Ishmael. We waited outside while Mariamme entered his office.

When she hurried out less than twenty minutes later, she stated without smiling that Ishmael had purchased five of her products and wanted to buy fourfold that amount if they could be delivered within the month.

"But that sounds like wonderful news! Why don't you seem happier?" I asked. "And it will give you an even better chance with your future customers."

Mariamme nodded, but said nothing.

Amos punched me, so I handed Mariamme's small bag of balsam products to Amos and asked, "But Mariamme, then what is wrong?"

Mariamme tightened her jaw and looked away. She said very little on the way home. The following day we received a written message delivered to our door from the synagogue in Tiberias.

> *"To Mariamme of Magdala, Purveyor of Oils and Perfumes:*
> *I hereby terminate and cancel all orders made with you yesterday. I no longer have need of your oils or other balsam products.*
> *(signed) Ishmael of Tiberias"*

Mariamme read the note aloud to Amos and me, then sat silently and closed her eyes.

"But Mariamme, how could this happen? Ishmael was so positive about the purchase yesterday?"

She finally said, "Darmud was there."

"He was what? There in Ishmael's office? In Tiberias?"

"Yes."

"What was he doing there?"

"I have no idea," she said. "But he was sitting there drinking a cup of wine."

"Sounds like they are good friends," I said, "probably because of his connections at the Temple in Jerusalem." Then I guessed what might have happened. "Do you think Darmud poisoned Ishmael against you?"

"Yes, probably."

"But why would he do such a thing? It doesn't make sense! Why he just had dinner at our house a little while ago."

"I don't know," said Mariamme. "He literally sneered at me with contempt on my way out of Ishmael's office. But I don't know why he would stoop to such cruelty."

"I don't either. He has accepted our hospitality. He knows you've been struggling. He knows how much you depend on getting your business going."

At this point Amos started making signs and gestures. I couldn't understand what he was trying to say, but he had reminded me of something.

"Mariamme, Amos and I never told you about this, but about six weeks ago Darmud came by to see you and knocked on our door. Amos and I would not let him in. We were rude to him. He asked where you were, and what you were doing at that hour. We would not give him any information, and we declined to let him wait there for you. I'm afraid he acted irritated, and insulted."

"Hmmm, you should have told me, but I think I understand why you didn't. Nevertheless, that's not something that would have made him turn on me—"

"Think again," I said. "What if he stuck around? What if he saw you come home?"

"Well what of it?" said Mariamme.

"I think that was the night you had dinner with Ruth and Josiah, your friends from the marketplace. Didn't Josiah escort you home?"

"Well, yes . . ."

"Mariamme, I've hated to tell you this, but now I am going to speak frankly. Darmud from the beginning has been a manipulative worm. When he feels you are escaping his grasp, he runs after you.

He makes sweet romance to you, then discards you for months on end. He insults you in front of mutual acquaintances. He treats you like a disreputable woman. Is it possible his jealousies were inflamed by seeing you (if he did) with Josiah?"

"But—"

"Is it possible he concocted some story so that Ishmael would have to cut your balsam deal off cold?"

"But how could he do that?"

Amos and I both stood in front of Mariamme. Amos crossed his arms and shook his head vigorously up and down as I said, "He could do that."

"But *why* would he do that?"

"To destroy you."

Mariamme closed her eyes tightly, grabbed the ledge next to her, and sat down. But she remained silent.

After a few minutes I raised the question about what should be done regarding the prospective synagogue customers in Bethsaida and Philippi. I feared the slander Darmud initiated in Tiberias might eventually spread there also. In the end I decided—with Mariamme's silent assent—that we had to make the trip to those cities anyway, at the risk of being turned down. We went to bed that night exhausted.

The following morning the marketplace was buzzing with news of the special messenger to Mariamme, purveyor of oils and perfumes, from Ishmael of Tiberias. Everyone seemed to know what was in the letter, and exactly *why* the deal had been called off. I noticed that Mariamme's approach was greeted with snickers by some, while other so-called decent people simply turned away from her. She continued to hold up her head and walk with dignity, but I could tell that each laugh, each mumbled comment, each cold look, each refusal to talk to her was a blow to her gut.

By planting himself quietly and anonymously among several vegetable stalls, Amos was able to get an ear load of what was being said. He confirmed to me with signs and gestures later that even the synagogue in Magdala was aware of the accusations against Mariamme, and believed they were true. The accusation of course was prostitution. No one had any evidence, but just about everybody was inclined to believe it anyway. Some noted that Mariamme had been seen one too many times walking alone with that nice man Darmud. Someone else had seen her heading to the olive groves along the lake with an unidentified tall man, at night. The stories started to increase exponentially.

The material upshot was that Mariamme's perfume and ointment business completely dried up. Her local customers were afraid to talk to her. The farther-away synagogues in Philippi and Bethsaida—by the time we got to them with our products—shut the door in our faces. It was over.

But that was not the worst. The worst was that Mariamme seemed to blame herself—not Darmud—for the whole disaster. Darmud's vision of Mariamme became Mariamme's vision of herself. Defeated, defiled, humiliated, and naïve. Someone who deserved being ground to powder. A worthless whore.

Mariamme spent most of her days sitting silently and most of her nights not sleeping, either tossing in bed or pacing back and forth in her room. Her face took on a ravaged, haunted look. If she ever had any anger in her, it was gone. All that was left was a small, lost person somewhere inside a rapidly desiccating shell of a human body that didn't eat, rarely slept, and hardly ever spoke. Amos and I were beside ourselves.

9 The Powers of Darkness

"You're just not very pretty anymore. You've grown thin and worn, and you are poor. Why would he look at you?" whispered a low voice.

"But I used to be the object of his affection!" she answered from her bed. She had not arisen to eat, or wash, in several days.

"Well that has changed. He scorns you now. And little wonder. You have fallen from such heights, and now you deserve to be covered in sludge. You are dirty, a disgrace. All those people back in Jerusalem saw it in your face, and called out the truth before you even knew it yourself."

"But Jesus didn't see it that way," said the woman, shaking her head from side to side and perspiring.

"Leave him out if it!" said the voice. "Ugh, I can't even say his name. An uneducated carpenter is very little help to you now. And anyway you've proven since that time that the crowd was right. Think of Darmud, and what you did with him. Letting him have you on the roof, letting him take you by the olive tree. Like any common

86

street whore. And right after you had sat there shiny-faced listening to the man from Nazareth! With a tear in your eye! You think *he* would approve of you now? Ha! What disloyalty, what faithlessness, what a slut. Darmud showed you exactly what he thought of you when he soured your deal with the synagogue in Tiberias. What he must have told Ishmael about you! It makes me shudder."

"Oh forget it," said another voice, louder and more assertive than the first. "Her main problem is not what she did, but what she lost, and what she left behind. I mean, good grief, she is a princess! Her family lineage, her education, her upbringing, her beauty! Why can no one recognize that now? They're all dolts, all idiots. Even Nainah and Amos are starting to doubt her."

"No they're not," protested the woman. "They are the only friends I've got left."

"Friends! Ha! Didn't you see the way they failed to defend you in the marketplace the other day? When people were whispering about you, and when those nasty young girls selling figs were looking at you with knowing smiles?"

"Well Nainah and Amos looked angry, and hurried on past!" said the woman, struggling to get out from under this thought.

"Oh ho, you didn't see how they smirked out of the corner of their eyes. Nodded knowingly. They didn't want you to see them, but Nainah and Amos were starting to side with the townsfolk, not you! And how dare they?"

"How dare they *what*?" asked the woman.

"Well you were Amos's keeper from the beginning. He owes you everything. You saved his life by leaving Sepphoris! And Nainah herself—don't you think she's profited from your presence in Magdala? Haven't you helped her meager pension by supplying her with food and clothing?"

"I did at first. But I haven't been able to do anything for her lately," said the woman quite honestly.

"That is as it should be. She is a useless old hag, childless and lonely. You brighten her life. She should pay *you*!"

"No that is wrong," said the woman.

"Not totally. At least she should defend you from the townsfolk.

Or make an effort. Instead, I think she's enjoying the whole thing. Out of jealousy. And Amos is no better."

"What do you mean?" asked the woman.

"I saw the way he watched those little girls at the fig stand. Sweating and salivating. They could have laughed you to scorn and thrown rocks at you. Amos would have come back later and cooed. He is just not worthy of you."

"All of you are full of shit," said a lusty third voice. "What Mariamme wants, and needs, is a man in her life. Preferably well-endowed. She *deserves* to be touched, and caressed, and kissed. Someone with a hard sausage at the ready, and a tongue to make things happen."

"Moreover," it continued, "there is nothing wrong with what she has done. She is a young, ripe, luscious woman. It is her destiny to be adored, to be fondled, to be worshipped. Sex is healthy, for pity's sake!"

"And I don't know what could be more desireable," it continued, warming to its monologue, "than that lovely stiff prick belonging to Darmud. Mariamme was made to sit on top of it, and ride! And to ride any others that come around. She's a woman!"

"Well, now you're talking," reentered the loud, assertive voice. "She is after all an aristocrat. Why should she follow the petty morals of the populous?"

"I knew we could work in tandem."

"Yeah, but you're forgetting something!" said an angry voice with petulant undertones. "She also has a right to get back at those who have hurt her. She has a right to be bitter, and to exact revenge."

"Yep, starting with Amos and Nainah," agreed the assertive voice. "Those were the most egregious insults. After all she's done for them."

"And don't forget her ancient, flaccid, perverted husband, who first neglected her, then kicked her out," countered the angry voice. "He needs to be hung by his diseased phallus, until dead."

"Well I've been quiet for the last several minutes," interrupted yet another voice that was deadly monotone and practical. "But to speak openly, how could her husband, or any man for that matter, accept her after what she's done? Not just for what they *thought* she had done in Jerusalem. But for what Mariamme *knows* she did recently, in Magdala. With Darmud."

"And by the way," it added, "the whole damned town knows about it too. They're ready to spit in her face. They saw her mounting Darmud's rooftop. They saw her walking with him to the olive grove. They suspect there are worse things hidden in her past. I think the best course of action is to lie low. Not stick her head out of the house. Give up her perfume trade for the time being. Hide."

"I have to agree," said that first low voice, which hadn't spoken for awhile. "She has gone further than any decent person should go."

"But I have to work, I have to eat!" feebly interjected the woman, still tossing and perspiring on her bed while this conversation took place.

"No you don't," said one.

"No you don't," agreed the others.

"It would serve them right if you just starved yourself to death. Yeah, that would show them. Then they could feel guilty and ashamed, just like you, for the rest of their lives."

"Actually worse than you, because murder is a much worse crime than the petty little offenses you've engaged in."

"Besides, you were born to a higher level. You didn't have to follow the same rules as everyone else."

"Somehow, I fail to see how this whole scenario gets back at Darmud. And he is one of the worst offenders."

"But didn't his cock make up for it?"

By this time Mariamme couldn't tell which voice was talking. But then a new one spoke up.

"Oh get serious all of you. She can't go against Darmud. He would strike like a snake. Mariamme is right to stay indoors, hide herself from the outside world. I mean, first it's whispers and giggles in the marketplace, but later it will be clubs and stones and the synagogue elders passing judgment. Don't think it can't happen here in Magdala. The way it almost happened in Jerusalem."

"You would have to bring that up," said a seventh voice, who was cagey and hard to characterize. "Do calm yourselves down—all of you—and remember what happened."

"I remember," said the woman, brightening slightly and trying to rise from the bed.

"My dear, I know you remember, or think you do. But your thoughts and emotions that day were overwrought. It did not happen as you think."

"You mean—?" she asked, now sitting on the side of the bed.

"Yes, I mean *that man* was not the barrier to disaster you thought he was," said this voice. "What, he? An ignorant carpenter? Dissuading the crowds? I doubt it."

"Well then what's the explanation? How did I survive it?" she asked, slumping slightly.

"The explanation is that it simply wasn't your day to die. You didn't see the whole scenario the way we did. There were Roman soldiers nearby. Some of the toughs protecting Jesus had alerted them of the disturbance. These men were worried of course not for *you*, but for what might happen to Jesus."

"And . . . ?" asked the woman.

"And the soldiers were squeezing inward while this was taking place. Jesus's men were looming on the outskirts, masquerading as Jesus's bodyguards and scaring the Temple elders to death. Stones were dropped because people were afraid of the repercussions. Not of *that man*."

"Yes, and a few of us had something to do with it," puffed the assertive voice. "We knew the Pharisees had a lot to lose if this came off badly—for instance, if Roman soldiers moved in and killed half the crowd. Or arrested them."

"We played on that fear," said Fear itself.

"And of course we let it occur to the Pharisees that their credibility might be damaged if bloodshed ensued. Not your blood, but theirs. So they backed off."

"That is why, my dear lady, that we are here to help you now," said the cagey voice, representing them all. "Put your trust in us, the powers of this world, and we will see you through."

"But I don't know who you are!" she exclaimed.

"Ah, but you do. We have been with you from the beginning, guiding your life, helping you through thick and thin. And we are here to see you through the rest of the way. We may disagree on the specifics, but that is part of the natural competition between our kind. Ultimately, we all want to achieve the same goal."

"And what is that?" she asked.

"Why your personal good, of course," said this voice, lying. "We represent everything the world can give you—money, power, success, respect and obeisance from others, adoration, worship, and all the sex you could ever want."

"But isn't there something else?" she asked.

"No there is nothing else. Everything else is a dream. Even your so-called friendships are dreams. You've got only yourself, and of course, us."

The woman looked puzzled, but lay back down on her bed. "If only I could remember what it was . . . what else I thought there was . . . in my life, I mean . . . but I'm so tired, so confused . . ."

She fell asleep while the voices swept back and forth in her room, through her mind. She awoke in the morning to the same soft, insistent mutterings. The tray of food placed beside her bed, day after day, took on an ominous glow, a bad odor, and day after day she refused to touch it. She felt incapable of raising herself off the bed. She could not take hold of any logical thought. The demons held sway and bored into her. She slipped into shades of deeper darkness.

10 Amos, Friend and Servant

My name is Amos, and if you could hear my tongue sing (the tongue which I used not to have) you would know about the ecstasy that has come into my life. He restored it to me, this man Jesus, who is really more than a man, and I don't know how he did it. But it happened. And now I can warble like a bird, I can yell to the mountains, I can express all that is trapped inside me since a boy of nine. But most of all, I can sing praises to the Lord.

But it didn't begin with me. It began with Mariamme. My charge, my lady, the kindest and most valiant young woman to walk in Galilee. She was on the point of death. Or worse, she was looking over the yawning face of hell, tormented by inner demons, driven into a continual nightmare with no structure, no logic. Nainah believes it was initiated by that cruel, oily Darmud, but really it had more to do with a long series of losses and disappointments and betrayals. The kind of thing that happens in every woman's life (from what I hear), but Mariamme got more than most. Not only had she been abandoned by her one true love Vitellius and chased into exile by her own family. But in recent days she was beguiled and betrayed by a glib-tongued seducer and excoriated as a whore. She lost her only source of livelihood, her very worth, and her old acquaintances now spit in her face.

Then came the fire. Mariamme was in her room as usual, listless, quiet, in a half-sleep, tossing restlessly. I had slipped out with Nainah to buy bread and fruit at the marketplace. We weren't gone very long, less than an hour, when I caught a whiff of smoke in the air. I motioned to Nainah and we turned to look at a tall pillar of black smoke rising from the direction of our abode, then a flicker of open flame. We dropped our business and went running.

As we approached the house we could see smoke streaming from the cracks around the door. We burst in and found Mariamme still lying on her bed, as in a trance, with her clothes starting to burn. We grabbed her and carried her out, rolled her in the dirt and patted her clothing with the palms of our hands until the flames were out. Others had come, thank Heaven, to help put the fire out. We were able to carry Mariamme over to Nainah's dwelling, and lay her carefully on the bed. She had burns on her face and over most of her body, and was only semi-conscious. We knew this was going to be the end.

It seems that several thoughtless young boys, listening to the gossip about Mariamme's so-called "profession," had taken it upon themselves to "punish" her by setting her house on fire. They were probably not aware that she was in it, or maybe they were. But the consequence of thoughtless evil is often the same as deliberate evil. Mariamme was dying. Even if her situation were not so grave, she had no will to live.

Nainah and I knew we only had a day or two before we lost her. We got down on our knees and prayed:

"Lord God Almighty, Creator of the Universe, restore our daughter Mariamme."

We prayed through the night. And then the sunlight dawned and came a knock upon the door.

I went to answer it, and a large tall man with a magnificent kingly head and a kind face asked, "May I come in?"

It was still early, early morning, but I motioned to him "Yes" with my head. He looked very familiar to me, as if I had always known him.

When Nainah, kneeling by Mariamme's bed, saw the tall man walking into Mariamme's room, she exclaimed "It's Jesus!"

I looked at him again, and realized it was the same man I had seen on one or two occasions from a much farther distance. I immediately relaxed.

Jesus was large and imposing. His figure seemed to fill the room, and yet he was quiet, almost shy in his demeanor. His face emitted strength. His hands were work-hardened and muscular. He walked over to Mariamme's bed and asked,

"How long has she been like this?"

"Her sickness of spirit has lasted for perhaps six weeks now. But the fire last night has finished her off, I'm afraid. She is burned all over her body," said Nainah.

"I think her sickness goes back several years," he said.

Jesus looked directly into her face and said "Mariamme."

Mariamme, who had been in a painful stupor until now, opened her eyes and looked at him. She became very still.

"Mariamme, do you have faith that I can heal you?" Jesus asked looking deeply into her eyes. His voice was kind, almost smiling, and I could tell there was a twinkle in his eye.

Mariamme answered, "Yes, Lord, I do. But I know that I do not deserve it. I am an adulteress. I have slept with many men."

"Yes, I know," he said. "Do you now see why I was worried about you that day in Jerusalem?"

"Yes, now I do," she said. "But how did you know? How could you have known so much about me?"

Jesus simply smiled. He put his hand on Mariamme's forehead. She immediately relaxed.

"Your sins are forgiven you. Sin no more."

"But what about us?" several grunting voices spoke up from deep within Mariamme's consciousness. "It is *we* who have been offended!" they squeaked.

"You're damned right. *Our* pride has been hurt!"

"Not so fast on settling scores! Her husband and those other fuckers deserve a comeuppance for kicking us out of Sepphoris! And those young bastards who set the fire deserve to be brutalized. We'll get back at them all!" said another.

"You think *you* have been offended!" said another voice. "How can I give up my craving, my physical *need* for a good cock whenever I want one? Who is to tell me that I can't have it? I am a free woman, I run my own life. Other women have these things. Why can't I? And they act so bloody superior."

"No way, you absurd bunch of sissies. The only way to get power, to salvage our pride, to assuage our anger, and to have all the delicious *sex* we want is to acquire money, success, obeisance from others. We will stop at nothing until we get it," said another voice, "because that will give us *everything* else."

"No no no no no. We should just die right here. What good are we? Let's give it up, refuse food, waste into the oblivion that is approaching us like a huge night shade. Only then will we get exactly what we deserve. Nothing can save us," said yet another voice. "We are just not worth it," it sighed forlornly.

"Well I think all of you are missing the point. What if those horrible boys come back to burn us again? What if there are other persecutors?" asked a more timid voice.

"Yeah," said another whining. "And who's going to look at an old crone, crusty with scabs, unsightly with sores and blisters. The only sweetness left to us is *revenge* on every last one of them—those sneaking murderous boys, our so-called friends, the whole town as a matter of fact!"

"You all have it wrong," spoke up two voices at once. "The only thing that can never be conquered is the shame of what we have done. Nothing can save us now, nothing. We are ugly. Ruined. A monster of burned flesh. Old forever. All there is left for us is to hate. Hate them, hate ourselves, and go down, down, down to suffocation. We deserve to burn."

I actually heard these voices and understood them. I cannot explain how or why. But Jesus also listened to these voices—which seemed to take place in a moment of time. His hand remained on Mariamme's forehead, and his other hand reached out and grasped Mariamme's right hand.

Jesus said in a firm and commanding voice, addressing these voices, "Come out of her." I heard a lot of noise and squeaking as Mariamme went rigid and shuddered, then there was a transformation in her face and all was silent. Her features relaxed, she exhaled very deeply and her body seemed to sink into the bed.

She said, "thank you," and looked directly at Jesus. Then she fell asleep.

"Let her rest for now, and when she wakes up, give her something to eat." Jesus stood up, and moved quietly towards the door. Nainah was speechless, and stayed put, but I accompanied him out.

Jesus stopped and turned to me at the front door. He put his hand on my shoulder. "Amos, you are a faithful and loyal servant, and not only to Mariamme. You have been selfless and kind, and God will bless you for that. Amos, do you believe in me?"

"Yes, Lord, I believe in you," I said out loud, as if I had been speaking with a tongue all my life. It seemed so natural that I let Jesus depart and walk silently down the deserted street, watching him from behind as he disappeared into the dawn light. It was only a moment later before I realized what had happened.

Jesus had restored my tongue! I don't know *how* he did it, but he did it. "Ooo-roo-roo-roo-roo!" I yelled to Nainah, and burst into the room where Mariamme lay. I saw then that the miracle performed by Jesus did not stop with the restoration of my tongue, or even the casting out of those evil voices from Mariamme. Her body and face full of burns had been healed. There were no marks from the fire, not any more, no blisters, no abrasions, no bloody lesions exposed. Just normal, healthy, soft pink skin. And there was Mariamme sleeping peacefully, and Nainah crying softly. And I was singing at the top of my voice "Ooo-roo-roo-roo-roo!"

God be praised!

We kept Mariamme in bed several days while she regained her strength with good food and rest. There was nothing amiss about her appetite now! And she was rearing to go, to walk outdoors into the sunlight, to run, to jump, to sing. She wanted to know all about my own dealings with Jesus, and how he restored my tongue. She asked to hear it over and over again. She didn't talk much about his restoration of her own health and her own mind. It was something she felt so deeply, she could not discuss it. But her joy and energy were unmistakable and we had trouble holding her back. Finally, at the end of four days—at Mariamme's insistence—we headed off to Capernaum, where we heard Jesus was preaching again. It was just a few miles away, but we took food and blankets for the journey because we didn't know how long we would be there. Mariamme didn't want to return home every night. She didn't want to miss a word.

When we got to Capernaum the whole town was buzzing about the scandalous teachings of Jesus at the local synagogue.

"There's strange teachin's comin' outa the synagogue," one old woman exclaimed as she sat down to rest next to us in the shade. We had been walking for a couple of hours, and had sought out some shelter so Nainah and Mariamme could rest and take a drink of water.

"What do you mean, strange teachings?" Mariamme asked.

The old woman looked around and gave us the once over. "I see you folks is not from these parts. Well, they've got that man Jesus there teachin' 'most ev'yday. I ain't heard him m'self, but mah son and mah nephew been there t'other day, part of the men's talk after the readin'. They claim Jesus talkin' 'bout bein' the 'bread of Heaven' or some such thing."

"Well I'm sure he meant it figuratively," ventured Mariamme. "Like his teachings can be spiritual food?"

"Oh you heard him b'fore, has you? Yeah he talks like that, kinda makin' compar'sons. That what you mean by 'figatively'?"

"Yes," said Mariamme.

"Well that's what I said to mah son, 'cause I di'nt think 'twas that bad, and I 'member all the healin's he's done. But then it got worst and worst. Jesus starts talkin' 'bout people needin' to 'eat his flesh' and 'drink his blood' in order to live!"

"Hmmm. What do you suppose he meant by that?"

"Nothin' other than he gone offen 'is head!" exclaimed the woman.

"Was there anything else?" asked Nainah.

"Well, he claimin' to be sent from God. I's thinkin' all the people believe that part, least ways up t' now. Not the Pharisees o' course, but us people did. But after the flesh eatin' and the blood drinkin', people fin'ly start t' listenin' after them synagogue leaders. Lot of 'em, like mah son and mah nephew, stopped their ears and walked out. Outta the synagogue. Jesus left there all alone with his men."

"Where is Jesus now?"

"Don't know," said the old woman. "They left Capernaum yest'yday. They prob'ly walkin' round Galilee now, lookin' for somebody to listen to 'em!"

"Which way were they heading?" I asked, still surprised that I could speak at all.

"South t' Magdala," she said.

"But that's where we just came from! We didn't see anybody like Jesus on the road!" said Mariamme.

"May be. But if I was them, me, I'd stick t' the wild parts, the desert. There's some has some pretty mean feelin's 'bout 'em, 'specially 'mong the synagogue folk. Jesus may be crazy, but he ain't stupid," said the old woman. "Well, I be goin' now. By t' way, what's your business in Capernaum?"

"Finding Jesus," I said decisively.

After the old woman walked off, we decided to walk on in to Capernaum and get any additional news we could on Jesus. We got an earful. Most people were shocked, even repulsed by his 'flesh and blood' teachings, but a few—a very few—seemed to understand and not to be offended. From those last people we learned that some of our leaders wanted to kill him—out of envy, and because he was undermining their position with the people. These same Jewish leaders rejoiced over the scandalous language Jesus used in the synagogue at Capernaum because it helped turned the people against him. Jesus was last seen heading in a southerly direction. He and his disciples might be somewhere on the shores of Lake Gennesaret, or we might look for him in his hometown of Nazareth.

I noted silently that if we got to Nazareth, we would be just a short walk away from Mariamme's hometown of Sepphoris.

After a refreshing repast in Capernaum, made up of the food we had brought with us, we headed back towards Magdala. We approached Gennesaret, less than a half hour's walk from Magdala, and noticed unusual crowds gathered on the seaside of the main road. We turned off and our hearts leapt, because it was Jesus. He was sitting on the bow of a boat (I hear he often did this when speaking), and talking to the assembled crowd of maybe two hundred people. He showed no signs of a dampened spirit, or discouragement over his so-called rejection at the synagogue in Capernaum. We got close enough to see his face very well, and his eyes danced with merriment as he expounded on the ways of God. In fact, he seemed to embody the Spirit of God himself, as he sat there and spoke in his calm, masculine, kindly voice—a voice that was clear and audible no matter where you sat—and uttered the words of Truth. Both Mariamme and Nainah seemed to breathe in every word. Mariamme's face was shining. The day was worth it.

With only a day or so interruption every once in awhile to replenish our food and water supply, we followed Jesus and his small band of followers around Galilee for the next several weeks, listening to his every word, growing in faith in God, and living in a peacefulness that we had never experienced. This was one of the happiest periods of my life.

We also covered a lot of territory. I think Jesus meant to preach to all the major and minor villages in Galilee. It was one day in early summer that I realized we were skirting very close to Sepphoris.

We had stopped by the side of the road to rest under a small shade tree when we encountered a tradesman whom I recognized by sight. He used to sell fine fabric at the marketplace closest to the Roman amphitheater in Sepphoris. He did not recognize me (who was I? A nothing, a slave, a servant at the time) and for that I was thankful.

I wrapped my cloak about my face and asked, "What news in Sepphoris, good man?"

He had always been good-natured in his business dealings, and so I hoped that attitude would carry forward to a supposed stranger. It did.

"Funny you should ask. There was a death recently, a death in a once-great family. The man who married Judah bin Asher's granddaughter."

"I think I've heard of him. How did he die?" My heart jumped.

"The guy was a derelict, threw out his wife for alleged transgressions, then went on to commit a thousand-fold more. Dissipated his vital juices. Drank too much. Died after passing out in his own vomit. Serves him right, I say."

"But what of the family? Were there any children?" I asked.

"No, not in Sepphoris. The family, or what's left of it, is scattered. The granddaughter—the one who got tossed out—was barren. Her brother and sister have left town. The mother-in-law is still there, Judah's daughter, but she's old and weak. She still has her mind. No one knows what happened to all the money. Jeremiah probably spent it all."

"Jeremiah?" I asked innocently.

"The guy who died. Died in his vomit."

"Well, God has strange ways."

"True. Anyway, I have to be moving on. Business to do. You on your way to Sepphoris?"

I looked around at Nainah and Mariamme chatting in the shade. "Maybe, after Nazareth."

"Well, I wish you well. Stop by my stand in the marketplace, near the amphitheater. I mean if you get to Sepphoris. I'll make you a good deal."

"Thank you," I said. "Travel safely."

I kept this bit of information to myself that evening, until I found an opportunity to discuss it with Nainah. Being a woman, Nainah immediately agreed with me that we had to tell Mariamme, and we had to see Mariamme's mother. Everything else, we would leave to God.

We spent the rest of the day and evening in the small company of followers walking with Jesus, and slept in Nazareth that evening. On the morrow we told Mariamme everything I had learned. She didn't want to depart immediately; she wanted to pray about it.

Mariamme went off into the hillsides outside Nazareth and walked. When she returned, she was in the company of Jesus and two of his disciples. Jesus had apparently been walking all morning, and Mariamme encountered him on her way back. She must have discussed her decision with Jesus and gotten his blessing because she looked very much resolved and at peace.

We set off for Sepphoris. The old house was in an uproar when we arrived. Servants were running this way and that, and nobody seemed to know what to do, or who was in charge.

The gatesman looked at me with disdain, but snapped to when Mariamme, with a sparkle in her eye and a command in her voice very much like the old imperial tyrant she used to be, said, "I am Mariamme, granddaughter of Judah bin Asher. I demand to see my mother."

"Yes ma'am," he responded, and stood back to let all three of us enter.

We marched directly up to the second floor rooms of Mariamme's mother, whom we found quietly sitting in her chair looking out the window, the book in her lap unread.

Mariamme walked across the room, stood in the full light of the window, and said, "Mother."

Her mother looked up, opened her mouth, and cried out, "My daughter!"

"Oh Mother!" she said as they embraced.

"Daughter, where have you been?" She cocked her head back and looked at Mariamme sternly. "Where have you lived all this time? As soon as Jeremiah died, I sent out messengers to search for you. They are right now combing all the villages nearby and faraway in Galilee. We have needed you so."

"Well I am home, thanks to Heaven above, and I am healthy. And what makes me truly happy is to find you here, alive and well. How was it with Jeremiah as head of the household? Did he treat you well?"

"What do you think?" responded her mother. "Fortunately he

was so obsessed with fleshpots and other escapades in the Roman quarter that it detracted from the time he might have spent beating the servants or plaguing the rest of us. He never raised a hand to me, except once. But I mostly kept out of his sight. I never wanted to take a chance, especially when he returned from one of his debauched evenings."

She got up from the chair and walked briskly over to a cabinet. "I especially didn't want him to find these." She reached in the cabinet and held out a stack of letters to Mariamme.

"What? What are these?"

"So you did have a lover?"

"Well, I, but Mother. That's a long time ago and so much has happened. I don't really want to . . ."

"Mariamme, I couldn't care less. I would have done the same, with a husband like Jeremiah." She smiled. "Where is he now? I mean, your lover?"

"I . . . don't know. I thought he had completely abandoned me. In fact I had despaired of ever seeing him again. I . . . I didn't know about the letters. And—"

"Did you let him know where you could be found after you left Sepphoris?"

"Perhaps not . . . I didn't know exactly where. Maybe I didn't think to do that . . . I can't think why I didn't . . ."

"Well I've looked at the letters—I haven't opened them—but they seem to be from all over the world. It's a miracle that my servants managed to intercept them when they arrived, and deliver them directly to me. They still come about once a month. This man is determined!"

"Mother," Mariamme said taking the letters, "I will tell you all about him, but later, please later, when we've had a chance to catch up with each other." She smiled as she clutched the letters close to her, then seemed to wake up. "But what about the rest of the family? My sister Elizabeth, my brother?'

"Elizabeth and her family are in Athens, with your brother. They are fine. I thought it best for them to remain as far away as possible. Your brother has been a great help, even at long distance."

"But what of our money? Has Jeremiah run through it all?"

"He would have if he could have found it. But he never paid much mind to business, so when I took over the bookkeeping—"

"You took over the bookkeeping?" Mariamme exclaimed.

"Of course. Who do you think taught you everything you know? When I took over the bookkeeping, I was able to fool Jeremiah on a number of things. I kept him on the shortest financial string I could, without his suspecting foul play, and I managed to hide or invest the rest. In ways that he would never discover. That's where your brother was a tremendous help. He has made sound business contacts in Athens, and has managed to increase our fortune twofold."

"Mother, you're a marvel! That is wonderful. But why, with the uncertain danger of Jeremiah around, did you not go to Athens yourself?"

"For one thing, I wouldn't be able to retrieve your letters. And somehow getting them made me feel closer to you. I always believed a miracle would happen, and you would be allowed to come back. It was my principal hope."

"And a miracle did happen. More than one, in fact. And it was only by chance that we heard about Jeremiah's death. While traveling to Nazareth."

"What were you doing in Nazareth?"

"Mother, that is a long story. There is a man, a prophet, called Jesus. I . . . and oh by the way, this is my friend Nainah from Magdala, and of course you remember Amos, our old servant."

"How do you do?" she addressed each of us politely and warmly.

"We are most pleased to be here," I spoke boldly, and smiling.

"But, but I thought Amos was mute!" she said, astonished, and looking at me.

"Yes madam. I was a mute, without a tongue. But this man Jesus restored my tongue, and restored my voice, and restored me."

"And restored our friend Mariamme, too, who was on the point of death after a fire," added Nainah.

Mariamme's mother was speechless for several seconds as she looked quickly from Mariamme to Nainah and back to Mariamme. "You will have to tell me more about this man Jesus," said

Mariamme's mother. "I have actually heard something about him—
good things—although not from our synagogue leaders. I do not
know that he has visited Sepphoris."

"Mother, we will tell you everything we know about Jesus," said
Mariamme as she hugged her mother and kissed her on the cheek.
"And I hope we can even bring you to see him."

"My dearest daughter. I am so glad you are home."

"Yes Mother. So am I. And I have many joyous things to share
with you."

And so the conversation ensued, until it was suppertime, and
we ate, and were exhausted, and slept to the next morning. Then we
got to work. It would be a number of months before Mariamme had
straightened out the mess left by Jeremiah. But the thing that put a
new light in her eyes and brought roses to her cheeks was the letters
from Vitellius. She sat down first thing the morning after our arrival
to write to him.

PART II

THE
Gospel
According to …

11 Nicodemus, Sanhedrin member

In all my years of teaching, and in all my years of exposure to the best minds of Judaism, I never met anyone who spoke the way he did. He explained the Law calmly and authoritatively, not with the frantic desperate pace of the lawyers seeking to prove a point. It was as if he had written the Torah and dictated the legal commentaries himself! He was patient with the slow to understand. He was frequently mirthful: his analogies danced and capered, then dove deeply beneath the surface. When Caiaphas planted goads in the crowd to challenge him, he stood his ground. At times he would answer them head on, as if he genuinely wanted them to know the truth. At other times his eyes sparked with anger and he named them for what they were: whitewashed sepulchers with dead men's bones inside. His explanations cut deep into the texture of the Law and inside the Law he showed us God's love. Not punishment. Not vengeance. Based on the company he kept—beggars, tax collectors, women of dubious reputation—he viewed most sinners with compassion. The ones who tried his patience and invited rebuke were the arrogant, the sarcastic, the willfully ignorant, and those who shut other people out. Unfortunately, these were mostly my colleagues, members of the Temple hierarchy, Pharisee or Sadducee. I could not help observing that he was harder on us Pharisees. I hoped it was because the obdurate pride of the Sadducees and their almost quisling status in relationship to Rome made them past redemption. But that was my own pride speaking.

Jesus was a carpenter by profession, and son of a carpenter. Or so I was told. But how on earth a mere craftsman from Nazareth had accumulated that much learning, that much understanding of the Holy Scriptures was beyond my comprehension. Yes, Jesus and his father might have spent extended periods in places like Sepphoris, a Greek city near Nazareth which Herod was rebuilding into a showplace. It needed woodworkers, carpenters, skilled craftsmen. Working there might have left Jesus with a veneer of sophistication. But this would not have included a course on the Law and the Prophets! And where did he get his ability to debate?

Jesus was not a Greek enthusiast. Like all of us he had been exposed to the Hellenizing influences so rampant in Galilee and Judah, and in the cities across the Jordan, but it did not seem to have tainted him, or even tempted him. He was thoroughly Jewish, thoroughly a son of Israel. Yet his orthodoxy did not extend to a strict interpretation of Sabbath Day law, and he was often caught being lax, or disregarding it completely. This was one of the chief arguments that my kind threw in his face. It didn't help that his laxness about the Sabbath was in favor of some poor soul suffering from a lifelong illness, and that Jesus's touch, sometimes his word alone, would restore the person to perfect health. That made my colleagues even angrier.

My first encounter with Jesus was not prompted by his healings, but by another unique event: the day he cleaned the Temple up. Got rid of the profiteers. Our Pharisaical faction saw the money changers as part of the foreign corruption seeping into our culture, contaminating our faith. Yet commercial activity was sanctioned by the Sadducees who controlled the business of the Temple. Caiaphas himself lined his pockets daily.

It was around the time of Passover, a couple of years ago. I was standing near one of the massive Corinthian columns of the Royal Porch, overlooking the Court of the Gentiles, when I saw a man striding deliberately toward a pair of tethered oxen with a look of fury on his face. Without asking anyone's leave, the man began untying the oxen and removing the cords from around their necks. The merchant in charge of them rose up from his perch yelling and gesticulating, making a terrible uproar. But the man continued calmly at his pursuit. With a pat he sent the loosed oxen wandering off towards the eastern gate. The leather oxen cords, he placed around his neck.

"Who is that extraordinary looking man?" I asked. He was tall, big, rustic and in his early thirties. The unusual thing about him was his look of grim determination and lack of concern about the merchant who was still yelling, and by now trying to pound him about the shoulders.

"Why, don't you know?" said one of my colleagues. "It's Jesus. From Nazareth. He's caused quite a sensation up there in Galilee. Caiaphas has had him followed for months."

"Well does he often come to Jerusalem? What's his business here?"

"I'm sure it has to do with Passover. Shhhh. Let's watch."

By now, the merchant's screaming had attracted attention and other tradesmen were standing up to help him. But nobody actually made a move because they were all fixated on Jesus's next action. He had twisted the leather oxen cords into a massive rope, and was now twirling it around his head. He strode briskly towards the booths of merchandise in the courtyard, and began turning them over with one hand, a table at a time, as he continued to whip the cord 'round and 'round with the other hand. Merchants were falling backward, coins were spilling all over the place, and moneychangers were ducking and fleeing to avoid the rotating weapon. Cages clattered to the ground and doves fluttered free. Bellowing oxen lumbered off in all directions. Frightened lambs herded together bleating and urinating. Young boys were scooping up loose coins all over the ground, while the merchants and moneychangers tried to chase them off. Guards ran this way and that trying to get at Jesus, but kept tripping over

four-legged animals and battling clouds of feathers. The entire courtyard was upside down.

"Take these things out of here. Don't make my Father's house a
house of merchandise!" yelled Jesus, over the din of shouting merchants and guards.

My colleagues and I, all Pharisees, stood transfixed, obscured
by the colonnade, and could barely contain our glee. We had wanted
the merchants and moneychangers scattered for a long, long time,
but had never had the courage. We began to chuckle mightily and
exchange comments. We sobered up when we saw members of the
Sadducee faction approaching with snarls of hatred on their faces.

When the Sadducees saw that the perpetrator was in fact Jesus,
they halted, stifled their rage, straightened their garments, and con-
ferred among themselves. Then they put on a look of cold reserve
and marched straight up to him.

"How can you justify what you just did?" they demanded.

Jesus still held the whip in his right hand, but was standing still
now, chest heaving. The crowd of onlookers (including the offended
parties of merchants and moneychangers) suddenly got silent, to see
what happened next.

Jesus looked the Sadducee party directly in the eye and remained
silent. Then he countered, rather enigmatically, something about if
they destroyed "this Temple," he would raise it up in three days. I
thought he meant himself because he tapped his chest when he said
it. But it wasn't clear. Then he walked out.

The Sadducees stood dumbfounded, not knowing how to respond. There was a hint of fear in their demeanor. Fear of Jesus? I
wondered.

From that day forth, and as long as Jesus remained in Jerusalem,
I gave this man special attention. He was in the Temple teaching almost every day, so it was a simple matter to observe him. The strange
part about it was that the more I listened to him, the more I wanted
to hear. I would arrive at the Temple early and stay late in order not
to miss him. I chose an inconspicuous spot, usually in the back of the
crowd, and I never asked questions or drew attention to myself. I just
listened. And the authority with which he taught was extraordinary.

12 Darmud, Temple Spy

Back in Jerusalem at last. It was the month of Tishri (late September) and my weary days of traipsing after Jesus in the countryside were over. I had done a decent job. I had kept my head. I hadn't been persuaded by his testimony, nor been left speechless and paralyzed after his so-called healings—like so many of my colleagues. I had reported faithfully on his activities, using (I thought) just the right amount of cynical detachment to appeal to the doubters in the Temple. What I believed myself, I had no idea. I had colored and slanted the truth in my own life so many times, in so many situations, that I seriously doubted the existence of anything called The Truth, or Purity, or the Greek Ideal. For me it was a constantly falling and rising ocean of infinite possibility, depending on where your little boat was situated at the moment, and which wave was about to crash upon you. Pshaw. There was no Truth. There was only expedience.

Still, I couldn't get rid of that gnawing sense of uneasiness whenever I saw the man, or heard him speak. I had watched Jesus in innumerable situations, hiding myself among the crowds on the hillside in Galilee, seated quietly in a synagogue, or even forming part of the background noise in a discussion at the Temple in Jerusalem. I couldn't help feeling at times that I was crushing something rare and innocent, or despoiling something beautiful as I passed my reports on Jesus to the Temple authorities. But then I do not believe in sentiment any more than I believe in Truth. So I would quash this alarming tendency with a round of women, wine and dissipation, until I had forgotten everything but my headache.

This was easier said than done in Jerusalem, with stricter standards than Galilee and with the Temple elite looking over my shoulder. But Jerusalem had its own rewards.

For one thing, it was a great place to observe the power structure. Theoretically Pontius Pilate ran the show. He was a Roman soldier and citizen of the equestrian class—meaning he wasn't as high a rank as he might wish—and the great Tiberius Caesar had appointed him Procurator of Judea (which included Jerusalem) and Samaria about five years back. But Pilate lived and kept about three thousand troops garrisoned in Caesarea Maritima, on the sea, and came to Jerusalem only for the major Jewish feasts—to keep order. In the meantime, in a peculiar arrangement of power-sharing jealously cultivated by the Temple hierarchy—and dating from Herod the Great's time—our very own Chief Priest Caiaphas held the power when Pilate was away. In the iron grip of his scrawny, veined hand.

I had come to Jerusalem with a set of misconceptions about the Temple hierarchy. I foresaw a tiresome and meticulous focus on the Law, and a self-righteous almost prissy determination in keeping it. Therefore I was astonished to find instead so much personal ambition, gamesmanship, and competition among my betters. I suppose I expected a quiet, humble faith much like my Uncle Philo's. But instead I saw a rapacious desire for recognition and deference. And this was often accomplished by diminishing—or even eradicating—the value of some other rival or pretender, usually a Temple colleague. In other words, dog eat dog.

Not to say that all were motivated by such things. Among the seventy-one Sanhedrin members, a good number refrained from fluffing their feathers, and seemed to do the quiet works of charity and prayer that our Scripture demands. But at the top of the heap were Caiaphas, his father-in-law Annas, and their supporters, and they were dominated by several competing realities. One was a sense that the Romans had to be placated, cultivated and snuggled up to in order to prevent the destruction of our nation. This allowed all sorts of foreign predilections and tastes to seep in since Caiaphas and his cohorts came to enjoy their social interaction with pagan circles and the preferences it gave them. Another reality was the fear and obedience Caiaphas needed from the simple people, the 'Am ha'arets. Fear and obedience not only kept the people in check when disturbances threatened, but it was life's blood to his ego and credibility as a Temple leader. For this reason Caiaphas believed the Law had to be enforced. Severely.

Overlying all of this, of course, were several centuries of Hellenism dominating most of the known world, including the Jews, with myths of Greek heroes, scandalous social and religious practices, and an arrogant notion of culture and sophistication which had little to do with the Jewish faith. Finally, there was Roman imperial power which for more than ninety years had controlled the Jewish nation, and could snuff it out in a moment's time. Ironically, it was the Romans—because of their begrudging respect for Greece's architecture, literature, and culture—who had extended the influence of Hellenism through trade and conquest. Consequently, the Jews—at a crossroads between Egypt and Assyria, between Rome and Damascus—could not hide from the constant barrage of attacks on their so-called ethical purity.

To their credit, the Temple leaders including Caiaphas worked hard to keep the Jewish nation intact. Whether their motives were self-serving is not for me to judge. I only observe.

Which leads me back to my old nemesis, Jesus. It was about midway through the Jews' Feast of Tabernacles. I was lounging in a sunny spot of the Temple courtyard, toying in my mind over the luscious foreign morsel I was going to enjoy that evening. There was a new shipment of slaves in from Attica, and I had spotted one nubile dark-skinned lass with ample bosom and tight haunches who attracted me considerably. I had private accommodations away from the Temple, having been able to allow myself this luxury with a little help from my distant uncle. And so I had made arrangements with the trader to purchase this almond-eyed girl, and to pick her up at twilight.

I was almost drifting off into pre-coital anticipation when a small commotion broke to my left and roused me from my reverie. There was Jesus—somewhat thinner than when I had seen him in Galilee, but still the striking erect figure he had always been, dressed in the same brownish-grey robe and striding briskly towards one of the porticoes. A small crowd followed him. It was getting bigger by the minute, though, as words were exchanged with other groups in the courtyard and they too joined the surge.

Frankly I was surprised to see him. Rumors were rampant that the Temple authorities wanted to kill him. People gossiped openly about it as far as Galilee. The rumors were true.

"But why would they want to kill him?" I had asked my synagogue contact Ishmael during my last trip to Tiberias.

"And why not? He's tweaked their noses every chance he gets. And our noses too, I might add. I told you about the encounter we had with him in up here in Galilee, didn't I? Where he stubbornly and even defiantly healed some old woman almost bent in half from an infirmity, who hadn't been able to raise herself straight for years? No? Well, when we questioned him on the propriety of doing such a thing on the Sabbath, he implied—no, stated!—that she was 'a daughter of Abraham' and that we valued our oxen more than this woman!" said Ishmael.

"Yeah, but what was the connection to the oxen?" I asked.

"Well, it was a little uncanny. Yes, I lead my animals to water on the Sabbath. We all do! But he acted like he knew more. You see, a week earlier I had had a little accident with my cart. I had to call a collection of townsfolk to help me pull both my oxen and my cart out of a roadside ditch."

"And that was on the Sabbath?"

"Well, yes. But how could he have known? He's got to have spies or something," Ishmael said.

"Perhaps. But I suspect a lot of things get passed around in the course of normal gossip. Jesus seemed to know something about *me* one time, and he's never met me . . . but I dismissed it as impossible. So get back to why they want to kill him."

"As in the 'daughter of Abraham' incident, my dear Darmud, Jesus succeeds in making us—the religious authorities—look not only ignorant, but arrogant and evil. The people lap it up."

"Especially, I bet, when it happens to someone in the Temple leadership."

"You mean like Caiaphas and Annas? Yes. But they never allow themselves to get that close. They send in surrogates to talk to Jesus, and he always demolishes them. Caiaphas hates that."

"But it would all be irrelevant, wouldn't it, if Jesus didn't have a big following?" I asked innocently. "I mean, if no one were listening to him—"

"There's the rub," said Ishmael. "The crowds keep getting bigger and bigger. Caiaphas and his gang feel they're being sucked dry. You know how much they depend on deference and respect from the little folk."

"Yes, I see. The so-called little folk are starting to see holes in the chief priests' arguments. Or their righteousness. Or both. In any case, Jesus is starting to undermine their authority."

"It's beyond that," said Ishmael. "The crowds who listen to him, who hang on his every word, could start to attract the attention of the Romans."

"Do you know for a fact that they already have?" I asked.

"Personally, no, I haven't seen it happening. But that's why Caiaphas uses people like you. It helps him anticipate such dangers, and circumvent them."

"So if the Romans haven't started to notice anything out of sorts, and are not about to come down on us, then Caiaphas might want to kill Jesus anyway, in advance, as sort of a precaution?"

"You might say that," said Ishmael.

My own analysis was that jealousy and hatred drove the Temple authorities more than fear of the Romans. Fear of a Roman crackdown might be used as an excuse for eliminating Jesus, but it wouldn't be the real reason. Like fat ticks on a dog's back, Caiaphas and his cronies were too bloated with the perquisites of power, praise, deference, and authority to allow themselves to be dislodged by some country bumpkin. In their heart of hearts they knew they were protecting themselves, not God. And Jesus had to go.

So here he was again. In Jerusalem. At the Temple. Bold as daylight. I watched as Jesus sat down in one of the porticoes of the Temple, and people gathered around him—most of them in hopeful anticipation, but some with their claws out. I was still a distance away from the crowd surrounding Jesus. I motioned discreetly to a Temple guard and told him to pass a message to Eleizer, my direct superior, saying, "Jesus is here. Come quickly."

I felt a little dirty passing this message, but thrust it from my mind as I moved in closer to get within hearing distance.

On the outskirts of the crowd people were commenting on how well Jesus could repeat the Holy Scripture, and discuss it. They wondered how this could be, seeing that Jesus never had any formal book learning that anybody knew about.

"Where does he get his understanding? Did he grow up in the Temple?" one old man asked.

"Nope, he was a carpenter, a builder. See his big hands? He's a sturdy fellow," said a second man.

"Yeah, but how does that figure? If he didn't train with our Pharisees, where did he get his words?"

"His words aren't anything like I ever heard from the Pharisees. Or the Sadducees. They're different."

"Yep. They plain and clear. Truthful. I ain't confused by 'em," said another.

"Shhhh," said another. "Jesus is speaking."

Jesus was saying that God was the source of his doctrine. Then looking directly at several men in the crowd around him, Jesus abruptly asked them why they were going about to kill him.

These same men (whom I knew personally as members of the Temple staff) looked startled, blanched white, and glanced left and right. They resembled someone caught with his hand in the Temple treasury. Then one of them scoffed,

"You have a devil. Who is going about to kill you?"

This was a disingenuous question, given that the Temple

authorities' desire to snuff out Jesus was *the* topic of the day. It was an open secret both in Judea and Galilee, and most people took it for granted that Jesus would *not* appear in Jerusalem this year because of this death threat.

Jesus looked calmly at the same men and ignored this question. Instead, he sought to show these men their error in condoning circumcision on the Sabbath, but questioning him for a Sabbath day healing. He told them not to judge superficially.

Comment: I think a lot of Jesus's effort was to get men to think more clearly.

Meanwhile someone whispered from behind me. He must have been a recent arrival. "Isn't this the one the Temple authorities want to kill? What's he doing here?"

"Yep, it is," answered someone else who had been standing there longer. "He's speaking loud and clear, and they say nothing to him. Maybe the rulers know that this man is the very Christ! Maybe that's why they don't nab him!"

Another person standing there from the beginning answered, "But we know where this man comes from. When the Christ comes, nobody's going to know."

It's uncanny how Jesus seems to know about conversations seemingly out of earshot, but he answered this last comment directly. He said they all knew him, and they all knew where he came from. Then he implied he came from God.

A whiff of blasphemy filled the air. Several people were shocked and made a move towards Jesus, as if to grab him and hold onto him. But others more favorably disposed acted as a barricade and pushed them back. The aggressive ones eventually settled down.

Others to the side of me, who were clearly on Jesus's side, asked, "Will Christ when he comes do more miracles than this man has?"

This was the last straw for some of the Pharisees listening. They and the chief priests had already stationed a group of Temple security guards on the periphery of this group, and kept them standing by, waiting. A unified weapon of muscle and steel. Now they sent the guards rushing in towards the center of the group, making an arrow for Jesus. The barricade of friendly people melted away, but Jesus sat there calmly, still speaking and expounding the Scriptures. When they got within several strides of Jesus, the guards stopped, stepped backward slightly, shuffled their feet. There were three of them. One sat down, and the other two just looked at the ground, then also sat down. People moved over for them.

Jesus finished his long discourse on the Scripture, and returned to the subject of his own origin and the source of his authority. He said that in a little while he would be returning to him who sent him, that people would seek him and not find him, and that where he was going they could not come.

This last pronouncement generated confusion, and there were varying opinions on what Jesus meant. Some thought Jesus would go to Jews living among the Gentiles (the people we sometimes call "Greek" Jews), and teach them. There was much discussion about this in the crowd. The day came to an end when Jesus and his small band of followers left the Temple, probably to have some nourishment and to sleep. Nobody knew where (but we were trying to find out.)

Finally, it was the last big day of the Feast of Tabernacles. Jesus had returned to the Temple almost every day, but had still not been arrested. Here he was standing in the Temple again, boldly speaking about himself in that poetic, cryptic way, indicating but not exactly stating that he himself was the source of people's salvation.

I looked over my shoulder and the same three Temple guards were back, standing on the periphery, this time sweating and looking fearful. No more the flash of brawn and muscle and steel, just three large burley men lurking sheepishly on the corners of the crowd and shifting from foot to foot. They made a pretense of not listening to Jesus, but I knew they were listening intently.

Jesus spoke for a long time on Holy Scripture that day, but I can't remember much detail because I was listening to and watching the swarm of people around him. Besides, there were others like me planted in the crowd. Let *them* take notes! Finally, Jesus said something that did stay with me: about if any man had thirst, let him come to Jesus and drink, and that same man would be a source of "living water." What he meant by this metaphor, I had no idea. It was odd.

But the people's response was troublesome. Someone argued that Jesus was the Prophet. Others said he was the Christ. Others again questioned whether Christ could come out of Galilee, as Jesus had, since he was supposed to be from Bethlehem, David's city close to Jerusalem. So there was arguing among the people, including some who advocated Jesus's arrest. Yet nobody laid hands on him.

I looked around again at the three Temple guards, who were still milling around the outskirts of the group surrounding Jesus. A shorter, swarthy man who looked like a messenger had just come up to them and was talking and gesticulating. They all turned and moved away in a group. I left the Temple courtyard and followed them to an inner office where Caiaphas was sitting, impatient and irritated, wanting to know why they hadn't arrested Jesus.

"You're still empty-handed! What's the matter with you? Why haven't you brought him?" one of the Pharisees demanded.

The guards were speechless. Finally one blurted out, "No man has ever spoken like this man!"

That was enough to put Caiaphas in spasms. He motioned for a gathering of the Sanhedrin—not everybody, just those he could count on, plus a few of us so-called observers who had been following Jesus's movements. We assembled hastily. Caiaphas was ready to jump down our throats.

"How are we going to do this?" he demanded.

"Do what?" several of us inquired carefully.

"Arrest the man, you fools! I want him arrested!"

One of Caiaphas's Sanhedrin cronies, named Yehud, responded, "We've got a little problem."

"Don't tell me we've got a problem. I know we've got a problem! You idiots. How are we going to fix it?" screeched Caiaphas.

"Well the way I see it," said my direct supervisor Eleizer, "we've got to redouble our efforts to discredit him in the eyes of the people. I questioned our three guards and . . ." he paused.

"Go on," said Caiaphas.

". . . and they are convinced that the people are too much on Jesus's side. They hang on his words. Our guards believe the people would not allow his arrest."

"Who cares what the people *allow*? Who's in charge around here anyway?" cried Caiaphas.

"But don't you see," said Yehud as he insinuated himself into the conversation again, "that we destroy our own credibility if we can't first convince the people that Jesus is crazy, or misguided, or hopefully evil?"

"That's what I've been trying to say," inserted Eleizer. "Call off the guards for now. We've got to engage him, prove him wrong, prove him to be on the devil's side."

"Yes. The people have to see it," said Yehud.

"Then we go after him. Anyway we can," said Eleizer, and gave me a sidelong glance to see if I grasped the subtlety of his evil intent.

On the following day, there were no guards in sight at the Temple. Everything looked normal, benign. But the scribes and Pharisees had been in planning sessions all night, and had contrived various lines of attack. I was in conference with Eleizer the better part of the morning, so was unable to witness the exchanges between Jesus and the different Sanhedrin members interspersed throughout the crowd—at least until later.

From what I learned, the exchanges with Sanhedrin members were pretty heated. In fact, it was a free-for-all. It began with discussions of Jesus's authenticity, where he came from, and who his father was. Jesus's interlocutors were put on the defensive. Jesus boldly accused them of seeking to kill him, asserted their father was the devil, and that they were in servitude to sin. They hurled equally virulent accusations back, claiming that Jesus was seeking his own glory, must be a Samaritan, and clearly had a devil.

When I got out of Eleizer's office I moved quickly to the Temple treasury, where I knew these discussions were transpiring. The crowd was tense, mumbling, especially around its outer borders. I spotted a few of my Temple spy colleagues, oily and unobtrusive as usual, making mental notes of whispered conversations. I saw three Sanhedrin members sitting close to Jesus and directly addressing him. One was on the same level as Jesus and the other two were on steps directly below him. They were leaning forward, ominous and snarling like a pack of jackals, as if they could happily lean over and take a bite out of his neck. Jesus on the other hand was seated at the top of the steps, leaning casually against a big marble column. He was as calm as a summer breeze.

The part I witnessed was apparently the climax. Jesus had artfully led the argument back to his own authenticity.

"Truly, truly, I say to you, if a man keeps my saying, he shall never see death."

One Sanhedrin member responded sarcastically, "Now we know that you have a devil. Abraham is dead, and the prophets also. And you say 'if a man keeps my saying, he shall never taste of death.' Are you greater than our father Abraham, who is dead? And the prophets are also dead. Who do you think you are?"

Jesus answered, "If I honor myself, my honor is nothing. It is my Father that honors me, of whom you claim, that he is your God. Yet you haven't known him; but I know him. If I should claim not to know him, then I would be a liar exactly like you. But I know him, and keep his saying."

He continued, "Your father Abraham rejoiced to see my day: and he saw it and was glad."

One Sanhedrin member licked his lips at this statement, ready to pounce. But another one jumped in first and asked in a raspy, excited voice: "You aren't even fifty years old, and you claim to have seen *Abraham?*" Proof of insanity! They knew they had him.

Jesus responded very quietly but very clearly so all the crowd could hear him. "Truly, truly, I say to you, before Abraham was, I AM."

This brought down the house.

You see, Jesus knew how to be enigmatic, misleading, and slippery all at the same time. The words "I AM" are the Jews' name for Yahweh, or the Lord God Almighty. The way Jesus said it, it sounded not only like God existed before Abraham (which everybody knew already), but that Jesus himself existed before Abraham. In other words, Jesus himself was God!

Immediately after these words I watched as the Sanhedrin members nearest Jesus leaned forward to grab him, and folks from the back of the crowd picked up rocks in the sandy courtyard to throw at him. I will never be able to explain what happened next. One moment Jesus was there, rising casually from a seated position. The next moment he was gone. He either melted into the crowd, or hid behind several nearby pillars, or some friend whisked him away. But he was gone. My fellow spies were rushing this way and that to find him. The Sanhedrin members were flinty-eyed and seething, clutching and unclutching their fists. The people looked bewildered and perplexed. And not a guard in sight.

That night Caiaphas called another emergency meeting. It was mandatory for all spies, all lawyers, and members of the Sanhedrin that he could trust. In other words, those selected to watch and report on Jesus. The three big burly guards stood just outside the doors. They knew they were in the hot seat.

Caiaphas sat silently in a purpling rage while Annas addressed the assembly.

"What the hell happened? Where were the guards? How did Jesus get away?"

Dead silence. Finally Yehud cleared his throat and said "Well, ahem, as you recall—"

"Yes?" said Annas, tapping his fingers.

"Well we agreed just the day before to call them off. The guards. We voted to discredit Jesus first."

"Yes," added my supervisor Eleizer. "We agreed to keep the guards out of the Treasury area."

"But from what I hear," said Annas while he looked at the three jackal-like Sanhedrin members who had leaned close to Jesus, "he did exactly that. Discredited himself. Jesus implied (didn't he?) that he himself was . . . was . . . I can't say it. He committed blasphemy."

"His blasphemy should have discredited him in the people's eyes!" said Yehud.

"But it didn't," said Eleizer. "My networks are reporting that many of the people think he actually *is* God, or close to it."

The Sanhedrin members gasped.

"Enough! Call the guards!!" said Caiaphas as he got up from where he was sitting. His delicate veined hands and long finger-nails formed into claw-like appendages as he beckoned the soldiers forward.

Three bumbling fellows—the same burley men who had been so awestruck in the presence of Jesus—were ushered in and made to stand in the center of the assembly. I was seated behind them and focused on the way their muscular arms and mountain-like shoulders prevented their hands from hanging the normal way. The palms of their big solid fists all faced me, behind them. I could see the sweat forming on their necks.

"What is your excuse," Caiaphas asked with exaggerated politeness, "for coming back empty-handed?"

The large fellows were mostly inarticulate as Caiaphas stalked back and forth in front of them, peering at them with the small beads of his eyes. He stuck his hawkish nose closer to one of the guards and looked up into his face. "Well?" he said.

This guard, whose name was Haman, was sweating profusely and flinched slightly, but he managed to respond what was in fact the truth: "We were barred from the Treasury area, sir. We were nowhere nearby!"

This gave courage to the middle guard, whose name I didn't know, to say, "We were told to back off, sir. We came running when they called us, but . . ."

"But what?" asked Caiaphas with milky sweetness.

"But it was too late," gulped Haman. "Jesus had disappeared."

Yehud jumped in. "It's true we had ordered the guards to back off . . . but there were plenty of the rest of you nearby." He looked at the three Sanhedrin members. "Why couldn't *you* grab him?"

These three, considerably less ravenous-looking than before, all looked at each other, then down. One finally said, "We still can't figure it out. He was right there. My fingers were within a breath of clasping his garment. His eyes were on me as I reached for him. I looked down for a split second to make sure I didn't stumble on the steps, and when I looked back up he wasn't there. It was uncanny."

"I'm supposed to believe that?" asked Caiaphas. He waved away the three guards, and stood there seething.

"Well I . . ."

At this point Eleizer spoke up, weighing his words carefully. "I think we need to look forward, not back. Jesus got away this time, but it won't be our only chance to catch him. Let's think this through. There might be another way. Darmud, do you have any ideas?"

All eyes turned to me. This was the first time that Eleizer had ever acknowledged in public that I might have something worthwhile to say. I mentally inventoried our various options with Jesus and decided to put forward my own inventive scheme. I wanted to shine.

"Well, we either look mean-spirited or inept when we try to capture Jesus in public. So let's take him in private."

"But *how*?" Caiaphas turned to look directly at me. He had a glimmer of a smile in his eyes.

"We are trying to find out where Jesus spends the night. So far we've had no luck."

"Why the hell not?" Caiaphas was getting angry again. "How hard is it to follow a band of twelve or thirteen men?"

"It's not that simple," I said. I refused to back down to the old buzzard. "Jesus and his men dissolve into twelve different directions once they leave the Temple. They disperse. Our men have chased down streets and alleyways following one or the other. But they always come back having lost the trail."

"Well don't the disciples get back together once they split up? I mean with Jesus?" asked Caiaphas. I could tell he had had training in this discipline.

"Yes, we believe they do. But they reportedly spend each night in a different place."

"Alright, so what's the solution?" Caiaphas asked impatiently tapping his claws together.

"We suborn a member of Jesus's gang. We find out where Jesus will be on a particular evening. Then we nab him," I said triumphantly.

"How far along are you?" asked Caiaphas, that light coming back into his evil eyes.

"We are working on it. We've got a contact."

"Tell me more." demanded Caiaphas.

"No sir, I will not. Rules of the game." I answered.

"*What?*" Caiaphas said, rising from his seat and stepping towards me, but Eleizer stepped in first.

"He's right. We can discuss the details in private, after this assembly," said Eleizer, ushering Caiaphas back to his seat. Then he bent down and whispered something into Caiaphas's ear which seemed to calm him down.

Naturally I was not invited to the private briefing of Caiaphas. Eleizer did the honors. But I knew that the plan I proposed, and which Eleizer would relay to him, would raise my status in our pecking order. Even if it was a long shot.

What had transpired was this. A young maiden who helped her father operate one of the money changing stands at the Temple had been observing a repeat customer. He guarded under his robes a sometimes sizeable bag of small coins which he came to consolidate into larger denominations whenever in Jerusalem, usually during the major feasts. He was clearly from the country. The maid found him terse and monosyllabic in his dealings with her, but supposed this was due to his own notion of propriety. She thought nothing further until several months ago she happened to observe this man in the company of Jesus. The two were talking confidentially. On another occasion she spotted this same man in a conversation with several of Jesus's known followers. (Jesus was well known to Temple regulars because of a notorious incident early in his ministry, when he drove all the merchants and moneychangers out of the Temple with a whip! It was still being talked about.) Anyway, putting two and two together the maid suspected that the man—whose name was Judas—might be part of Jesus's inner circle, the so-called disciples, and that the moneybag he handled contained the group's pooled resources. In other words, Judas functioned as treasurer. (It wasn't clear where Jesus and his vagabonds got money in the first place. Foreign supporters?) But if all this were accurate, Judas was our means of getting to Jesus. Our access agent, to put it concisely.

In subsequent debriefings the maiden assessed Judas as a nervous man, anxious, always on the go. He was exceedingly intelligent but he always seemed to be dissatisfied. With himself? With his situation? She didn't know. But he didn't seem content, and he couldn't seem to settle down. Also, he was very meticulous about the money he kept. He counted every transaction twice.

It wasn't clear why Judas kept coming back to the same moneychanger, possibly out of habit, possibly because the proprietor cheated less than others, or possibly because the maiden (a sweet pretty little thing named Daria) looked at him with such warmth and adulation. In any case, the contact had infinite possibilities, and as soon as we got the report we went to work.

My idea of course was to develop a penetration of Jesus's inner circle. Nothing better than an agent (or informant) with direct, intimate access, who spends every waking hour with the principal target. We only had second-hand assessment from Daria, but my gut instincts told me Judas would be ripe for the plucking some months hence. But first, we had to meet him.

We were in the process—when the Caiaphas meeting took place—of putting one of our more pliable and crafty men in direct contact with Judas. It was a difficult undertaking and required immense coordination and luck. But on the fourth try our man Niam—a ranking member of the Sanhedrin—had "casually" wandered by as Judas stopped to change money and chat with Daria, and the introduction was made. Niam spoke familiarly with Daria and her father, then artfully spent several moments in conversation with Judas, managing both to convey his lofty position and disparage the notion of power. This impressed Judas, no doubt torn between the simplicity of his master and the sheer might and consequence of Temple authority. Niam waved his finger at Daria and her father, telling them to treat Judas well, then offhandedly told Judas to look him up if he needed anything. Then he was off.

For a first encounter, we considered it very successful. But success would depend on follow-up contact over a period of time. Caiaphas would have to be patient. This could take several months.

Eleizer relayed these details to Caiaphas and the delicacy of pulling this fish in slowly. Caiaphas huffed and stormed at the delay, but was subtle enough to understand that Judas had to come to us willingly. So in lieu of a better idea, the chief priest pursed his lips and held his tongue. Besides, within hours another crisis had come to the fore. Jesus had healed a blind man.

13 The Blind Man

Suddenly I felt the presence of someone stopping, and standing before me on the steps. There was a hush of voices, then someone asked, "Master, did this man sin? Or was it his parents? What caused him to be born blind?"

My name is Micah. When my parents realized I had been born without sight, they named me after the prophet who said "Rejoice not against me, O mine enemy: when I fall, I shall arise; when I sit in darkness, the Lord shall be a light unto me." My parents knew my blindness was a result of their sins. Naming me Micah was their way of asking God to be my light.

And He had become my light—despite my darkness. I knew He was there, protecting me. He also gave me acute hearing and better understanding than a lot of people. For instance I could detect treachery in a person's voice. I didn't have to see him to know what he was thinking. I could also detect kindness and truth. And that's what I heard in Jesus's voice.

I will never know how he found me that day. I was like a small grain of sand on a dark desert night. The Temple loomed up behind me, so massive it would take a man like me twelve daylight hours to feel my way around it with his hands and feet. Like the other beggars, I sat safely on the grand steps leading up to the Royal Portico built by Herod. I arrived there every morning, and left every evening at sundown. This was how I earned my keep. My parents and I lived in a little home south of the Temple. I was twenty-two years old. I had done the same thing every day for the last fourteen years.

Well, almost every day. There was one day when I was age nine, after I had been begging for a little over a year—367 days to be exact. I was determined to assert my independence, to show how capable I was, to show I was a man. My parents were later than usual picking me up so I proceeded to walk home by myself. We did not live far, just a little beyond the pool of Siloam to the south, and I was certain I could make it at least that far. So I started out. But somehow I got off path and fell into some kind of depression or construction pit and hit my head. When I came to, I could feel it was night. The air was chill and damp and everything was quiet. I managed to climb out of the pit, walked about twenty paces very carefully, and came in contact with a massive wall—which I assumed to be the south Temple wall.

Now I knew I had to be cautious because my parents had warned me that parts of the Temple were still in the process of being built. Consequently there were many holes or pits next to its walls used for storage of building materials. There were also trenches for drainage and other excavations for underground stables. So I clung to the Temple wall and inched my way along it to the left. This was how I knew how massive it was. Each individual stone required ten to twenty paces to move past, with my left and right arms outstretched and my right cheek pressed against it. I knew I had gotten to the end of a stone when I felt a break, and the next stone started. I traversed three gargantuan stones in this manner before I got to a turning, a corner. I let go of the wall and continued walking in a straight line to the left until I came to what I sensed was a stairway. The stairs to the Royal Portico! My home base for begging! Thus reassured and not willing to give up on my nighttime adventure, I turned blindly to my right and marched forward until I found the corner of the Temple again, and headed north. In the same manner as before, I slid with my right cheek and my chest pressed against the wall, and my arms outstretched, up the west side of the Temple until I reached a small stairway, and four massive stones beyond that, another grander doorway. I counted the stones so I could remember my bearings.

By the time I was twenty-one years old, I had encompassed the entire Temple several dozen times in this manner. I knew every nook and cranny, the dimensions of every stairway and entrance, what they were called, and where the shifting construction pits were. Since I would take a day or two off of daylight hours every month or so to do this, I apparently became a well-known phenomenon around the Temple. I was referred to as "the blind man" or simply "that sinner." I got no help in my journeys around the Temple, and sometimes boys played tricks on me. But I persisted. It was important to understand my own world, in the only way I could sense it. Touch, smell and sound. Also taste: the grit of dust was constantly in my mouth.

Fortunately my parents didn't mind this distraction from begging. They also seemed to understand my need to do this. I got so good at finding my way around, that with few mistakes I was able to get between home, just past the Pool of Siloam, and back to the steps of the Royal Portico by myself. This relieved my parents of the responsibility to escort me daily, and gave them (strangely) a wondering respect for me.

I had just turned twenty-two and it was during the Feast of Tabernacles that I first heard Jesus speak. Normally I do not go inside the Temple, but since I already knew the exterior wall so well, I had taken to exploring the Court of the Gentiles. I had heard about Jesus's healings and signs from the other beggars on the steps. A lot of them scoffed, but some thought he might be authentic. I wanted to find out for myself. On that day I heard Jesus was speaking in Solomon's Porch. So I felt my way up the steps, traversed the Royal Portico, located Solomon's porch, and sat down between two strangers.

That was the day I knew Jesus spoke the Truth. He talked about God's light, God's mercy and loving kindness. He said God's Kingdom had come to earth, and would be victorious over the powers of darkness. By that I took him to mean not only my own individual darkness of sight, but man's internal darkness. Sin, despair, and death. Jesus didn't seem to speak the way my namesake Micah or any of the other prophets might have spoken. He didn't screech, he didn't raise his voice, he didn't use rhetorical rant. He spoke quietly to us, as if he were speaking to his best friend. And his voice sparkled with mirth, joy—I could feel it. I could feel he was speaking Truth.

Jesus frequently taught in the Court of Israel—farther to the interior of the Temple—but I was not allowed in because I was blind. (Blind persons and other sinners were even barred from the Court of Women!) But as many times as I could get close to his teaching, I listened to every word.

So the Sabbath Day came, and there I was sitting on the grand steps leading up to the Royal Portico, waiting for alms from passersby. It was then that I sensed Someone had stopped in front of me. And I heard a voice ask: "Master, did this man sin? Or was it his parents? What caused him to be born blind?"

Jesus's voice (which I recognized immediately) responded that it was neither I, nor my parents who had sinned. "But that the works of God should be made manifest in him."

Then he spoke about his need to do God's work in the daytime, before the night falls. I knew he was talking about the nighttime of sin and darkness. And he spoke again about being light itself: "As long as I am in the world, I am the light of the world."

Then he did something strange. I sensed Jesus lower himself to my level, perhaps squatting, and I heard him spit on the dust covering the steps. The next thing I felt was his rubbing a mixture of wet clay and spittle on my eyelids. Then he told me, "Go, wash in the pool of Siloam."

I got up immediately, left my cherished spot on the steps, and made my way to the pool. I knew how to get there, and I could scarcely breathe in my excitement. My only thought was to do what Jesus said. I washed, and lo and behold, my eyes opened and I saw light. At first it was blurred, with flashes of brightness that I couldn't make sense of. But after several minutes it became clear. I blinked, and saw the world for the first time. It was glorious. Bright with sunlight and color and movement. I turned, and there was the Temple looming behind me. Bigger than my fingertips had ever imagined. Taller than my own height by twenty times. People next to it were as grains of sand. I saw even more than before my own insignificance, and wondered how and why Jesus had taken the trouble to find me. I began to sense that what he represented was even more glorious than the Temple itself.

All this flashed through my mind as I stood by the pool of Siloam, trying to understand what had happened. People had stopped to stare. I felt I might know them if they spoke to me because I recognized people by their voices (and sometimes by their smell). So I began running from person to person, asking if they knew me. I thought some of them might be my neighbors.

One man (whom I didn't know personally) looked at me with astonishment and asked, "Is not this he that sat and begged?"

Another, who was our butcher and knew me well, answered, "This is he!"

But another said, "No it's not. He is only like him." This man should have recognized me because he lived three houses down.

But I said, "I am he."

Several exclaimed, "Then how is it that you see?"

I told them what Jesus did, anointing my eyes with clay, and telling me to wash in the pool of Siloam. "And I went and washed, and I received sight."

"Where is Jesus now?"

"I do not know," I said.

It was the Sabbath Day, as I mentioned earlier, and several of the people in this gathering around me thought it was important to show me to the Pharisees. They escorted me back to the Temple.

The Pharisees asked me the same questions my neighbors had asked. I answered with the same facts, but some of them got angry.

"This man is not of God, because he doesn't keep the Sabbath day," one said, referring probably to the fact that Jesus had made clay with dirt and spittle, and had therefore "worked" on the Sabbath.

Other Pharisees disagreed. "How can a man that is a sinner do such miracles?"

There was shouting and sharp dispute among them.

Then they turned to me. "What do you yourself say of Jesus, the one you say opened your eyes?"

I said simply, "He is a prophet."

Several of the Pharisees hissed at this response, and dismissed me.

The next thing I heard— no, saw!—was an older couple rushing up the steps to the Royal Portico. Someone nudged me: *they were my parents*! They had been summoned by the Pharisees. When they saw me and realized that I was now seeing, they hugged me and fell down and praised God. They asked how it happened and I told them. Fear came upon them when they learned it was Jesus, because it was common knowledge that the Temple leadership hated him. They gave me one last hug and soberly approached their interview in the Temple.

I wasn't there, but my parents tell me that the Pharisees asked them to confirm that I was their son, and that I was born blind. They confirmed it. Then they were asked how it happened that I could see. My parents looked at each other, then back at the Pharisees. It was clear to them that their answer was extremely important. Any misstep could get them cast out of the Temple. Finally, my mother spoke up and said, "We don't know. Our son is of age; ask him; he shall speak for himself."

So the Pharisees called me in again. I bounded up the steps rather cheerfully and approached the interview with a spring in my step until I saw their sour faces.

"Give God the praise: we know that this man is a sinner," one Pharisee said angrily, speaking of Jesus.

I answered, "Whether he is a sinner or not, I don't know. But one thing I do know, which is I was blind, and now I see."

They asked me again, "Well what did he do to you? How did he open your eyes?"

I looked at them in astonishment, and again noticed the exasperated and dismissive manner some of them displayed in dealing with me. "I have already told you, but you did not hear. Why do you want to hear it again? Are you interested in becoming his disciples?" I asked impudently. I didn't care. They had asked for it.

The Pharisees in the front of the group practically barked back at me, "You are his disciple. But we are Moses's disciples. We know God spoke to Moses, but as for this fellow, we don't even know where he is from."

Not to be intimidated, I calmly spoke back, "Why here is a marvelous thing, that you don't know where he is from, and yet he has opened my eyes! Now we know that God doesn't hear sinners: but if any man is a worshipper of God and does his will, God hears him. Since the world began, it has never been heard that any man opened the eyes of one that was born blind. If this man were not of God, he could do nothing!" I wanted to add that the only blind people here were the Pharisees, but I stopped short.

In clear outrage several of them responded, "You! You were altogether born in sins, and do you try to teach *us?*" Then they cast me out of the Temple, for good.

Hours later, I was sitting on the steps of the Royal Portico with my colleagues, the other beggars, telling them over and over the story of what Jesus did, and what the Pharisees did in return. Word had gotten around fast that I had been cast out of the Temple. My fellow beggars wanted to hear how I had stood up to the Pharisees.

Suddenly I saw a tall large man in rough-hewn clothing coming down the steps towards me. Following him several steps behind was a small crowd of well-dressed personages—Pharisees, I thought. I didn't know who the man was until he stopped in front of me and spoke.

"Do you believe on the Son of God?" he asked quietly. I recognized his voice and my heart was thundering. I was certain that the group following him was out of earshot.

"Who is he, Lord, that I might believe on him?" I asked in return.

"You have both seen him, and it is he who is talking with you now," he answered very simply.

"Lord, I believe," I replied, beaming. I somehow knew this all along. God had been with me all my life, and now He was standing before me. In the flesh. I fell on my knees and worshipped him. The well-dressed personages had by now reached the landing on the steps just above Jesus and witnessed this scene in horror. But they could do nothing. I had already been cast out of the Temple.

Now more loudly and clearly for all to hear, Jesus turned to this group and said, "For judgment I am come into this world, that those which see not, might see, and that those which see might be made blind."

One of the group on the landing asked, "Are we blind also?" It was one of the Pharisees I recognized from my interview, one who had *not* scowled at me, but had remained silent during the questioning.

Jesus answered him, "If you were blind, you would have no sin. But you insist that you see. Therefore your sin remains."

Jesus then sat down on the steps with me and the other beggars—the lame, the halt, the blind, the abandoned women, the small dirty children, all the other insignificant grains of sand that got squashed underfoot. He sat down with us and taught us about the Kingdom of Heaven. It was then that we knew that we mattered, and that God had not forgotten us. It was the happiest day of my life. The Pharisees on the other hand, not wanting to sully themselves with the dust of the steps, nor to stoop to sitting with beggars, edged up the steps coldly and silently, and disappeared into the Temple.

From that day forward I joined myself to Jesus, and followed him. We spent most of our time out of Jerusalem, until the Feast of Dedication.

14 Nicodemus, Sanhedrin Member

Jesus also did, during that first Passover, what I would term miraculous healings of several men who came to him. I could not say in every single case that my perceptions were accurate. I did not know the persons involved, and for all I knew, they were not sick in the first place—just acting like it. Also, I was standing at too much of a distance (for discretion's sake), and therefore couldn't swear to what I saw. But in one case, I did know the man, a poor soul covered with sores who had been begging at or near the Royal Gate of the Temple for the past five months. I remembered him because his wounds were so ghastly, ulcerated and bleeding, and I always wondered how he survived from one day to the next. I would drop a coin into his pouch each time I saw him. This very man, whom I recognized immediately, was carried into the Temple courtyard on a pallet by friends, and set right in front of Jesus. The crowd got silent. I watched as Jesus spoke something to the man, laid his hands on him—right on his ulcerating sores—and looked up to Heaven. This lasted for several minutes. After that there was a low roar of voices which got louder and more excited.

People in front of me craned their necks and crowded inward, blocking my line of sight, so it was a few moments before I saw the same man, the former beggar with sores, emerge from the crowd with an ecstatic and tearful smile on his face. He was walking upright. He was completely free of sores. I would swear to this event.

It was one day after this healing that I made up my mind to seek out Jesus and speak to him. It was long before he was in any danger from the Temple crowd, so the place of his nightly abodes was not a secret. Using a few of my secular contacts, I was able to find out where Jesus spent the nights, and I went to see him. I told myself that I chose nighttime because I wanted a private conversation. The closer truth is that I did not want to stir up the suspicions of my Sanhedrin colleagues. Jesus was a controversial figure. Associating with him openly would place me in a precarious niche and I wasn't ready to risk it. But I did want to get to know him personally.

First a word about myself. I was a member of a faction within the Sanhedrin that most people considered the good guys. It was we Pharisees who were trying to keep Israel on the straight and narrow, steering clear of the foreign influences which had come so near to bringing down our nation. But everything seemed to be going wrong. The Sadducees, our opposing faction, were too enchanted by aspects of Greek culture and too cozy with the local Roman hierarchy. The simple folk were impressed by the Temple's grandeur and too mentally lazy (or subservient) to see through the vanity of its rulers. Our chief priest Caiaphas had only perfunctory interest in the meaning of the Law. His religiosity was really a love of severity and control. Even my fellow Pharisees sometimes failed to teach the people, strutted vaingloriously, and utilized their learning to shut others out. Gossip, pedantry, personal rivalries and hairsplitting prevailed during serious assemblies. I was disgusted by all of this and in fact there were days when I hated everybody.

So I carefully prepared my conversation before going to see Jesus. I was keenly aware of our differences in status and, while I respected him, I wanted the satisfaction of bestowing my favor upon him and having him grateful for my attentions. Therefore I thought the best approach, starting off, was to flatter him. Something like this:

"Rabbi, we know that you are a teacher come from God: for no man can do these miracles that you do, except if God is with him."

Jesus would respond, no doubt, with appreciation and openness, especially in view of my position in the Sanhedrin and the fact that I had taken the initiative to come to him.

I would continue: "We Pharisees have a very positive view of you! We were enormously impressed that day you chased out all the moneychangers and merchants from the Temple courtyard! We've been wanting to do that for a long time."

This, I hoped, would generate curiosity in Jesus, such as, "You don't say. I thought that particular event wasn't too well received by members of the Sanhedrin."

"Well, by certain factions, no. But by most of us Pharisees, yes," I would answer. "We've been trying to rid our religion of foreign influences for years! We've made incremental steps, but nothing as dramatic as this!"

I would continue with: "I watched your healing of the man with sores yesterday in the Temple. That was most extraordinary."

Jesus would be gratified.

"But most of all I have been impressed by your teaching. I have listened to you almost every day since Passover."

Jesus would be flattered.

"All of which is to say," I would continue, "that I would like to know more about you. Please tell me about yourself. Where did you study Torah?" And I would take it from there. This would at the very least establish a relationship between us, and I might have the opportunity of meeting him again, privately of course, until I decided what I wanted to do. I told myself valiantly that I was fully prepared to support Jesus openly, in front of the Sanhedrin, provided he was worth it. But that was always at some future date. Not now.

So I approached Jesus that night with my conversational agenda memorized, and feeling completely in charge. I barely got through the opening line.

"Rabbi, we know that you are a teacher come from God: for no man can do these miracles that you do, except if God is with him."

"Truly, truly, I say to you, except a man be born again, he cannot see the kingdom of God."

What was he talking about? This was a total non sequitur. But thinking he might be leading into some legalistic argument of which we Pharisees are so fond, I ventured politely, "How can a man be born when he is old? Can he enter the second time into his mother's womb, and be born?"

"Truly, truly, I say to you, except a man be born of water and of the Spirit, he cannot enter into the kingdom of God. That which is born of the flesh is flesh; and that which is born of the Spirit is spirit. Marvel not that I said to you, you must be born again. The wind blows where it will, and you hear the sound of it, but cannot tell from where it comes, or to where it goes: so is every one that is born of the Spirit," answered Jesus.

This was definitely not from the Torah. Born of water? Was he talking about John the Baptist? What did this have to do with me? Wasn't being a member of the Sanhedrin all the credentials I needed? Still, I bit my tongue. I hoped I could get the conversation over to my planned agenda, and I didn't want to alienate him. So I asked again, "How can these things be?"

Jesus answered, "Are you a master of Israel, and do not know these things? Truly, truly, I say to you, we speak what we do know and testify what we have seen, and you and your colleagues receive not our witness. If I have told you earthly things, and you believe not, how shall you and your colleagues believe, if I tell you of heavenly things? And no man has ascended up to heaven, but he who came down from heaven, even the Son of man which is in heaven."

I was speechless. My prepared conversation hovered in the air and blew in all directions like so many shreds of tattered parchment. Jesus had directed our engagement from start to finish, in fact had done circles around me, and I had not been able to get past my first piece of mild flattery. In a second I saw it all before me: my own trivial, self-focused, rule-abiding pursuits, narrow, fearful, plodding and precise, versus something Else, something bigger, which Jesus was trying to make me see. And in all my earthbound blindness, I couldn't see what it was, what he was driving at. But I knew it was important. In fact, I felt that my very life my depended on it.

I smiled at him, rather shamefacedly, and shook my head to signify that I still didn't understand. He put his hand on my right shoulder, and smiled back. It was like sunshine, that smile. I suddenly felt encouraged, even though I knew no more than I did before. In fact I felt exuberant, and chuckled. He chuckled back, and before long we were both laughing heartily and slapping our knees as if we had been friends for years on end. That brought the evening to a close. There was nothing more I knew to say. I gave him a silent friendly nod, turned around, and made my way back to my home, still shaking my head, still smiling, still trying to understand what it meant to be born of the Spirit.

15 Judas Iscariot

I am a precise man, a meticulous man, an honest man. I like to be in charge of the details because no one else sees their importance, and frankly no one else is capable. That is why from the very beginning, Jesus put me in charge of the money. And that is why under normal circumstances he would have trusted me, and only me, to prepare the upper room for that last dinner before Passover. He knew that only I had the foresight, the discretion, and the ability to do it in absolute secrecy. Instead he chose Peter and John. I'm sorry to say that these two—though full of God's love—were bumblers in this regard.

Unfortunately, I wish I had been fuller of God's love, and more of a bumbler! But let me tell my story.

The beginning of my troubles was a surprising, if flattering, meeting with a member of the Sanhedrin. He was a kindly looking grey-haired man with (it turned out) a backbone of steel. Our first encounter took place at a moneychanger's booth in Jerusalem. It was fall. The Feast of the Tabernacles. I was there to consolidate our bag of small coins—donations mostly—and make it lighter and more portable. I always went to the same moneychanger inside the Temple walls because he cheated a little less than the others. And his daughter was modest, quiet, and shy the way a well-bred young woman should be. We had exchanged a few words about the weather, or other trivia, each time I visited their booth and in this manner I got to know Daria (the young woman) and her father, the proprietor. But the real cataclysmic event came on the day I met Niam.

Niam was not what you would expect for a Sanhedrin member. Yes he was urbane and sophisticated, well-spoken, and from all observations highly educated. But he had this self-deprecating manner about him, and a tendency to make jokes at his own expense, which I found charming. I always loved people who belittled their own importance.

"How often do you come to Jerusalem?" Niam asked.

"Not as often as I would like. It must be quite stimulating to be part of the Temple hierarchy?" I ventured, once I learned he was part of the Sanhedrin.

"Yes," he smiled, "it is one of the jolliest groups I have ever been acquainted with."

"What on earth do you mean?" wondering if I had misheard.

"Oh you know. All these characters overwhelmed by the majesty of their own importance." He looked both ways in the courtyard, then put his finger to his lips. "But don't tell Caiaphas I said that!"

"Caiaphas! You know Caiaphas?!"

"Well, not well. We're not cozy. One of his nieces is married to my son. Not that it's done *me* any good," he smiled more broadly.

"That's amazing. Do you know Daria and her father well?" I asked, looking back at our two moneychangers.

"I stop by quite often *just to keep them in line!*" he said more loudly, in the direction of Daria and her father—both of whom smiled.

"Listen," Niam said, "I am due at a council meeting in a few minutes. Look me up next time you're in the city, and we can drink some wine together. I will show you my decrepit office. It's the only one Herod forgot to renovate when he rebuilt Solomon's Temple. Hey," he waved to Daria and her father, "take care of this good fellow. You are lucky to have such honest customers!" And he was off.

This chance meeting with Niam, try as I might not to let it flatter me, flattered me to hell. I couldn't help thinking that he had been as charmed by me as I was by him. The cut of my brow, my palpable intelligence, my solemn eyes—I didn't know what. But to make an invitation like that after a few short minutes of conversation—well, I was pleased. This could be a valuable contact for our little band of wanderers. I thumped my breast. I said silently with a glance upward at Heaven, "Lord, let Jesus know what good I can do him! Let me come back into his good graces! Let him see me as I really am!"

Well Jesus did come to see me as I really was, but not in the way I intended. When we returned to Jerusalem at the Feast of Dedication—it was wintertime—I looked Niam up. We had already been in Jerusalem for about a day. Jesus was sitting in one of the Temple courtyards surrounded by the usual herd of rapt attendees, while Pharisees, Sadducees, and other religious authorities stood warily around the rim. I slipped quietly away from that group. At first I had thoughts of buying provisions, or doing some other errand which required the moneybag I kept as treasurer. But as soon as I left the spell of Jesus's teachings, I thought of Niam. I didn't know how to "look him up," so I did the best I could. I asked one of the Temple guards.

To my surprise, the guard knew immediately whom I was talking about, and walked me down long steps and a labyrinth of internal corridors to his office. A cubbyhole no better, no worse, than Niam had said, but pleasant and dry, lit with a bright oil lamp. Niam was writing. He lifted his head as soon as he heard commotion at the door.

"Why Judas! What a pleasant surprise! How long have you been in town?"

"Not long. We . . . ah, I just got here." For obvious reasons I was reluctant to admit to Niam—or to anyone from the Temple—that I was part of the group following Jesus. So I thought it best to comport myself as a singleton.

"Do come in. Let's have a drop. Do you like a good Rhodian?"

"Well I . . ."

"Sit down. Let me pour you some. The Greeks may not be good for anything else, but they do make good wine. Here." He handed me a cupful.

"This is quite an establishment. I had no idea the Temple had such a maze of offices and rooms below its principal courtyard!" I said, making small conversation.

"You have no idea," he responded. "It goes on forever down here. Sometimes even I myself get lost." He paused and smiled that beguiling smile, "No doubt there are some here who wish I *would*. I mean, *get lost*."

"Hard to believe," I said and tried to smile back.

"Now what brings you to Jerusalem?"

"Well, I . . ."

"Oh the Feast of course. That is what brings everybody this time of year. And things are so sprightly and cheerful with all the lights. Say, did you know that man Jesus is teaching in the Temple today?"

"Yes, I was aware," I said with feigned indifference.

"Then why aren't you listening to him?" he asked encouragingly. "Everyone else is!"

"Except you," I answered pleasantly.

"Well true. Too much work to do, I'm afraid. Listen, I'd love to get your thoughts on him. You, I mean, as one of the 'people,' so to speak. We in the Sanhedrin talk too much among ourselves. We get inbred, insulated. Jesus from what I understand is quite a force to be reckoned with. He exudes power and authority. I have been arguing with my Sanhedrin colleagues for some months now that we need to *understand* what he teaches, *fathom* what his appeal is, instead of always trying to trip him up. After all, he may be a prophet in disguise. We don't want to be working against God Himself."

I thought this was a quite convincing argument. Niam seemed sincere. Yet I remained cautious and noncommittal. "Yes, Jesus's teachings are unusual. Based on what I have heard, anyway."

"Well what about dinner tonight? We can talk this over more. It will be perfectly enlightening to get a firsthand account of the people's perspective, which I'm counting on you to give me!" he said hopefully.

I played this over in my mind and quickly decided that a private audience with Niam could be useful. Useful in getting a positive viewpoint of Jesus across, useful in persuading a member of the Sanhedrin to be more receptive to Jesus's ideas. Who knows, this might be the means to getting an inside track in the Temple. If Jesus could be accepted and acknowledged by the Temple hierarchy, then nothing could stop him.

A tiny, ugly voice reminded me that Niam could also be *my own* road back into Jesus's good graces. I used to be Jesus's favorite, and it was my deepest heartache to think that somehow in some way I had disappointed him. I saw it in his eyes.

All these thoughts occurred in a split second, before I turned to Niam and said, "Yes, I think I could get away for awhile after dark. Where shall I meet you?"

"Come to the Golden Gate. Ask any guard—no, ask the one named Rubin—to take you to my chambers. How nice of you to accept! I shall look forward to it."

I hurried out to get back to my fellow disciples before I was missed. Somehow I didn't see my way clear to telling any of them what I had been up to, or my stratagems for the future. They wouldn't be able to keep their mouths shut anyway, and it would be all over the neighborhood before I'd put a stop to it. I knew Jesus would understand. He understood everything, and far better than I. But Jesus was the last person I wanted to tell about my meeting with Niam, or my supper later that night. For reasons I couldn't fathom, I had a sneaking sense of shame about it. I worried Jesus might suspect me of doing something underhanded. Or the disciples would think so. So I kept it to myself. Better to present to them the entire plan on how Niam could help us, a plan to be conceived by *me*. The gleam of envy in my fellows' eyes, the spark of delight in Jesus's, would make it all worth it.

The evening with Niam was what one might expect. He plied me with wine, olives, cheese, tasty nuts, fish and tidbits I had not seen since my childhood. I felt pampered. We even had an aide, or servant, at our beck and call. Niam was extremely kind to the servant, never dismissive, and always thanked him sincerely after each small attention. This naturally gave me a feeling that Niam was a person I could trust. The other persuasive factor was that he hung on my every word, as if I were a person of value.

"So what is your candid opinion of Jesus? Is he the real thing?"

"Not to be disrespectful, Niam, but you must tell me what you mean by that."

"Do you think he really has the authority of God behind him?" Niam asked innocently.

I probably said more than I should have on this first evening, but I told Niam in simple practical terms why I thought God was with Jesus, and in Jesus. I told about the healings I had seen. I told Niam about Jesus's modesty, his unwillingness to pound his chest, his shyness about inserting himself into a person's life unless invited.

"But that doesn't track with his challenges to some of my Pharisaical colleagues in the Temple of late. For instance, back during the Feast of the Tabernacles."

"Well true, but the one thing I have seen Jesus get angry about, combative about, is hypocrisy. I think he sees hypocrisy in some of your colleagues. Also snobbism, and the desire to shut other people out. He hates that."

"You are very insightful. I think you are right. I have seen it too."

Was he confirming the hypocrisy of his colleagues? Or affirming my insights into Jesus?

To clarify I added, "I have even seen it against myself. His anger." Then I realized I had gone too far. I had indicated a personal relationship or contact with Jesus.

Niam simply raised his eyebrows and waited. Seeing that I was on the brink of clamming up, he coaxed further conversation out of me by changing the subject.

"Speaking of hypocrisy, how do the 'real' people see our Sanhedrin leadership? What's the general attitude? Are they regarded as wise, learned, good men? Or as people in bed with the Romans?" Here Niam was getting down to brass tacks.

"Do you want me to be candid?"

"Yes, I do," he said.

"Well, to tell you the truth, the Temple leadership does not have a perfect reputation. Many people do regard them as hypocritical, as too attached to their power and authority, as too protective of their own privileges." I paused.

"Go on," he said, "I assure you this is for my ears alone."

"And many wonder if they are simply jealous of Jesus."

"Hmmmm. Now that's interesting. Why would the Sanhedrin by jealous of *Jesus?*" he asked.

"Well not you, of course. But some of the others. Because he is drawing the people away from them. Undermining their authority. And his power to heal the sick is real."

"Yes, I see your point. The healings do carry a lot of weight with the people. Hard to deny that."

"Yes, it is." Suddenly I felt very protective of Jesus. I had this cold fear in my chest that I had walked into very dangerous territory. I was not sure my scheme to convince Niam—and therefore the Sanhedrin—of Jesus's goodness was working. I felt like a small squirming animal surrounded by cats. Suddenly I needed to get out of there, and fast.

"I have to go."

"Oh, so quickly? Well I certainly understand. Look, this may simply be the idea of an old man who no longer thinks straight, but I am more convinced than ever before—because of you, Judas—that Jesus is someone the Sanhedrin needs to listen to more carefully, perhaps more personally and privately. It would do the Sanhedrin good, and believe me, there are some good and holy men among us. It would not fall on deaf ears."

"I know that. I didn't mean to imply . . ."

"Yes, yes, I know you didn't. But anyway, my idea is to have Jesus meet with a few members of our group, perhaps in a private session. Perhaps if they could talk to him face to face, without the crowd distracting them. If you know of any means—or anyone who has the means of bringing this about—please let me know. It would be very helpful to us all."

I stared at Niam for a second, looking for any sign of disingenuousness. I saw none. His face was plain, simple, truthful; his eyes sparkled with admiration for me. And respect. I saw *respect*. In this manner I was reassured, and felt I had not done any harm to Jesus or my compatriots by talking to Niam. Who knows, maybe I had done some good.

"Good night, Niam. I will remember your request, and if it turns out I know anybody who might help you, I will let you know. Thank you for dinner." I left. I took a roundabout way back that night, in case I was followed, and arrived at the room where Jesus and our group were staying on the outskirts of Jerusalem. I said nary a word to Jesus or my other companions about what had transpired with Niam. It was too early. I had to think. I had to give things a chance to work. But I was certain that somehow, some way, my new, influential contact would be key to recapturing my former status among the disciples. And of course to helping Jesus with his mission.

It's funny now to think how my "status" was so important then. When I first met Jesus—I was on a spice-buying trip to Galilee—it was his lack of status that appealed to me. He was merry, funny, personable. He looked at me with a twinkle in his eye, and sight unseen before that moment said, "Come on Judas, let's go eat."

Several other fellows were with him, just as unpretentious as Jesus, and I said, "Yes, let's. Who are you?"

He did a sweeping bow and a flourish of the hand, saying "Jesus. Let's go."

So off we went, laughing and joking down the road to the home of one of his followers' mother. Of course I had heard of Jesus previously. His teaching in the Galilean synagogues. His healings, which were hard to credit. The sensation he had caused in Cana by creating vintage wine out of nothing but water. Anyway, I was fascinated by these stories. Some said he was a prophet. Some said he was the Messiah. Some felt he had been sent by God to save Israel. Many having met him said he was more than a man, sort of a "god-man"—that is, a miracle worker of divine origin. I wasn't sure what to believe, but I was anxious to hear him myself, to appraise him myself, to judge whether there was any truth to the stories about him. And I'll admit, I was flattered at being singled out by him on that first day. His invitation to "eat" was so jocular, so matter-of-fact. No protocol, no fanfare, just simply something between us guys.

I felt Jesus paid special attention to me that day, and for a long time thereafter. He asked my opinion. He listened to me carefully. He seemed interested in what I had to say. He seemed cognizant of my intelligence, and even told me once how "insightful" I was. He would turn to me in the middle of a discussion with the other disciples, and ask, "Judas, what do you think?" as if my own opinion had greater weight with him than anyone else's. I loved him for this.

I had come from a family that never paid me much mind. My mother was too busy raising her brood, all girls but me; my father Simon had his head in his business, spices, and was always trying to make ends meet. Perhaps from him I got my love for small things, details, and for keeping accounts. But he never really appreciated my talents and stashed me in the back room to deal with the money because I was bad with customers. My deepest thoughts I shared with no one. In my father's opinion, it was only making money, feeding your family, surviving that made sense. And this is the mindset I lived under, until Jesus.

Jesus never worried about money, as far as I could tell. When one of us (most often, me) questioned him about provisions he said, "our Heavenly Father will feed us," shrugged his shoulders, and refused to worry about it. And he was right. Small coins would slip into my bag unsolicited—from family, friends, even the poor. People would feed us when we passed through their villages. A few wealthy supporters also helped. I never knew where it came from, but my money bag was rarely empty. Our little group always, always had enough to eat, a warm enough place to sleep, and shelter over our heads when we needed it. When it was a warm summer night we had the stars as our ceiling. And it was splendid. All of it. For the first time in my life I had a happy, robust group of men with whom I could mostly be myself. Like brothers. I was a little stiffer than the rest of them. I brooded a lot. But I found that their playfulness, their glee, and their absolute devotion to Jesus—the most playful and gleeful of them all—was intoxicating. I became one of them. After sending word to my mother, I never looked back.

In my meaner moments I thought it served my father right. I had wasted years trying to elicit a smile from the old man. But now, a star far brighter had appeared.

My sense of exhilaration over the next three years was hard

to explain. I had always believed in God, but He was more of an intellectual experience. He had never gripped my gut. I was never convinced He would bother, personally, with the likes of me. Jesus changed all that. He showed us what God was really like. In some ways Jesus even resembled God, but not how you would guess. Yes he had authority, understanding, insight, and unworldly intelligence. He was absolutely fearless and unconcerned about his image or reputation. But he was also humble, even shy. He looked pained when you didn't understand him, but he didn't rebuke you. He was patient, quiet, a good listener. He saw the best in you. To the point that you would go out of your way not to disappoint him. Letting him down caused greater grief to me than you can imagine.

And that is what happened, quite by accident, not long after I started walking with him. It was near Sychar, in Samaria. We were passing through, and Jesus sat down at what is known as Jacob's well—a famous spot—to wait while the rest of us went into the neighboring village to buy some food. A woman, a Samaritan woman, had just approached to draw water there.

When we returned from the village and were still far off, we saw that the woman and Jesus were talking together. We were astonished. She had her hands on her hips and seemed to be flirting with him. At one point we heard them both laugh! As we got up closer we could see that the conversation had gotten more serious, but we were still dumbfounded. We wanted to ask him about it but no one said anything. And then we ended up staying another two days in Sychar so Jesus could preach to the woman's townsfolk. She had dragged them all down to the well just to see him!

"But Jesus, think about it. Who was this woman?" I asked a day after we left Samaria. I was the only one of the disciples courageous enough to bring her up.

"What do you mean, Judas?" he asked with a smile.

"What I mean is, she was disreputable. She was living with a man not her husband! And he wasn't the first!"

"Yes, I know."

"And on top of that, she and all her townsfolk. They were Samaritans!"

"Yes."

"Well we Jews don't talk to Samaritans! They're degenerate! Heretics! They've intermarried with pagans! They've used statuary in their temple!!"

"But Judas. Think what you are suggesting. Are the Samaritans not in need of God's word? Would you deny them that?"

"They don't even know who God is. They worship something else, they're not sure what. You are wasting your time."

"Judas, all time belongs to God. Those people opened their hearts to us. They invited me to teach them."

"But the woman herself. Forget she's a Samaritan, forget that. But what are you doing to your reputation by talking to her, by laughing with her? No woman should comport herself that way with a stranger. People will think your own character questionable."

"They already do."

"Well that's why I've brought this up. I feel obligated to protect you, shield you from filthy tongues. But I can't do so unless you listen to me."

"And do what you say?"

"Well . . . sometimes it might make sense . . ." I faltered.

"Judas, Judas. You will never stop wicked tongues. Even if we all did what they wanted."

"But that woman was not worthy of you!"

"Judas, all people are worth something to God. He will come into whatever heart is willing to hear him. Our job is to help people hear him. Don't be like the Pharaisees, shutting people out."

And then I was ashamed. I looked over, and noticed several of the other disciples—James, Philip—listening to our conversation and shaking their heads. They had quickly disavowed any worries similar to my own, and pretended to approve of Jesus's behavior, even though I had heard them questioning it earlier. Resentment rose within me. My ears grew hot, and I got up quickly and moved away from Jesus and the other disciples. I kept to myself that evening—sulked, more like it—and caught Jesus looking at me several times, sadly.

The next day was sunny, with things more or less back to normal, except that I distrusted some of my companions more than before.

But Jesus, I loved more dearly, achingly. I saw he was right, but could not come down off my proud horse and admit it. I made him pay for our estrangement several more days before I lightened up.

This was the first of Jesus's and my misunderstandings. The second major rift came much later in his ministry and had to do with a woman known as Mariamme of Magdala. This woman was reputed to be a slut, but one from an upper-class Hellenized Jewish family, so she was in an odd category. She appeared out of nowhere, accompanied by a hefty older woman and an ageless-looking bald-headed man who had a permanent look of happiness on his face. They simply attached themselves to our band of followers, slept under the starlight with the rest of us, and hung on every word that Jesus said.

Normally I would not have made a fuss. But after I made the usual inquiries (one could not be too careful), I uncovered an unsavory background in Mariamme herself. Her husband had booted her out because of adultery. What is more, she had been publicly exposed and brought to shame because of an adulterous incident in Jerusalem. That is when Mariamme and Jesus first crossed paths—in Jerusalem. Jesus had valiantly saved Mariamme from being stoned, I fear at great cost to his own reputation. I was not there, and a good thing for her, because I would have brought Jesus to his senses and let her take the punishment she deserved. But now, scarcely a year later, here she was again, wantonly traveling without a husband and keeping company with us men.

"She is very intelligent, Judas. And she is seeking God's truth just like you," he said.

"I know, I know. But there is something improper about this. Even if Mariamme didn't have the reputation she has, which even you acknowledge, it is just not fitting to have women, *women*, sleeping out here in the wild with us."

"I'm not sure what you mean." He was so naïve.

"You know exactly what I'm talking about. She is a sinner. Her presence will make *you* look bad. And us of course."

"But that tax collector, Simon, was also a sinner. And you rejoiced just as I did to see him turn from his corrupt ways and back to God. Mariamme has also repented."

"Alright, you can say that. But what if she is here for other reasons? She likes men, that's obvious from her past life. Suppose she becomes a temptation to one of us?"

"Judas I think you need not worry."

"Jesus, I think you are being careless. Stubbornly so." I was getting anxious. I was failing to convince him of the risk. I looked over and noticed some of the other disciples now listening to our conversation, and it became all the more incumbent upon me to prevail. I tried one more time.

"Why don't I talk to her? I could ask her—very graciously—to take her companions and at least reside in some neighboring town every evening. In order not to compromise your mission. She would understand."

"Let her be, Judas. Mariamme is welcome to stay with us as long as it suits her. I need her."

"You need her?" I gasped. "What do you mean you need her?"

"Just what I said. God has a purpose for Mariamme, just as He has for all of us."

I slunk away defeated, but caught a snicker coming from the direction of James. This was not my day.

As it turned out, however, Mariamme and her companions departed in a few days for Sepphoris, her native city. I made the normal inquiries and learned that her estranged husband had died, and her relatives had asked her to return home. Good riddance I thought. That was early summer, in the month of Sivian. We did not see her again until deep winter, in the month of Tevet, just after the Feast of Dedication when she and her companions returned to our company looking much better fed, and better dressed. Mariamme had apparently come into some money. By that time we were hiding out in a place beyond the Jordan, near Bethabara, where John had first baptized. I say hiding because Jesus unfortunately had made so many enemies among the Temple ruling class in Jerusalem that it was actually considered unsafe for him to be there. I wasn't sure. The rumors were that they wanted to arrest him and kill him, but these rumors conflicted with the story I had gotten from Niam, my Temple contact, who professed the desire simply to talk to him. I felt hysteria had taken hold among the disciples. It was all the more necessary for me to bring Jesus together with members of the Sanhedrin so that they could understand his devotion to God, believe his power, and not be appalled by his authority. In other words, I was sure I could fix things if given the chance. All I needed was to convince Jesus, then work with Niam to bring this about.

Convincing Jesus was easier said than done. I had not yet spoken with him about Niam. In fact, I had spoken with nobody. I still had this fear in my belly that Jesus wouldn't understand, or that he would think I was deceitful for having kept Niam a secret for so long.

Anyway, I was just screwing up my courage to talk to Jesus about Niam and a proposed conversation with the Sanhedrin when Mariamme of Magdala (or Sepphoris) came back into the picture with her two companions, the old woman and the bald fellow. I suddenly felt eclipsed. Jesus started to spend longer hours in conversation with Mariamme than I thought proper. Of course her two companions were also there, and we disciples were within a stone's throw, but their laughter and enjoyment of each other's company made me nervous.

"Mariamme is *not* one of the boys. This should not be." I knew this was a sore subject between us, but I couldn't help myself when I finally got Jesus alone in Bethabara.

"Whatever do you mean, Judas?" he asked innocently. I would say impudently, but impudence was not part of Jesus's personality. He simply said what he meant.

"We've talked about this before. I know I shouldn't bring it up again, but—"

"Judas, there are now other women in addition to Mariamme who follow with us from place to place, and sleep under our protection in the open air."

"Yes, I know, but she is just not the kind of person we need hovering around when we return to Jerusalem."

"Oh, and what will we be doing in Jerusalem that Mariamme and her two friends cannot be with us?"

"Well, supposing you wanted the Sanhedrin members to take you seriously? Supposing you wanted to have a discussion with them? We don't need ex-whores flitting in and out—"

"Judas, remember your own life, your own failings, and your own sins. Do not become obsessed with someone else's. It will be the unmaking of you. We *all* need God's forgiveness," he said pointedly, looking me straight in the eye.

And I was ashamed, knowing the things I had kept from him— my plans with Niam, my subterfuge in hiding this contact, and somewhere at the bottom of it all, the pride which motivated me. In a brief flash of truth, I knew that it was my own standing in Jesus's eyes I was trying to redeem, and my own position in relation to the other disciples that I was trying to elevate. Jesus's protection, Jesus's success were not my primary consideration. I ducked my head, and turned from him. I could feel his disappointment, his sadness concerning me, but I didn't have the guts to come out with the truth. After that we scarcely exchanged two words until my next outburst in Bethany.

16 Darmud, Temple Spy

"Impact, impact, impact!" I told Eleizer. "You've got to look at things in context! For all the influence that blind fellow had, Micah, whatever his name was, Jesus might have healed the local mule instead."

"His parents had a trade. They had neighbors. They'll talk. And remember, his parents still have access to the Temple," said Eleizer.

"No they won't talk. Did his parents talk when we brought them in front of the Sanhedrin? They're scared little rabbits. They know what the penalty is."

"You may be right. But their son—what kind of damage could he do?"

"Who cares? Among the cripples on the Royal steps? Who listens to beggars?"

"I see your point. And Micah no longer has access to the Temple, so he's limited."

"I think what we've got to do," I said, "is look ahead. We've got

155

to get Jesus back to Jerusalem. And we've got to get Judas working on our side, even if he doesn't realize it."

"By the way, where is he now?"

"Who? Jesus? Judas?"

"Both."

"We're not sure. We're trying to find out. But we're pretty sure they're not in the city."

Several months passed after this conversation with Eleizer. Fall turned into winter, and Caiaphas was again at boiling point. Jesus had not returned to Jerusalem, and more importantly to me, neither had Judas. Niam was ready and willing, but first Judas had to come back, take the bait. Niam's first successful encounter with Judas back in September was beginning to look like a fond dream.

Then it happened. It was wintertime, the Feast of Dedication, and suddenly Jesus was back in the Temple. Teaching, daytime, surrounded by a crowd. As reported later, Judas apparently took this opportunity to seek Niam out. They had a five minute chat in Niam's office, and Niam adroitly followed up with an invitation to dinner that night. It went exceedingly well. Wine, food, exhilarating conversation. I've watched Niam work, and he is able to apply that artful mixture of erudition, haughtiness, and devil-may-care attitude so that an insecure target finds him irresistible. Then he showers that same target with deference and respect, only tying the knot tighter. It worked well with Judas, who apparently felt himself worthy of high-level company but was under-appreciated and starved for attention. He was extravagantly grateful when he found it.

Niam's report of the encounter acknowledged that Judas was not stupid. He kept watching Niam for signs of deception, or for Niam's probing into areas that endangered Jesus. Judas seemed to feel protective towards his master, and clammed up once or twice when he had exceeded his own boundaries of caution. Also, he left rather suddenly, but Niam was able to smooth over any rough spots and felt certain that this would not be their last contact. He counseled patience. Caiaphas of course remained at boiling point, but his only choice was to wait.

The next cataclysm occurred in Bethany. Jesus had not returned to Jerusalem since wintertime. He was reputed to be in the area of Bethabara, across the Jordan and northeast of Jerusalem in that remote place where John Baptist used to draw crowds. And then suddenly he showed up in Bethany and the earth exploded.

Jesus, it appears, had raised a dead man to life again. Lazarus was his name, the only son of a prominent family in Bethany. Lazarus had friends in Jerusalem, living only a short distance away, and many had been present for the event. The story could easily have been dismissed as a hoax, had we had time, or had we heard about it sooner. But by the time the story got to us it was absolutely drilled into people's minds—and many witnesses attested to the fact—that Lazarus had been in the grave for four days, wrapped in grave cloth, and was stinking like a dead animal when Jesus got to him. The prevailing belief was that Lazarus had really been dead, and that Jesus had really raised him. All of Jerusalem was talking about it, and hordes were tromping up to Bethany to see Lazarus. Not to mention that the crowds professing belief in Jesus were growing into raucous, excited, talkative bands of pilgrims waiting for his arrival in Jerusalem.

Caiaphas demanded a council. The Pharisees and chief priests convened a meeting and I attended with Eleizer. At this gathering there was no attempt to debunk the raising of Lazarus. True or not, we had to deal with the perception of truth.

"What do we do?" someone asked, almost wringing his hands. "This man does many miracles. If we let him thus alone, all men will believe on him. And the Romans shall come and take away both our place and nation." My secret suspicion was that this man belonged to Caiaphas, and had been planted up front to say these very words. In truth, there was no hint anywhere that the Romans were riled up about Jesus, or that they had even noticed him.

To the handwringer Caiaphas responded, "You know nothing at all. Nor do you consider that it is expedient for us, that one man should die for the people, and that the whole nation perish not."

With this statement and subsequent discussion, everyone understood—including those of the Sanhedrin outside Caiaphas's trusted circle—that it would be Caiaphas's intention to put Jesus to death.

And for the pure, patriotic reason of defending Israel. Otherwise, the Romans would come in and stamp us out. Or so Caiaphas wanted us to believe.

The chief priests later insisted that Lazarus should be done away with also, since he himself constituted the only material proof that he was alive. I found this rather silly.

In any case, from that day forward the planning intensified regarding Jesus.

Unfortunately he made himself scarcer than ever. Word was that Jesus escaped from Bethany after the Lazarus event to a city called Ephraim, near the wilderness, and remained there with his disciples. Expectations for his next return to Jerusalem pointed to Passover. Niam was primed. Caiaphas was primed. I was anxious. All of us waited. The only thing we needed was Jesus in Jerusalem and our penetration of his group, the honorable Judas Iscariot, to fall into the pit.

17 Judas Iscariot

We were in Ephraim. I was still shaking, dumbfounded over the raising of Lazarus. For the first time the possibility had occurred to me that Jesus was not only the Messiah, but God Himself, come to earth. You see, I had read the prophecies. I knew them by heart. I had discussed them with Jesus. His answers to my questions were clear, but elusive. I was often not sure what he meant. But he had referred to himself with astonishing frequency as the Son of Man, and this was a mystical figure in the Book of Daniel who at the end of time would come on the clouds of Heaven with the holy angels of God. Jesus was clearly something more than a mere man. The raising of Lazarus, after four days in the cold, stinking grave, had proved it. My heart was thundering still. I couldn't settle down. The other disciples were the same. We could barely look at Jesus without the urge to fall down and worship him.

Word of the event got back to Jerusalem. No surprise, since Bethany was close to Jerusalem and Lazarus had friends in Jerusalem. As the days passed I started to wonder why we remained in Ephraim.

We should go up to Jerusalem! Because of Lazarus, Jesus's fame would precede him. The Sanhedrin would be even more desirous of talking with him. Niam would welcome us with open arms. I began to go over in my mind how I would explain to Jesus what he needed to do next. This would entail my coming clean about my contact with a member of the Sanhedrin, but I hoped to do this in private, without the other disciples gawking about. If Jesus got accepted by the Temple authorities, *then all of Jerusalem would acknowledge him.*

A few days later we left Ephraim and were on the road, heading towards Bethany. It was only six days before Passover and I was sure Jerusalem was our final destination. I began to look at the Lazarus event solely in terms of how we might exploit it. It wasn't that I was in any less awe about what had happened, but my soul couldn't survive at the heights it had soared to. I was intentionally confining myself to practicalities.

Lazarus's two sisters Mary and Martha had dinner waiting for us in Bethany. Theirs was a wealthy household, and the sisters never stinted on food and wine whenever Jesus came through. Especially so now, after their brother Lazarus had been restored to them. As usual, Martha hurried around and busied herself with the cooking and the serving, wisps of hair caught in perspiration on her forehead and cheeks flushed from the kitchen fires. Mary on the other hand sat quietly, even indolently, along the wall of the room listening to every word of our conversation at table. Every time Jesus was in town she seemed to forget her role as woman, and while not exactly engaging in the discussion, seemed to feel she was a part of it. Lazarus her brother, who reclined at table with us, did not rebuke her.

"Judas," Jesus turned to me reclining just to the left of him at table and asked, "who is Isaiah referring to when he says, 'Yet it pleased the Lord to bruise him; he hath put him to grief: when thou shalt make his soul an offering for sin, he shall see his seed, he shall prolong his days, and the pleasure of the Lord shall prosper in his hand'? Who is being bruised and put to grief? Who is becoming an offering for sin?"

This was my element. I loved it when Jesus addressed me directly and asked me to expand on portions of the Holy Scripture. Especially in front of the other disciples. Most of them had little but rote knowledge of the ancient texts.

"Well, references in Isaiah to the unknown 'him' could either refer to Isaiah personally or to Israel as a nation. Most of the time in my opinion they refer to Israel's promised Messiah."

"And how about this passage?" asked Jesus.

"It's hard to say. The fact that the passage speaks of suffering and death—an offering for sin in the Temple means the death of the animal sacrificed—seems to narrow the possibilities. Surely God does not mean Israel to die. And even though we believe Isaiah may have died violently, I don't think he's referring to himself in this passage. Otherwise, several verses earlier, Isaiah wouldn't have associated himself with the 'we' in 'All *we* like sheep have gone astray . . . and the Lord hath laid on *him* the iniquity of us all.' Clearly Isaiah considers himself part of the sinful 'we.' The 'him' is someone else. Who do you think the 'him' is? Who becomes the offering for sin?"

"The Messiah," answered Jesus.

"Well hardly! Isaiah refers to Israel's Messiah in his prophecies numerous times, but it is always as a King, a Counselor, a mighty warrior who will conquer."

"But Isaiah does refer repeatedly in his prophecies to a suffering servant. Who could that be?"

"Well, usually I think it is Israel, suffering as God's chosen servant. Sometimes it may be Isaiah referring to himself, since he experienced great tribulation in bringing God's word to the people."

"But the suffering servant in Isaiah is not only described as dying, but as a willing, obedient victim. 'He is brought as a lamb to the slaughter, and as a sheep before her shearers is dumb, so he opened not his mouth. . . . He hath poured out his soul unto death.' Would this meet our understanding of Isaiah when he was sawn in half? Did he offer himself willingly?"

"Well I don't know . . . I suppose not . . . not exactly."

"And again speaking of the suffering servant, the same passage states that 'The Lord hath laid on *him* the iniquity of us all. . . . For the transgression of my people was he stricken.' Isaiah is again distinguishing between himself—one of the people, one of the transgressors—and the 'righteous servant' who takes their iniquities upon himself and becomes 'an offering for sin.'"

"But this sin offering. If it's not Israel or Isaiah himself, the only other choice is Israel's Messiah. But how could it be the Messiah? He's not supposed to die! Other prophecies say he will live forever!"

"Judas, look across the table. Whom do you see?"

"Our good friend Lazarus, looking sprightly and in the prime of health after . . . after—"

"Exactly."

"After he was dead."

"With God, all things are possible, Judas. A short time ago, Lazarus was in the grave. He now lives. Would that not also be possible for Israel's Messiah?"

"But why would God have the Messiah die?"

"'When thou shall make his soul an offering for sin, he shall see his seed, he shall prolong his days, and the pleasure of the Lord shall prosper in his hand.'"

"You mean the Messiah has to die in order for his seed to live? But how horrible!"

"God's plan for your salvation is much bigger, and much deeper than you might think, Judas."

"Yes, I . . ."

"The suffering servant is one and the same with the conquering Messiah." He paused and looked around the room. We stared at each other with perplexity.

"Judas has shown exceptional understanding for Scripture. But it is time all of you began to look deeper," he said to us, and with that, the conversation ended.

I felt vindicated by Jesus's last words, even though they were more out of kindness on his part than intellectual prowess on mine. But I still couldn't fathom what he meant. The Messiah die?

Nevertheless, it struck me as a very good moment to draw Jesus into a conversation about the Sanhedrin. I could at least introduce the topic, reveal my ruminations on the advisability of such a contact when we got up to Jerusalem, then get into the more embarrassing details about Niam later, when I could talk to Jesus privately. Martha was clearing the plates and vessels away. The other disciples were still reclining, refilling their cups of wine. It seemed like exactly the right time to—

I heard a slight brushing sound to my right and behind me, and noticed that Mary had gotten up from her seat at the wall and had ensconced herself embarrassingly on the floor at Jesus's feet. She had broken a bottle of ointment, spikenard I think, and *expensive*, and was anointing his feet with it. This caught everyone's attention. Though we were all still leaning back on pillows, some of the disciples actually sat up and stared.

Jesus didn't even blink. He took the service done to him serenely, naturally, as if it were the most normal thing in the world. Still reclining at table, he reached over and plucked another grape from the bunch in front of him.

Mary by this point was weeping uncontrollably. She had brought no towel to wipe the oil from Jesus's feet afterwards, looked around only slightly for one through her tears, then proceeded to undo her hair—rope upon rope of long silken tresses—and to use that magnificent rippled mane to wipe away the oil from Jesus's feet. At least in this manner, the ointment had a dual use: Jesus's feet, Mary's hair.

Needless to say, I was furious.

"Why was not this ointment sold for three hundred denari, and given to the poor?" I lashed out. My complaint was beside the point, of course. What really bothered me was that Mary had *interrupted* me when I was on the verge of addressing something delicate with Jesus. She had scuttled my opportunity. Her embarrassing impropriety was secondary. So was the money.

Mary looked up through her hair and her tears, but bent her head back down to Jesus's feet and kept crying. Jesus said, "Let her alone; she has done this against the day of my burying. For the poor always you have with you; but me you have not always."

He was right about the poor, of course. Now I know how puny my criticism must have looked to the other disciples. Some of them thought I was primarily interested in the money, the stupid money, because I was treasurer. Some thought I nicked from the money bag, and regretted the loss of this fine sum. I didn't care. I was honest as the day was long with the money. The thing that concerned me most was her damned timing. How dare she! Once again I looked like a sour, small-minded fool. I ducked my head and refused to say anything to anybody the rest of the evening. I knew I had spoiled it for them all. I could feel Jesus's eyes upon me, but could not bring myself to look back.

Now in retrospect, I see very clearly what was behind Mary of Bethany's emotional reaction. She, a mere woman, had listened to our discussion and hit upon the truth. I, through my rage, saw nothing.

18 Darmud, Temple Spy

It started bad. A lot of people in Jerusalem had heard about the raising of Lazarus up in Bethany, and a lot of them had even been there to see it! The common people, the rabble, were in an uproar. Even some of our Temple leaders were agitated, and starting to doubt their own good sense. Then we heard the rumor that Jesus was on his way from Bethany to Jerusalem right now. In the wake of this rumor a group of small tradesmen, farmers, fish sellers, bakers and other simple folk had plucked palm branches from the trees and set out to meet him en route. What we witnessed from the Temple mount was astounding. First we heard the noise, the shouting coming from the east. Then we heard the music. Someone was playing a flute, as if it were a festival. We climbed up to Solomon's Portico overlooking the western slope of the Mount of Olives and there we saw them descending towards Jerusalem, heading straight for the Temple.

"What the hell do they think they're doing?" asked one of my colleagues.

"It's not a feast day," said someone else. "Who's that poorly dressed figure at the center of it all?"

"Jesus," simultaneously responded several of us, who had been charged with following him all over Galilee.

"Are those palm branches? See what they're waving?"

"Yep, we see it. And that's an ass he's riding on, to make matters worse."

"Ha ha ha. Is that the most glorious mount he could find? What a joke."

"It's not a joke," I said. "It's very serious." I was one of the few among my colleagues who understood this point, not because I had studied the scriptures deeply, but because my uncle Philo had mentioned it once or twice, and somehow I remembered it.

"Based on the prophet Zechariah," I continued, "it is the sign of a King to come riding mounted on a donkey. A horse would signify a conquering King. A donkey means a King who comes in peace. This is probably deliberate."

"Pshaw, what do you know?" said one of my colleagues. "This isn't your area of expertise. I think he couldn't find anything better than an ass! Ha ha!"

"You're right. It isn't my expertise. And you're right again, to most people he looks silly."

"But not to them out there! Look! The crowd is getting bigger! What are they shouting?" asked another colleague.

"Shhhh. Let's listen. 'King,' I caught the word 'King,' and wait, wait, 'Son of David'! What could that *mean*?" asked another.

"I think they are calling *Jesus* 'King' and 'Son of David,'" answered someone else. "But shhh. Let's listen. They're getting nearer—and look, some of the Pharisees have infiltrated the crowd."

"They don't look too happy."

"Yeah, but maybe they'll keep order."

"Look, there's Azar. He's addressing Jesus."

Later we learned that Azar had commanded Jesus to rebuke the crowd, silence them from shouting that he was the "Son of David." Jesus's response was if he silenced the crowd, the very stones would cry out! He had an acute ability to twist a Pharisaical beard with the very scriptures that beard could quote from memory. The "stones crying out" of course was a reference to the prophet Habakkuk.[1]

After Jesus's disastrous (for us) entry into Jerusalem, we set to work with even more determination to get to Judas. As it turned out, it was not all that hard. He came to us.

It happened the evening after Jesus's return to Jerusalem. According to the account given to us, Niam played it coolly. Meaning, he refrained from acting overly pleased or enthusiastic about Judas's sudden appearance at his door, out of breath. Niam was working on some reports required by the Sanhedrin, so fortunately was still in his office at an hour later than usual.

"I had hoped I would find you here. Am I interrupting your work?"

"Why Judas, what a pleasant surprise. I haven't seen you in months! Where have you been keeping yourself?"

"Oh, in various parts of the hinterland. Frankly I am glad to be back in Jerusalem, in civilization."

"Sounds as if you've been wandering in the wilderness! Why are you out of breath?"

"Oh I'm sorry. I only have a few minutes. I, er, I have another engagement."

Niam raised his eyebrow, but said nothing.

"I mean I am expected somewhere in a few minutes. I simply wanted to say hello and—"

"Well surely you have more than a few minutes for me! You so rarely get to Jerusalem! How about stopping by at the same time tomorrow evening? We can have supper."

Judas gave a faint smile, but it was clear he was pleased at Niam's invitation. "I'll see what I can do. Thank you."

Niam is a master. Based on his report, Judas showed up promptly the next evening and Niam made no mention of Jesus. He did little more than entertain Judas with amusing insider stories about the Sanhedrin, ask his thoughts on scriptural points, and flatter him with rapt attention. Niam's words were like a caress. Judas was aglow, almost drunk by the end of the evening with the notion that

---

[1] Habakkuk 2, 11

he was being taken seriously, and valued. Had he lacked this kind of reassurance among Jesus's followers?

"Well, Judas, I am sorry to say goodnight, but it is late for me, while you are a young man and have the whole night ahead of you. Do you have many friends here in Jerusalem?"

Judas froze momentarily, but looking into Niam's face judged the question to be well-intended. "Oh a few," he said.

"Well if you are so inclined, you are welcome to bring one or more of these friends with you the next time. I always like company, especially at this time of evening. It diverts me from my work. And I'm sure being as intelligent as you are, that you have chosen your friends wisely."

Judas swallowed, no doubt thinking about his friendship with Jesus and the disciples. "Thank you Niam. That is very kind of you, and I will keep your invitation in mind." And he took his leave.

On the morrow, Niam made it a point to be close by in the Temple courtyard when Jesus passed through with his disciples, including Judas. Niam made it very apparent to Judas that he had seen him, and doubly apparent that Niam made the association of Judas with Jesus, and Jesus with Judas.

Judas looked shocked at seeing Niam, then quickly grasped what Niam must be thinking: Judas had lied. No words were exchanged until later that day.

At dusk Judas found his way again to Niam's office. He was glistening with sweat.

"Niam, may I talk to you?"

"I don't know," Niam responded, shaking his stylus and not even looking up. "I'm rather busy right now."

"But I wanted to explain . . ."

"You need not explain, Judas," he said looking towards the man. "I see that I have been foolish myself, by thinking we were perhaps friends. But really, I do need to get back to work," he looked down again at his papyrus.

"No, I need to explain about Jesus!"

"Judas, I now understand, and confirmed it by doing some checking, that you have been an associate of Jesus of Nazareth for a very long time. Almost three years to be exact." Niam's eyes narrowed.

"I was nervous, afraid about telling you. When you asked that time. I wasn't sure of your intent, or rather the Temple leadership's. You know there are so many tales of their wanting to kill him."

"Well of course you'll always believe what you want to believe. Now really, I must get back to work. May I have someone show you to the door?" he asked coldly.

"No, I can find my own way. I'm sorry, Niam." Judas bent his head and started to trudge off.

"Wait a minute," Niam said as he raised himself from the table and came over to the door. He put his hand on Judas's shoulder, and gave him a kindly smile and a wink. "Let's just regard it as a mistake, shall we? We'll see each other soon."

Judas brightened, but still walked off quietly and hesitantly.

This was of course the hot-cold formula that always ensnares a person as insecure as Judas. I have used it successfully myself. Niam knew Judas would be back, and if we handled it right we would have Jesus too.

A few days later, Judas did scuttle back. It was two days before the Passover. He appeared unannounced at Niam's office, his hair wet with sweat and his eyes with a pained, almost yearning expression. At least this was how Niam described it in his report.

"Well Judas. So here you are again," said Niam, trying to remain as expressionless and non-committal as possible.

"Yes Niam. I am back. To make amends," he offered.

"Yes?"

"What I mean is, I would like to offer you the chance—you and the Sanhedrin, that is—of speaking with Jesus. Privately."

"Yes."

"I'm sorry I didn't offer this opportunity before. I, I, I didn't know whether I could trust the . . . er . . . situation."

"You mean, whether you could trust me?"

"Well. No, not really. I don't know. It just didn't seem right."

"And what changed your mind, Judas?"

"Well I got to thinking that Jesus might be going down the wrong path. He has always aligned himself carelessly, almost exuberantly, with the wrong sorts of people."

"You mean beggars, prostitutes, lepers, tax collectors?"

"Yes. You knew? I didn't think it was so—"

"So widely known? We at the Temple may be isolated, but we're not idiots. And people do talk to us, you know."

"Of course. I guess I underestimated you."

"Perhaps so."

"Anyway, Jesus is wasting his time with those people, it seems to me. I thought instead that if Jesus were known to the Sanhedrin, the Temple leaders, really known to them, really conversant with them, that you, too—as a body—would be as convinced as I am, as we who follow him are, of his intelligence, his good intent, his ability to work with you, not against you, for the sake of Israel. Essentially, you see, he is on the same side as you are."

"I am sure of that. That is why I made the suggestion in the first place, many months ago (remember?) about our meeting with him. Tell me, Judas, is Jesus willing to talk to us privately? Have you broached this with him?"

"Well, ah, no not yet. I meant to, I wanted to, but the circumstances never presented themselves—"

"So I take it, Jesus is not willing to walk into the Temple tomorrow for an announced meeting with the Sanhedrin."

"No, he is not."

"Well, then let's deal with the situation we've got. Jesus doesn't know your plans for him, but somehow you think he would be willing to speak with us if the idea were presented to him?"

"Yes, that's sort of it."

"And you, naturally, would like us to be the ones—not you—to broach the idea with him?"

"I guess so, yes."

"Alright, then let's put our heads together. You see we have a little problem broaching the idea in broad daylight, on the Temple grounds."

"Why would that be?"

"Well, Judas, you know as well as I that Jesus could refuse to meet with us. In front of a crowd of his admirers at the Temple, it makes it ten times as bad. Caiaphas would be mortified. It would be the thousandth time Jesus had twisted the beards of the Sanhedrin, but the first time for Caiaphas personally. We'd like to avoid that if we can."

"Well what else is there to do?"

"Let me see. I'm thinking."

"Maybe I could—"

"Wait! I've got it. You, Judas, know where Jesus stays in the evenings, don't you?"

"Yes," said Judas guardedly.

"Well, it would be a simple matter to lead one of us, or a few of us to him after dark, wouldn't it? So if Jesus refuses to meet with the Sanhedrin and tells us to get out of his sight—"

Judas gasped, "But that wouldn't happen!"

"It could happen. So if Jesus rejects our invitation to meet with the Sanhedrin, at least it wouldn't be in public, in front of the crowds at the Temple. Only his small group of followers need know."

"Well I see your reasoning . . ."

"You would be doing an immense favor to Caiaphas by handling it discreetly this way. Because if it didn't work, we would be saving embarrassment all around. Also, Caiaphas would be enormously indebted to you personally."

"How do you mean?"

"Well Caiaphas has been wanting to speak directly to Jesus for a long time. Privately, man to man. He feels sure they would see eye to eye on many things, and instead of continually being adversaries, could join forces for the good of Israel. If this works, Caiaphas will be ready with a nice sum of money to support Jesus's mission—"

"No! Jesus wouldn't take it. He's not concerned with that sort of thing."

"Well you can always turn it down, it's of no import. Caiaphas just wants to show his appreciation. I'm sure he doesn't intend to offend anyone. So, where were we? Do you have any questions?"

"Yes. If I agreed to lead you to Jesus after dark, who would be in the group I would lead?"

"Oh just a few officers from the Temple. We'll keep it small."

"By officers, do you mean soldiers?"

"There will have to be a few, for the protection of the Sanhedrin members that come along. They would insist on that. But don't worry. I will handpick the group myself."

"You won't be part of the group yourself, Niam?"

"No Judas, it is more fitting that I await you at the Temple, as part of Jesus's welcoming party. But of course you will be with him the whole time."

Judas remained silent for a few moments, with his eyes transfixed on the candle on Niam's desk. The circles of sweat under his armpits had traveled almost to his waistband, and his forehead was soaked and shiny. He looked up at Niam and croaked, "Yes, I think it can be done. I will come back tomorrow night. I will lead you to Jesus's location."

Niam put his hand on Judas's shoulder and pressed it in a friendly manner. "Until tomorrow night, then."

19 Judas Iscariot

I had just been to see Niam. I had offered to put the Sanhedrin in touch with Jesus. I had been too cowardly or maladroit to tell Jesus about this beforehand. Perhaps I was afraid he wouldn't like the idea? The disciples' reaction would be brutal. So I had agreed to lead members of the Sanhedrin to Jesus, so they could ask him privately about an audience. I didn't understand why the topic had to be broached under cover of nightfall. I understood Niam's concern about avoiding embarrassment to Caiaphas, in case Jesus refused. But why was I thinking about Caiaphas? It boiled down to myself. I wanted to please both parties. I dreaded rejection by either. So I would act merely as a go-between, the guy with bright ideas who made things happen.

I woke up with a headache the next morning and stormed silently about the next several hours conversing with no one. No matter. The other disciples hadn't spoken to me in days. Jesus himself seemed preoccupied. My outbursts and hurt feelings had already placed obstacles between him and me. And now, my slightly shady connection with Niam all these months had matured into a full blown *plan* which would be hard to explain. I carried the guilt of that thought as we walked together to a small house in Jerusalem, where we were to have dinner. It belonged to one of Jesus's followers.

It was still light when our little band marched up the steps to that private room. It was springtime, and just before Passover. The room was small, so none of the women was there—just us men. I was too twisted inside to want to eat. As we entered the room I stayed close to Jesus.

"Judas, sit here," he said, and motioned to the cushions just to the left of him. John was on his right. I kept trying to get Jesus's eye, but it was difficult the way we reclined because the back of Jesus's head was to me, and his face was to John. During supper Jesus was mostly silent. I couldn't get him to engage in any discussion of Scripture. Then when supper was over he did the oddest thing.

He got up from the table and took off his robe and his cloak, and laid them aside. Then he grabbed a towel and wrapped himself in it, like a slave or common servant about to perform a chore. Then he filled a basin with water, got down on his hands and knees and proceeded to wash the feet of John, and in succession each of us men! After cleaning each foot he wiped it with the towel he was wearing around his waist. It was a messy, dirty job, the kind only a menial would do. I wanted to stop him from demeaning himself in this way but fortunately, before I made a fuss, Peter did it for me.

"Lord, you are washing *my* feet?" asked Peter, abruptly sitting up when Jesus kneeled in front of him. John and several disciples ahead of Peter sat there dazed.

Jesus pulled one of Peter's feet forward by the ankle and dipped his own hands in the basin preparing to wash it. He looked up momentarily,"What I'm doing you won't understand now, but you will understand later."

Peter jerked his foot backwards and away from Jesus's hands. "Nope, you shall never wash my feet," he said shaking his head.

Jesus gently pulled Peter's foot towards him again and said, "If I don't wash you, then you have no part with me."

Peter looked alarmed, quickly stuck both of us feet out and

extended both hands palms up. "Then Lord, not my feet only, but also my hands and my head!"

"He that is washed needs only his feet washed to be clean all over. And you are clean, but not all of you," Jesus said, looking around generally. His eyes settled momentarily on me, and a dagger went into my stomach.

I was last in succession. When Jesus came to me, I sat mutely while he washed my feet. His face was quiet and determined. When he finished, he looked at me kindly for a full second, then dried my feet with the towel and got up from the floor.

Then he put on his clothes again, sat down at the table, and explained what he had done for us. He told us that if he, our Lord and Master, washed our feet then we ought also to wash one another's feet. "The servant is not greater than his lord." He was laying down an example for us. I had tears in my eyes. I saw at that moment my own immense shortcomings in this area. I was always bristling over someone's slight, offended over someone's remark, jealous of my own personal dignity. Jesus had tossed his own personal dignity aside like an insignificant crumb, in order to show us what true majesty was.

Then rather abruptly Jesus announced that "one of you shall betray me."

We all looked at each other, wondering whom he could mean. I would have punched any man in the face who betrayed our master! I would be ready to kill him! I looked at the faces of each of my compatriots with the same wondering, suspicious eye that they looked at each other, and at me. There were murmurings and whisperings all around the table. I saw John say something to Jesus, and Jesus respond. Then Jesus leaned over to me and offered a piece of bread soaked in the last delicious droppings of fat. Almost like a peace offering. It made me smile, because he had probably noticed how little I had eaten that night.

But then he said to me, "What you have to do, do quickly."

I got up immediately, I'm not sure why. I grabbed my bag and left the house. Outside on the stoop, I paused to think. My gut contracted. What had Jesus meant? Had he known all along what

I was planning for him, for his benefit? He was more than intelligent, more than insightful. He had God's gift of prophecy. He had invited me to sit next to him at dinner. He had looked at me kindly and even dipped a morsel of bread for me. He seemed to be showing me favor again. So it was not hard for me to convince myself, as I walked along, that Jesus knew what I was up to, and had given his consent. He had even allowed me a graceful exit to go see Niam at the end of the meal.

I now enter the part where I can make no excuses for myself. I've given up on that. Only shame and horror drive me. I am determined to finish this account in the hope that my own failings will be known, and avoided, by others. I myself do not deserve to see tomorrow.

It was night. The Temple was looming before me in the darkness and for the first time appeared like a huge crouching bug, all its legs tucked under it. I entered via a small door on the western side, where Niam's man Rubin was watching for me. I found my way through the labyrinth of underground corridors and descending stairways to Niam's office. He was there waiting for me.

"Come on, let's go," he said when he saw me. "The others are waiting."

He walked me briskly to an upper level, where I saw a lit room with twenty or so men standing around. More than half of them were soldiers with swords and staves and unlit torches. I halted, and would not go in.

"What's this about? You said only several Sanhedrin members and a few guards!"

"Look, Caiaphas is there. He's getting impatient. He's already been waiting an hour or two," Niam said as he took my elbow and pulled me forward.

Suddenly I faced a chorus of voices pounding in my ears. It was somewhere between angels' song and the screeching of hell. Caiaphas was addressing me, but I couldn't understand what he was saying. Niam nudged me from behind.

"I'm sorry, sir. Could you please repeat what you just said?" Why was I being so polite? I wanted to turn and run.

"We are so grateful that you have come to us tonight, Judas," said Caiaphas stepping forward. "We have already been waiting several hours, but no matter, you are here."

"Yes, sir." Again I was being so civil!

"We understand that you will take us to Jesus's location tonight, in preparation for his talk with the Sanhedrin. Is that correct?"

"Well, I ah I'm no longer sure."

"What do you mean, not sure?" Caiaphas asked with an oily smile barely concealing the gritting of his teeth underneath. He clenched his claws.

"Well," I said, trying to put together some courage in myself though my knees were giving out and my ears were still pounding with that hellish chorus. "I thought the group I would be leading to find Jesus would be much smaller," I looked around at this armed band. "I thought there would be Sanhedrin members among them, and there are none."

"Yes, Judas," he said gently. "We had to change plans. There have been reports about, disturbing reports of persons wishing to assassinate members of the Sanhedrin. I cannot allow the leaders of our nation to take that sort of risk, especially at night and on the eve of Passover."

"But will you not send even one Sanhedrin member along? Niam, for instance? That was after all the plan."

"But why is that necessary, Judas?" Caiaphas still spoke softly and patiently to me, as if I were a backward child. "You will be with the group. You yourself can explain to Jesus what it is we want."

"*I? I can explain?*" I thought to myself how I had been unable to explain this escapade with Niam to anyone for the last six months!

"Yes, of course you can." Caiaphas looked at Niam standing slightly behind me. "Niam has told me how remarkable you are, how intelligent. I'm sure you can find a way."

"Well then if it is up to me and me alone to broach the topic," I asked daringly, "then why do I need the soldiers?"

"Do not be impudent," snapped Caiaphas. "You forget whom you are speaking to." Caiaphas's face now got very stern and expressionless. "You need the soldiers to escort Jesus safely to the Temple for the interview, and safely home again. You are also aware that there are death threats out against your Master?"

"But wait a minute. Isn't this a total reversal?"

"What do you mean?" Caiaphas asked unsmilingly.

"I mean, that as it was described to me, by Niam, simply the question was to be put to Jesus. The question of whether he would agree to talk to the Sanhedrin. The meeting itself was not to occur until later."

"This is taking entirely too much time," said Caiaphas dismissively. "It is late in the evening, and you have already kept us waiting for almost two hours. And now you have the audacity to tell us how and when would be our best time to meet with Jesus?" He turned and started to walk away.

"Wait just a minute!" said Niam rather forcefully. "Caiaphas, let me speak to Judas."

Niam huddled with me and turned on the old charm. "Judas, I know you're upset. Caiaphas damn him has his gruff, disagreeable ways. But he is really a good, simple man in his heart. He thinks you are throwing up unnecessary obstacles, details which you are insisting upon which are really secondary. The main thing is getting Jesus together with Caiaphas. Then everything will be resolved."

I felt myself weakening in front of Niam's silken voice. "But this is not what you described to me," I said, trying to reason.

"Well if it makes you feel any better, they switched the plans on me, too. I'm not at the top. I'm not privy to everything. But believe me. Caiaphas himself is a good man. He has Israel's best interests at heart. He is anxious to be aligned with Jesus. How he goes about it . . . well, he has his own ways."

"I guess . . ."

"But whatever you do, Judas, don't offend him. Caiaphas has a long memory. How you handle the next few minutes could have long-term repercussions for not only you, but for Jesus and all of the people who follow him."

"I can see that."

"Come let's go back to Caiaphas, and try a more conciliatory approach," Niam said as he gently took my elbow and led me to Caiaphas who was now seated, tapping his fingers, looking unhappy.

"Caiaphas, sir," said Niam. "Judas would like to try to work out some agreement between yourselves. He knows it is in the best interests of his country, and of himself," he said patting me on the shoulder.

I swallowed, feeling the old desire to please, and the old fear of rejection. "Caiaphas, sir, I would like to cooperate if I can. But you must assure me that no harm, no harm whatsoever, will come to Jesus."

Caiaphas smiled broadly and leaned forward, "Why of course, Judas, that is why we are sending the soldiers. Precisely to protect Jesus from harm."

I was afraid to push the alternate suggestion of why didn't I—all alone—go to Jesus and get his consent. They had put such planning into this meeting, the details they had put together already had physical momentum. Caiaphas was impatient, Niam was urging me forward, my need for approval was palpable—for those silken words and those pats on the back. Everything compelled me in some uncanny way. I looked at the faces before me. At Caiaphas, Niam and others I recognized from the Sanhedrin—all dignified, handsomely robed, lofty in authority—and they were looking back at me respectfully, expectantly.

"Alright." I set my teeth and was now determined to get this over with as quickly as possible. It would be a blink of an eye, and we would get Jesus back to safety. I suppressed my worries about the danger of this enterprise, the soldiers, the secret meeting with the Sanhedrin, and instead concentrated on the good it would reap. Soon we would be laughing about it as we marched again around Galilee.

Niam put his arm around my shoulder, and said, "Good boy."

"Wait one second," said Caiaphas raising his finger and with the other hand motioning to one of his aides. "Consider this a token of the total support we will be able to provide your group in the future." An aide placed a small heavy bag of coins in my hand. "And for the trouble you have gone to yourself, Judas."

"But—" I said, about to raise another protest.

"Come on," hurriedly whispered Niam. "Let's not embarrass him. You can give this back later if you don't want it." He ushered me out the door and asked me which Temple exit I wanted to use. I motioned to the one looking out towards the Mount of Olives. As we walked, I looked back and counted fifteen Temple guards following us.

Niam faded out at the gate. "Good luck," he said.

I was so upset about the image of this band of men following me, soldiers all, carrying lanterns, torches and weapons that I forgot to hand back to Niam the bag of money given me by Caiaphas. I was also suddenly aware that the question which I had avoided addressing with Jesus for the longest time, about his audience with the Sanhedrin, was now exclusively up to me. I would have to tell him, confess my long contact with Niam, *and* explain what an armed group of fifteen Temple officers was doing standing behind me—all at the same time.

As we marched up to the garden where I knew I would find Jesus, on the slopes of the Mount of Olives, I tried to think what I would say. I could not come up with any words.

We came to the spot, but must have created a lot of noise in our approach because Jesus came forward out of a grove of trees to meet us. He saw me immediately and looked me directly in the eye as he said, "Whom do you seek?"

This was the moment for me to explain to him why I was there, backed up by soldiers, and that despite the appearances, our intentions were benign. Instead my tongue froze. I couldn't move my legs or my arms.

One of the soldiers yelled back, "Jesus of Nazareth."

When Jesus answered, "I am he," the whole company of soldiers took several steps back and fell to the ground, as if in awe or fright.

Jesus asked again, "Whom do you seek?"

Another soldier croaked from his place on the ground, "Jesus of Nazareth."

"I have told you that I am he: if therefore you seek me, let these others go their way," Jesus answered as he motioned to his followers cowering nearby behind the foliage.

A few soldiers stood up and started approaching Jesus gingerly. Then Peter came from off to the side, drew his sword and attacked one of the men, a servant of Caiaphas himself, and cut off his ear.

Jesus moved forward and told Peter to put his sword away. He said, "shall I not drink the cup which my Father has given me?"

That episode propelled the other armed men into action. They got off the ground and rushed forward. There was shouting and confusion as some of the officers scuffled with the disciples. Three soldiers grasped Jesus by the arms, held him by the hair, and bound him with tight leather straps around his neck and wrists. The disciples scattered. I stood frozen in place yelling at everyone, at the guards as they shackled Jesus, at the disciples as they ran in every direction, at God. It was at that moment, when they bound him and all his friends disappeared but me, that I realized the sinister intent of this venture.

The soldiers started moving down the hillside with Jesus marching in the middle. They were pushing him and laughing as he stumbled. I ran after them, and thought of muscling my way to the front and yelling that they had confused their orders, that Jesus wasn't supposed to be a prisoner. But in horrible hindsight I knew I was wrong. This is what they had intended all along. My role had been played and God forgive me I had even been paid.

At that moment, just as I remembered the bag of silver in my pocket, I noticed two men following us stealthily from behind. It was dark, but the way they walked and their silhouettes in the shadows resembled Peter and John. Overcome with shame I tried to hide myself among the group of soldiers. I didn't want Peter or John to see me and ask what the hell I was up to. We reached the bottom of the slope, crossed the brook of Cedron, and headed towards the high priest's palace.

"Who is this fellow? He doesn't look like one of you," the palace gatekeeper said when we got to the door, motioning at me.

"He's alright. He's our 'associate,'" said the head officer sardonically.

Once inside the palace, they dragged Jesus to Annas first. I say dragged, because they had rushed Jesus down the Mount of Olives at breakneck speed, and since his hands were shackled, he was exhausted and bleeding from having fallen several times.

Annas was the father-in-law of Caiaphas and a crusty old soul reputed to have a knife for a tongue. Seeing Jesus, he almost immediately waved his hand in dismissal and said, "Take him to Caiaphas."

Caiaphas's eyes sparkled as he watched Jesus being pushed into the room. He smothered a look of triumph then asked Jesus, in strictly neutral tones, to tell him about his doctrine and disciples.

Jesus did not kowtow the way I had. He looked directly into Caiaphas's eyes and responded, "I spoke openly to the world; I always taught in the synagogue and in the temple, where everyone can listen. I have said nothing in secret. Why ask me? Ask those who heard what I said. They know what I said."

"You dare to answer the high priest in this manner?" shouted one of the officers and slapped Jesus square in the face with the palm of his hand.

Jesus was almost knocked sideways by this blow, but righted himself despite the shackles. "If I have spoken evil, say what evil I have spoken. But if I have spoken well, why do you hit me?"

I was getting frantic by this point. I had not yet seen Niam as part of the so-called "greeting party," so I searched for him in the crowd standing around Caiaphas. There he was at the back. I moved around to the side and to a point where I was directly behind Niam (who didn't see me), and where I had a direct view of Jesus's face standing in front of Caiaphas. Jesus was still standing erect, meeting the gaze of Caiaphas without flinching. I tapped Niam on the shoulder.

"Niam we have to talk. Please. Now," I said urgently.

Niam looked around with some surprise. "What are you doing here? You're not supposed to be here!"

"You've got to stop this," I whispered. "This is not what I intended!"

"Shhhh," someone said, since Caiaphas was addressing Jesus.

Niam grabbed me by the shoulder looking irritated, and walked me hastily out the door. "Judas, this is not the time to discuss things. I need to be in the room with Caiaphas."

"But it is sounding like a trial! Not an audience! And the way they bound him and brought him down off the mountainside! And all my friends, his followers, have run away."

"Yes, and he's alone in front of Caiaphas," said Niam with a smile he couldn't prevent.

"What . . . what are you smiling about? This is in direct violation of what you and I agreed upon, what we discussed several nights ago. What Caiaphas even affirmed! *That no harm would come to him.*"

"Judas, I have to go now," his eyes were very cold. "You have your reward, so hang onto it. Those silver coins may come in handy now that—"

At that moment the doors opened and a large company of Temple officers marched Jesus out, followed by Caiaphas and his coterie. After they passed, Niam grabbed the arm of one of Caiaphas's servants who was bringing up the rear.

"What transpired in there? Where are they taking the prisoner now?"

"*Prisoner?*" I gasped.

"He committed blasphemy," said the servant excitedly. "Right in front of the high priest, in front of multiple witnesses. They've condemned him to be guilty of death!"

"But our Law. It doesn't permit an execution," said Niam, still holding onto the servant's arm.

"Pilate will do that," he jerked his arm away and looked back over his shoulder as he ran after the departing group. "Pilate will put him to death."

My heart stopped beating. At that moment I saw what would happen, and what I had done. I had brought it about. My cursed desire to please everyone, to be everyone's darling, my pride, my self-imposed isolation, my intellectual arrogance, my touchy dignity. I dug the bag of silver coins out of my pocket and flung it at Niam. He caught it.

"What am I supposed to do with this?" he asked, and handed it back to me.

"I've sinned, I've betrayed innocent blood!" I shouted at him.

Several of his colleagues standing nearby overheard this exchange, and chuckled. Niam looked over at them and smiled. They knew exactly who I was.

This little exchange infuriated me even more, so I flung the bag across the room towards them, where it landed spilling on the stone floor. One of them scoffed, "Who cares? That's your problem."

Others laughed. Niam turned from me and walked over to them.

I ran out of the room, out of the Temple. I fled physically but I couldn't flee my guilt, my horror. I still cannot. Today, two days after Jesus's trial, I sit alone in this room with the shutters drawn, the doors closed. I am down to my last two candles as I complete this treatise. I haven't conversed with anyone since I started. The landowner of this wreck of a house in which I sit knows to take this manuscript to my father Simon, in upper Judea, when it is finished. My father at least deserves to know what became of me, and about the sycophantic pride and desire for praise which ruined me. Most of all he deserves to know—as does my whole family—of the Light which I followed, and which I killed. Now all that remains is for me to kill myself.

20 Pontius Pilate

T he road was brutal. Ninety-five years under Rome and this wretched country had little to show for it. No engineering achievements. No decent highways. No architecturally graceful bridges. Nothing laid out meticulously straight in an east-west fashion. Just a dusty little backwater with labyrinthine cities, sheep's paths, rock-covered trade routes, and silent, resentful people. You'd think they would have welcomed us. But no, we were dirt under their feet.

"Bring the troops in closer. We'll camp here tonight." I pointed to a mound of grassy ground with a few olive groves scattered at the top. A small, unsullied rivulet wound its way along at the bottom.

"Aye, sir. And your wife?"

"Give her and the boys that shady spot at top. Set me up next to her." I imagined Claudia was tired. We had started out early the day before, leaving Caesarea Maritima at an ungodly hour before sunrise. I hated these treks to Jerusalem. We still had another day's march to go.

The sun was sliding toward the horizon and I stopped my horse for a moment to feel the cool breeze that was coming up. In some ways Judaea reminded me of my native Samnium, taming my father's horses, riding over those hills from dawn to twilight. It had the same green softness in the spring.

But Passover was an ugly time to go to Jerusalem. Nothing but trouble, year in year out. Claudia Procula (my wife) was more understanding of the Jews. She respected anyone who practiced religion earnestly. Even if it wasn't her religion! But I detested them—their dead seriousness, their fervor, their self-righteousness. As if they actually believed what they said!

"Prefectus, Sir," he saluted, "we are setting up camp. Shall I take your mount?"

"What? Oh yes," I said, somewhat surprised that someone was speaking to me. I dismounted, grabbed my soldier's pack and blanket, and walked up the hill towards my family.

Claudia was unpacking our household gods, which she always brought along when we travelled. She handled these with great care. She wouldn't let the servants touch them.

"Ave, my husband. How goes it?" she smiled.

I smiled back at her as the two boys—twins—rushed to my knee and vied for the best position. They were muscular little creatures at two and one-half, and would make fine warriors one day. They were the apple of my eye.

"Boys, boys, let your father be! He's had a long day," she said as she gathered them together and gave me a kiss on the cheek.

"Claudia, I am still concerned about you and the little ones. I do not normally like to bring you along with me when I travel, but I hesitated leaving you in Caesarea alone for such a long time." I shook my head. "I don't know how long I'll have to be in Jerusalem. There are mad men cropping up all over the country. Like flies on ripe fruit they swarm the capital on holy days."

"I am very happy to be with you wherever you go, Pilate," her eyes sparkled at me. "It is no hardship. And the boys, well—they think they are on an adventure!"

"Yes, yes I see that. Hey you hellions, come over here! Don't bother the men when they're setting up camp!" They came racing back to me, laughing and pushing each other. They were ready for battle. The little animals would get riding lessons when we got back to Caesarea. Their mother wanted to wait until they were three, but they were big for their age. We'd see how strongly our equestrian blood ran through their veins.

"I noticed you received news today," Claudia looked at me sideways while still unpacking "her gods" and setting them on a perch inside her tent. One for the hearth, one for the harvest, one for human fertility, all homely earthen figures, squat and fat. "Was it from Rome?" she asked.

"The news? Yes it was," I answered. "I'll have to tell you about it later—"

"Sir!" A tribune—Sergius—had just approached and saluted me. "Some of the boys have, ahem, requisitioned animals from a neighboring flock. May we have your permission to prepare them?"

"Of course," I said. "But keep the maximum number of soldiers on watch. All night, you understand? We are a small company." I looked back at my wife's tent. "And put two additional men up here next to my wife's tent."

"Yes, sir!" He saluted and walked briskly off.

"Well how about now?" Claudia said, returning to our conversation. "Anything new on the Sejanus affair?"

"Shhh. We'll talk inside, after the boys are asleep."

We waited until the men had eaten, and my boys had been fed and put to bed. Then I asked Claudia to join me in my ceremonial tent. This was reserved for affairs of state, discussions with my advisors, and review of maps. No one entered this tent without my invitation, and soldiers guarding my family's tent next door knew not to get close enough to overhear our conversations. Not if they valued keeping their ears attached and tongues in place.

"The missive from Rome was not good news," I began, once inside.

Claudia looked at me silently, and waited.

"They are still arresting former friends of Sejanus. Most recently, an entire family got rounded up—including sons and daughters and babes in arms. Tiberius's suspicions know no bounds." Sejanus had been Tiberius Caesar's regent in Rome, appointed when Tiberius retired to live in Caprea. Sejanus had become overweening in his power grab and two years ago Tiberius executed him.

"But where does that leave *you?* Sejanus secured your appointment! He . . . *he lobbied Tiberius on your behalf.*"

"Yes, yes I know. But keep in mind that was six-seven years back. Sejanus hasn't done anything for me since and I can't see his chirping favorably of me to Tiberius. Not in the later years anyway. Sejanus was much too concerned with his own advancement to concern himself with the likes of me."

"Well maybe it will help if Tiberius simply forgets about you."

"I'm not sure that will occur, because I send in regular reports concerning Judaea. I'm sure Tiberius reads them."

"But—"

"But what would help is for Tiberius to forget my connection to Sejanus. Sejanus was extremely busy after the emperor retired from public life. He was setting himself up as Tiberius's successor. He might not have thought even to mention me more than once or twice."

"Let's hope. But how can we know?"

"And remember. Tiberius is partial to those of equestrian rank."

"Well that's small comfort. But why is he so suspicious of everyone? Why is he killing so many people off?"

"Claudia you know as well as I do that he is old, decrepit. Maybe his mind is going too."

"But he's the Emperor! The next thing to a god!"

"Pshaw. That pansy?"

"Pilate!" she said in horror. "Someone might hear you!"

"Just a minute," I stepped quietly outside the tent, and circled around it. No one was close by. Two soldiers sat on either side of our family tent. Each kept a cautious eye on my adjacent tent, but neither was close enough to hear anything.

"We're okay," I said upon re-entering. "If I had caught anyone listening in, not to mention napping, well they know the penalty. But fortunately, no one was."

"Anyway," she said inquiringly. "Why—?"

"Claudia, you've seen corruption at close hand. You know the temptations of unlimited power. He is merely a human being. Akin to all the other groveling, cowardly, sniveling, perverts around him. And when his position is threatened—"

"Yes, I see. It sounds silly, but I often wish there were some human that *was* a god, that *acted like* a god, that had the dignity and bearing of a god. Instead all we've got are despicable old-age adolescents. Spewing evil."

"I hope you don't include *me* in that crowd!"

"Don't be silly. You know you're the only one I ever trusted. The only one I ever will."

"That's dear of you to say, Claudia," I kissed her on the forehead. "But I know you also trust in our Roman deities. Otherwise you wouldn't carry them with you on our trips to Jerusalem. I know you rely on them to protect our small boys."

"Yes I do. Even though I think in my heart that there is something bigger behind them all, protecting us."

"What on earth do you mean?"

"I can't explain it. Sometimes I get a feeling—" She looked in the direction of the boys' tent. "I've got to go. I have to pray before I go to sleep. I have to check on the boys. Come to me when you are free. I will wait up for you." She kissed me tenderly on the lips and walked out.

My wife Claudia was, admittedly, superstitious. But I had to respect her devotion to what she thought was good, what she thought was the truth. She may have had doubts about our household gods but until something decidedly *more* true came along, she would stick with the best she had. On the other hand, I was a practical man. I believed in power, might, brutality. These got things done. I left religion to my wife. It couldn't hurt.

I sat down and poured over incident reports—soldier scuffles with Judeans, occurrences of insolence, minor rebellions—for about an hour, until midnight, then walked over and joined Claudia, sleeping soundly.

The next morning was noisy with the bang and clatter of camp breaking up at dawn, on my orders. I was traveling with two centuries for safety reasons. Half these men would garrison with me in Jerusalem. The remainder would return to headquarters in Caesarea Maritima. The regular Jerusalem contingent numbered about twelve hundred, and represented a visible projection of Roman power in the Jewish capital all year 'round. It reminded Caiaphas who was in charge.

I had a strange working relationship with the Temple hierarchy. Caiaphas—a slithering serpent if I ever saw one—had been appointed chief priest by my predecessor Vitelius Gratus. He had worked out reasonably well, knew whose hand he had to eat out of, etc. And so I kept him on. But Caiaphas was not beyond conjuring up little tricks designed to embarrass me—always with the hope that something would get back to Rome, or worse, to the new Roman legate in Syria, Pomponius Flaccus, and there would be hell to pay. I had to watch his every step, especially when he exhibited those yellowing teeth and fawning countenance and pretended to be doing me a favor.

For instance, I indirectly had Caiaphas to thank for the almost-disaster of the Imperial Eagle incident, in which I came within a hair's breadth of murdering several hundred Jews come to petition me in Caesarea. And for the aqueduct debacle, where a number of them did bite the dust. The old fox misled me on both counts. I had no idea the Jews took their religion so seriously. Still, the old man could generally be relied upon to support Roman interests. Especially when I reminded him of the penalties for not.

We were approaching Jerusalem.

"Tell my wife to look out her curtain," I said to the aide riding next to me and motioned to Claudia's litter. "I don't want her to miss this sight."

The sunshine dazzled and played on the marbles of the Temple Mount in the distance. I was always astounded that this mere backwater of a city had put together a structure that rivaled Rome. In size it was magnificent. It covered almost one-fifth of Jerusalem. It was Hellenistic in design—huge columns, cloisters, courtyards. And covered ceiling to urinal in white marble. But because of its Asian provenance the marble had a slight rosy tinge when it hit the sun.

Either that or the golden vine—a surprisingly elaborate and finely wrought piece of work that adorned the front of the temple and hung down from an immense height above the entrance doors—gave the marble a soft pinky hue that reminded me of Rome. It had grapes as tall as a man! Odd to think the Jews had such taste for opulence. Or the resources to pull it off. They were a scruffy, inelegant lot, so long-faced and serious. They couldn't appreciate the artistry of a Praxiteles or a Polyclitus because human forms were not allowed. Our fine Greek sculptures were lost on them. Obscenities, to the Jews. Nor did they want any part of our lively mosaics depicting gods and animals. But they did allow one mammoth piece of plain white glistening architecture to honor their own god. Inside of which was an empty altar and a *candlestick*. The Jews were odd people.

"Almost there," I said to myself as we approached one of the western gates of the city. There was no cheering. There never was. Just sullen crowds of people—tradesmen, travelers, simple folk—who stopped to watch us coldly as we marched past. I halted my horse and waited for the litter carrying Claudia and the boys. They pulled even with me and a few minutes later we entered Herod's palace gate together.

The palace of Herod Antipas in Jerusalem was ours whenever we wanted it. He knew he had to get out during festivals. It was situated in the western part of the city, some distance from the Temple Mount in the eastern part. Fine with me. The farther away my wife and children could be from any disturbances, the better.

Herod was a half-Idumean, half-Samaritan non-Jew who ruled as tetrarch of Galilee and Peraea, on behalf of Rome. He inherited the position from his father, Herod the Great, who had lobbied his way into Caesar's good graces. Herod and I didn't have to deal with each other often, thank the gods, because we had different jurisdictions. Why did I despise him? It wasn't because he kept sending his agents to penetrate my household staff. I expected that. I had one more to crucify when I returned to Caesarea. No, I despised Herod because he gave Rome a bad name. He was ineffective, flippant and lazy. He had unnecessarily alienated the Jews by fucking his brother Philip's wife, and continuing to fuck her. He used tax collections to build glorious cities as monuments to himself. True, he feared Rome and worked well with Caiaphas, but unlike the Chief Priest, Herod lacked the moral authority to keep the Jewish population under control. Caiaphas was much smarter about it. In any case, at every Passover, we generally found ourselves together in Jerusalem—Pilate, Caiaphas, Herod. Each member of this love triangle hated the other. I not only hated them both but distrusted their mean, wormy little ways and had spies in strategic positions reporting on them. Not to do so would have been suicide.

"I think it's time to get some rest," I said to my wife as she supervised the unpacking of our things. "Let's have a light supper then send the boys to bed." I looked over as they were chasing each other around the room, looking out the tall windows, pointing at the Temple in the distance, and throwing cherry pits at the soldiers below.

"Enough!" shouted Claudia to both of them. "Let's get you washed up! Come over here, *now!*" She then proceeded to wash their faces, hands, and ears while giving instructions to the servants for our nighttime repast.

I sat down to read the stack of reports that had been brought to me by an aide. Zealots, minor scuffles near the Temple, bigger crowd for Passover than usual, lodging scarce, lots of people sleeping in the streets, anticipated rowdiness because of it. The usual problems. Oh, and a new so-called "prophet" had marched into the city on an ass several days before—what a laugh! Dressed like a workman, his garment slightly soiled, his feet in crude sandals. His followers—described as raucous, loud, excited—strewed palm branches in his path and called him a "King"! So what? Poor beggar couldn't even commandeer a horse. Probably a crazy. I looked at the author of the report: the Temple, meaning that old rat Caiaphas. Why was he so hot and bothered? Didn't he have *real* issues to worry about? I set the report aside and joined Claudia and the boys for dinner.

"And don't mention it to anyone. I will tell Pilate myself," said Claudia to her servant Rulia just as I came in.

"Tell me what, darling?" I sneaked up to plant a kiss on the back of her neck.

"Oh! I didn't know you were back. I met the most extraordinary man today!"

"*You what?*" This did not sound like Claudia, the most circumspect of Roman matrons.

"What I mean is, I didn't meet him, I just saw him. And he helped me with my bundle . . .

"*He what?*"

"I mean when I dropped it, he picked it up. That was all."

"Where were you, dear?" I asked, trying to be patient with the confused way my lovely wife told a story.

"In the marketplace, of course. With Rulia and three of your soldiers. These Jews have fabulous things to sell—balsam, myrrh, frankincense; silk, wool, amber, pepper! And I wanted to get a closer look at the Temple. The market is near the Temple."

"Why don't you start from the beginning, dear. Tell me about this man you met," I said, sitting down and pouring myself a goblet of wine. I knew this would take awhile.

"Well there wasn't much to it. Rulia and I were making our way towards a produce stand at the far end of the market, near the Temple (because someone here had told us about their good quality bananas) when we saw a crowd of people moving towards us. They were led by a rather large man in a dingy-looking garment. Sort of workman-like. The garment I mean."

"Go on."

"Well the man reminded me of what you read about in those Greek stories. A philosopher king. He was tall, dignified, and everyone in the crowd following him was trying to get his attention, hanging on his every word."

"How big was the crowd following him?"

"I can't judge. The market place was already full of people. But I'd say fifty to seventy-five men and women. Oh, and among them were crippled people and blind, also old people. Not the usual philosophy students. Oh, but also there were some people who appeared to be wealthy, maybe lawyers or rich merchants. They were up front, nearest the man. The other people, poorer looking people, lagged behind."

"What happened then?"

"Well, Rulia and I had spent the good part of the morning buying bread and produce. We had two large baskets full, and I carried one of them because you know how heavy they can get. Rulia couldn't do it all."

"Why didn't you get one of the soldiers to . . . oh, never mind."

"And then in watching the crowd surge forward, the crowd led by our 'philosopher king,' I realized they were coming straight for us. I lost my composure. I dropped my basket, laden with a whole morning's work of purchases. Fruits, vegetables, berries, fish, special exotic nuts—rolling all over the ground."

"And?"

"Well at that point, the man in the dingy garment stopped suddenly. He caused the crowd behind him to stop, too. In a flash he was down on the ground, down on his knees, retrieving my basket under somebody's booth, then gathering up my lost produce. The people following him were astonished. 'But Master!' they protested 'this is not for you to do! Master! Stop!' But there he was in the dirt gathering up my purchases. I stood there in amazement. By this time the whole market place was silent. And watching."

"What happened then?"

"Then he stood up, dusted himself off, and handed me the full basket. He smiled at me, nodded his head, and walked on. The crowd surged around him like a river around a rock, all talking at once. I think they went into the Temple."

"And that's all? Who was this man?"

"I don't know who he was. But he was clearly some kind of teacher, some person of renown, despite his dress."

"And why did you find him so extraordinary? I mean other than his politeness."

"It was his face, Pilate. The way he looked at me. It was so odd."

"Claudia! Was he being impertinent? Was he leering?"

"No! Nothing like that. Look, I know the Jews hate us. But he looked at me with kindness. As if he had known me all me life."

"Uh huh. Was he handsome?" I asked suspiciously.

"Somewhat. Perhaps. In a rugged way. He wasn't a pretty boy. He reminded me of a soldier, or someone used to manual labor. I felt as if I knew him from somewhere."

"Hmmm."

"I felt this peculiar sensation of total peace when he smiled."

"Darling, your imagination is running away with you." I got up and kissed her forehead. "As long as you promise not to run away with *him* and leave me and the boys to fend for ourselves!"

"Oh Pilate, you're being ridiculous!" she smiled at me. "I hope you yourself get to meet him. You would see what I mean!"

I walked back to my study where I had a pile of reports to read. But I vowed to have my Temple team (spies, all) identify the man and keep an eye on him.

Within less than a day they had reported back to me. The man's name was "Jesus." He was an unschooled Galilean, poor as dirt. A carpenter by trade. He was one and the same with the so-called "prophet" who had ridden into Jerusalem on an ass several days before. What a crock. The one Caiaphas was so up in arms about. Pshaw. I knew I could sleep soundly that night after all.

Pounding. Pounding on my door. Voices on the street. Torch lights.

"What the hell is going on?" I yelled as I made my way to the door, barefoot, feeling the cold stone underfoot. Claudia was still in bed, moonlight shining on her hair. It was dark. I looked out our chamber door to see one of my tribunes, sweating and saluting.

"My apologies, sir, it is urgent. There's a crowd of Jews outside the palace. That old fart Caiaphas is at the head of them. Says he needs to see you, *now*. They've got a prisoner."

"Jupiter's balls! It's the middle of the night. Can't this wait 'til morning?"

"Apparently not, sir. We suggested the same. Come back at a decent hour, we said. But they started to raise an uproar, almost a riot."

"How many of them are there?"

"I'd say, at the moment, about one hundred fifty. But others are joining the mob, so I don't know what it will be by the time you get down there."

"Who is the prisoner?"

"Some poor beggar. Hard to tell. He's pretty beat up. They didn't say what the charges were."

"Alright, say I'll be down shortly."

"Yes, sir!" He saluted and hurried off.

I took my time to dress correctly. Tunic, sandals, equestrian ring. I called a servant to drape my toga praetexta, and another to carry my curule chair. I would not receive that prick Caiaphas without the full authority of my office. As an extra precaution I took along with me several sturdy soldiers and my Jewish interpreter.

I walked in a leisurely fashion down to the Judgment Hall, paused at the entrance for effect, then strolled inside. It was empty. There was one lone figure standing there at the bottom of the steps—a large man in a rough garment, his hands bound in front, his face pummeled, his hair soaked with sweat. I supposed this was the prisoner.

I walked down the steps, past the prisoner towards the other end of the Hall. There was a massive gate leading to the street. I had a soldier open it, and found a crowd of angry excited faces standing outside, like a dam ready to burst. They were headed by Caiaphas.

"Why don't they come into the Judgment Hall?" I whispered to my interpreter, who understood Jewish customs. "Are they afraid?"

"No. It is shortly before the Jewish holiday of Passover. The Judgment Hall is gentile territory. They do not wish to be defiled."

"*Defiled!* Who do they think they are?" I whispered back. "Oh well, never mind, I'll address them out here." The prisoner continued to stand inside the Judgment Hall, near the steps at the other end. I guess they didn't worry about defiling *him*.

"By the way," I addressed my interpreter. "Who is the prisoner?"

"His name is Jesus."

"Jesus?"

"Yes, sir. Caiaphas has sent you several reports."

"Oh, *that* Jesus."

I had the gates to the Hall opened wide so I could speak to the mob while remaining mostly within the threshold. There were now up to about 250 to 300 persons outside. I didn't want to take any chances. My bodyguard stood stolidly behind me.

I stepped forward and asked Caiaphas (through my interpreter) what the charges were. He shoved back at me some syllogism about the guy being guilty or they wouldn't have brought him to me in the first place. I told the old goat he could take his prisoner and shove it—or words to that effect. Caiaphas and his swarm of sycophants responded that they needed him dead, but legally couldn't do it without my help. So now the Jew was defending Roman law!

I turned on my heel. Aphrodite's Ass! It was an ungodly hour in the morning and they couldn't even enunciate the charges! Didn't they know things had to be done correctly? I walked back inside to address the prisoner myself. I mounted the steps. Sat down in my curule seat. I had a headache.

Remembering Caiaphas's reports, I asked the prisoner standing below, "Are you the King of the Jews?" It was rather a joke, I thought, and I chuckled as I said it.

But he looked at me directly in the eyes and quietly engaged me in conversation. He asked where I had gotten my information. We then discussed whether I was a Jew, whether he was a King, other worlds beyond this one, and the meaning of Truth. I thought it rather interesting, but decided at the same time he was crazy.

On the other hand, I'd never had a prisoner address me with such composure.

I went back out to the Jews standing at the gate. By now there were about 450 to 500 people. I told Caiaphas I found the prisoner harmless. There was a rumble in response to this then a growing, growling roar, with people shouting expletives and rocking left and right in unison. I tried not to show my alarm while motioning Caiaphas to quiet them down. He did it by raising one gnarled finger.

I straightened to my full height and reminded them of the Passover custom about releasing a prisoner. I suggested releasing Jesus. No, that's wrong. I actually suggested releasing "the King of the Jews." And unfortunately smiled when I said it.

The wrong tack. Foreseeing that this might come up, Caiaphas had already circulated a name among the crowd. At his signal they started chanting for Barabbas. The option was absurd. Barabbas was a robber and had killed people into the bargain. I turned and walked back inside the hall without saying anything. I noticed I was sweating.

The prisoner was standing there quietly, calmly. Not weeping, not pleading, just doing his best to stay on his feet. He had been knocked around pretty hard. I suddenly remembered this was the same man my wife Claudia had encountered in the marketplace.

I had the prisoner scourged. (I heard no screams during this process. Unusual.) My soldiers covered him in a ridiculous purple robe (signifying royalty) and put a crown of thorny branches on his head. Then they sent him back out. I thought showing him to the Jews in this pathetic state would be enough to satisfy them. I didn't like to execute prisoners unnecessarily and this man's utter humiliation in front of the crowd was enough to destroy any revolutionary power he might have had. Caiaphas would know that. Lastly, I hated bending to Caiaphas's will, for any reason. It led to further impertinence and would loosen my grip on this damnable nation.

I walked out to the gate and announced the prisoner's approach. I again refused to condemn him.

But when he came out, more black and blue than ever, barely standing from the scourging, blood seeping through his royal robe, the crown lopsided on his head, some thought it comical. There were guffaws from the crowd. I guess I hoped some might take pity on him, but they didn't.

Instead, their reaction was to shout, "Crucify him!" It made me cringe. Finally in light of my continued refusal to condemn the prisoner, Caiaphas let slip the "real" charge: the prisoner thought he was the Son of God.

That did it. By the time this was translated I noticed the sweat was dripping down my temples and my heart was racing. I could hear pounding in my ears. I remembered my discussions with Claudia, where she speculated what a god, a *True God*, would be like if he walked the earth. Would he be anything like this man? I motioned to one of my guards to escort Jesus to the back of the Hall again, out of earshot, and I followed them.

This time I didn't mount the steps to my curule seat. I approached the prisoner at eye level, man to man, and demanded to know his origin. No answer. I reminded him that I had the power to crucify him, or to let him go. Why wouldn't he speak to me?

This is when he said, and I will never forget: "You could have no power at all against me, except it were given you from above: therefore he that delivered me to you has the greater sin."

This was not the statement of a crazy man. I looked at him carefully.

He was standing there in that ridiculous robe, the crown on his head poking into his flesh and causing droplets of blood to catch on his eyebrows and beard, his beat up face, his wrists bruised and bound in leather, his bare feet. But he was perfectly calm. Like a King waiting to give judgment. I thought again of Claudia. I tried to look at him with her eyes, and for a blinding second I really saw it. What if this man *were* from another world? What if he were a god?

I don't know how long I stood there without saying anything, just looking at him. Uncannily, I thought back to my boyhood days raising horses for my father in Samnium. And my beautiful stallion, Decus Celeritas. A graceful, intelligent horse, who loved me, who could sense my presence a mile off and would gallop over to me, his tail and mane flying. An innocent creature, he would gladly give his life for me. And I allowed him to be used in a Roman festival, which resulted in his death. I thought there was only a small risk, I didn't think my lovely Decus would end up as the October Horse. It was my pride that let him go, my pride of ownership, my not wanting to appear sentimental. So I allowed it. I didn't have to allow it. And he never came back.

Now here was someone standing before me who—despite his appearance—was full of dignity, intelligence. So certain of his power he didn't have to prove it. Was I facing a real King? A god? I'm not a superstitious man, but there was something frightening here. Something pure like light itself, but more personal. I was getting the same sick feeling I had gotten as a boy, before Decus went off to Rome. The dread of destroying something that shouldn't be destroyed. I had to fight.

I went out to the Jews numerous times after that. Arguing, re-monstrating, bullying, pleading. Jesus simply stood in the grand Hall and waited. He said nothing. But when I caught him looking at me several times, it seemed to be with understanding. Not with fear. Finally, over the course of this back and forth, Caiaphas saw my turmoil and sensed my weakest point.

He and several others finally asserted that if I let this man go, I was "not a friend of Caesar."

He hit his target dead on. This was my vulnerability, my greatest fear. I thought my bowels would give out. I beat back my thoughts about Jesus, about Decus, all the sentimental imaginative anxiety I had been fretting about for the last hour, and got back to the real world. The real world was this angry mob, its fists clinched, yell-ing curses from the gate. The real world was Sejanus's execution, Tiberius's paranoia, the supporters of Sejanus being rounded up and killed. It was Claudia and the boys, and the need to protect them. It was this rattlesnake Caiaphas, obsequious and dangerous standing before me. It was my own skin. I knew what I had to do.

I returned to the back of the hall, to the top of the steps, and sat down in my curule chair. Jesus stood at the base of the steps below me. I avoided looking at him.

"Behold your King!" I yelled to the crowd outside the gate. I'm not sure what I meant by this. I was no longer trying to gain the Jews' sympathy for the prisoner. I knew what their answer would be.

They again screeched for me to crucify him.

"Shall I crucify your King?" I yelled in response.

Caiaphas and the other top dogs immediately responded, "We have no king but Caesar!"

Completely resigned by now, I directed my soldiers and handed him over. They lined him up with two other miscreants, condemned the day before, and marched him off in the direction of Golgotha. My parting shot was the sign I got nailed up over his cross. Just to goad Caiaphas.

But that was small consolation. In my heart I knew I had failed. I had failed Decus all over again. I had failed Claudia, and failed myself. I was suddenly very, very tired.

21 Nicodemus, Sanhedrin Member

This morning, Jesus is on trial in front of Pontius Pilate. I am racing to the Hall of Judgment to be there to support him. I have had several meetings with him over the course of the past two years, but I have still not brought myself to the point of avowing Jesus openly, publicly. I am still a silent supporter. My disapproval of most of the Temple hierarchy, especially Caiaphas, is well known and that is perhaps why I wasn't notified of the secret, middle-of-the-night arrest and trial of Jesus in front of the Sanhedrin. He had a few friends there, but they were as silent as I have been these past two years, and were fearful of raising a protest at the proceedings. They tell me he was knocked around quite a bit.

The Hall of Judgment, where I have just arrived, looms before me. I see the gathered crowd waiting on the street outside and catch my breath. Have the proceedings already begun? There is Pontius Pilate, the Roman prefect of Judea and Samaria. He's standing just inside the doors to the Hall. Several sturdy looking soldiers stand behind him.

As I get up closer I see Caiaphas and his gang at the front of the crowd, nearest the gates to the Hall, but still standing in the street. Pilate addresses them through an interpreter.

After some back and forth I realize Caiaphas is neither bluffing, nor wavering on his intent to see an end to Jesus. Pilate turns around and proceeds back inside the Hall. He approaches a lone figure in white at the far end. The figure is standing at the bottom of some massive steps leading to a huge interior room of the palace. His hands are bound. I can no longer restrain myself. I force my way through the crowd and past the entry gates. I am now inside the Hall. A soldier stops me.

"I am a representative of the Sanhedrin. On behalf of the Temple, I have been appointed to witness Pilate's proceedings with the man called Jesus. May I enter?"

The soldier looks at me, motions for me to wait, then signals two soldiers at the far corner. I hear behind me a collective intake of breath and the following conversation from Caiaphas and his cronies.

"What is that fool Nicodemus doing? He can't go in there!"

"Well in fact he can, my lord. The Roman guards haven't stopped him."

"But the Sabbath!" he sputters. "He's contaminating himself before the Sabbath!"

"I don't think he cares . . ." I can't hear the rest. The two soldiers have come and are escorting me further into the Hall. I am ordered to stand off to the side, along a vast wall lined with offices that project onto the main Hall. I stand near the doorway of one of them. I am not as close as I would like to be to the proceedings, and I strain to see what is going on. Pilate is now seated in a curule chair at the top of the steps. The Prisoner stands at the bottom.

22 Baruch, Official Interpreter

Was he biding for time? I couldn't tell. His conversation with Pilate danced around the subject and never really hit the nail on the head. It was already clear what the Jews outside the Judgment Hall wanted. They wanted him dead. But Pilate went by the law. He was methodical. He would do this right.

"Are you the King of the Jews?" he asked the bound, roughed-up figure at the bottom of the steps. I tried to leave the irony out of his voice as I translated from Latin into Aramaic.

The prisoner responded politely in his native tongue. "Do you say this of your own accord, or did others say it to you about me?" I translated.

"Am I a Jew?" Pilate showed mild irritation and tapped his fingers on his thigh. As custom dictates, he was seated on his curule chair, one foot slightly behind the other. This was always the way sentencing was passed. He leaned forward to peer at the prisoner below him. "Your own nation and the chief priests have handed you over to me: what have you done?"

"My kingship is not of this world," answered the man, looking directly at Pilate. "If my kingship were of this world, my servants would fight, that I might not be handed over to the Jews; but my kingship is not from the world."

Pilate showed the slightest smile and rubbed his chin. "So you *are* a king?"

Still looking directly at Pilate, the man answered, "You *say* that I am a king. For this I was born and for this I have come into the world, to bear witness to the truth. Every one who is of the truth hears my voice."

The man's gaze must have been hard to take because Pilate broke eye contact and shifted his gaze. "What *is* truth?" he said forlornly, as if to the air. He then got up without a word, walked down the steps, past the prisoner, and towards the gates to the street. A noisy crowd waited just past the threshold. I followed him. The prisoner remained behind, still standing erect but almost sagging from fatigue.

"I find no crime in him," said Pilate referring to the man still standing inside. The crowd he addressed was mostly riffraff scooped up by Caiaphas and his cronies on their way to see Pilate. I recognized several members of the Sanhedrin up front.

"But you have a custom," continued Pilate, "that I should release one man for you at the Passover; will you have me release for you the King of the Jews?" I translated this into Aramaic, but left the sarcasm out of it.

The crowd immediately yelled out, as if prompted in advance, "Not this man, but Barabbas!"

Pilate shook his head when I translated this. Barabbas was a robber rounded up a few days earlier by our occupying soldiers on accusations of sedition and murder. He was a simple-minded vicious dog, from what I understood, and would cut out the heart of his own mother if there were profit in it.

Pilate went back inside the Hall where the prisoner was still standing, but swaying precariously. Pilate spoke to his chief guard, who nodded and motioned to two soldiers. They marched the prisoner off, still bound, to the palace courtyard. This meant that he would be scourged. I was glad no interpreter was required for this activity, because it was brutal.

23 Nicodemus, Sanhedrin Member

I am still at the side of the Hall and too far away to hear anything, but it looks like they are actually holding a conversation! Jesus is looking directly at Pilate and Pilate is looking directly at Jesus. As if they were equals. There is an interpreter there—a Jew in his forties named Baruch, I think—who facilitates the exchange. Baruch is a secular Jew who doesn't give a rap about the Temple, or our nation, but makes his living off his extraordinary gift for languages. I heard he could switch from educated Greek, to sophisticated Latin, to fluent Aramaic at the blink of an eye. Pilate found him in Caesarea on the coast when he arrived in Judea and hired him on the spot.

After a several-minute exchange with Jesus, Pilate leaves Jesus and addresses Caiaphas and his mob. I hear a bunch of yelling. Pilate walks inside again and motions to a guard. Jesus is led away. I follow (escorted by guards) to some kind of inner courtyard. I am allowed to stand off to the side while Jesus is stripped and tied to a stake. Two soldiers with whips in their hands loosen their shoulders and snap leather cords in the air.

To this day I cannot discuss the scourging. I am surprised Jesus did not die from it. In my abject cowardice I do nothing.

Two other soldiers have plaited a circle of thorns, and when the scourging stops they clamp it on Jesus's head. They untie his hands and he rolls into a seated position leaning against the stake. A soiled purple robe materializes from nowhere (probably stolen) and is draped around Jesus's back. They make him stand up for this. Others come up and bow with a flourish saying, "Hail, King of the Jews!" before striking him with their hands.

They are laughing and dancing around him in a circle when Pilate's man comes in and directs two of them to bring Jesus out into the Judgment Hall. Pilate is already there. They lead Jesus out as he is, purple robe and all. He is barefoot.

24 Baruch, Official Interpreter

After the whipping Pilate went back out to the gates and addressed the crowd. He had the prisoner brought up behind him, and repeated that he could find no fault in the man. I translated.

The eyes of the crowd shifted slightly to the left—to the bloody pulp in the purple robe. There were guffaws.

Pilate glanced over his shoulder at the prisoner and yelled, "Behold the man!" I translated.

Suddenly Caiaphas and his officers erupted with shouts of "Crucify him, crucify him!"

Pilate blanched at this, but stood solid. "Take him yourselves and crucify him," he challenged them, "for I find no fault in him."

Rather impudently, Caiaphas and two of his henchmen responded, "We have a law, and by that law he ought to die, because he has made himself the Son of God."

I have gotten to know Pilate quite well over the past few years. These words frightened him. He said nothing in response to Caiaphas but motioning with his eyes directed that the prisoner be escorted back to the other end of the Hall. I followed him.

Once there, Pilate did not ascend to the curule seat as was his wont. He walked up to the prisoner and looked him straight in the eye. His hands were crossed behind his back. To the unwitting observer he looked relaxed, but his jaw was clenched, his muscles tense.

"Where are you from?" he asked the prisoner peering directly into his face. I translated into Aramaic.

The man gave no answer.

Pilate asked again, "You will not speak to me? Do you not know that I have power to release you, and power to crucify you?" I translated.

The prisoner looked at Pilate directly with his one unobstructed eye. "You would have no power over me unless it had been given you from above; therefore he who delivered me to you has the greater sin."

Upon this, Pilate turned on his heel and walked back towards the gates of the Hall. I followed. The crowd on the street outside was still seething and rumbling. Pilate then made repeated attempts to convince them of the prisoner's innocence, and each attempt evoked a louder chorus of dissent. Finally one of Caiaphas's officers shouted, "If you let this man go, you are not Caesar's friend: whoever makes himself a king sets himself against Caesar."

When I translated these words to Pilate, he stiffened. He abruptly turned and walked to the back of the Hall, mounted the steps and sat down on the Judgment Seat. The prisoner still stood at the bottom. It was midday.

Pilate yelled to Caiaphas and his mob still standing at the gates, "Here is your King!" There was not a trace of irony in his voice. I translated.

The crowd as if one voice shouted back, "Away with him, away with him, crucify him!" I tried to keep their anger out of my voice as I translated, but it was all too apparent.

Pilate, showing no emotion in his face asked, "Shall I crucify your *King?*" His emphasis was on the word "King."

Caiaphas and his top echelon responded in a manner calculated to give Pilate no exit whatsoever. "We have no king but Caesar!"

With that, Pilate handed Jesus over to be crucified.

But first, he motioned to me and whispered that he wanted specific wording detailing Jesus's offenses. As was customary, this legal notice would be carried ahead of Jesus's procession then tacked to his cross. He told me to get it ready immediately, and to write it in three languages. I hurriedly went to work on a plaque of wood and had it ready for the soldiers preparing the massive crossbeam. I conveyed Pilate's instructions. In large white letters the titulus said:

"Jesus of Nazareth, the King of the Jews." (in Latin)

"Jesus of Nazareth, the King of the Jews." (in Greek)

"Jesus of Nazareth, the King of the Jews." (in Hebrew)

Caiaphas was still loitering at the gate waiting for the procession to Golgotha to begin, and noticed what was afoot. He and two of his supporters caught my attention and motioned to me to approach them. They had a message for Pilate.

The message was, "Do not write, 'The King of the Jews,' but, 'This man said, I am King of the Jews.'" I nodded and went straight to Pilate.

After Pilate heard my translation his eyes took on a cold granite color. "What I have written I have written," he said quietly.

I delivered the message to Caiaphas. He and the others backed off equally stone-faced, but said nothing. The procession was leaving, and they followed along to make sure everything happened as it should.

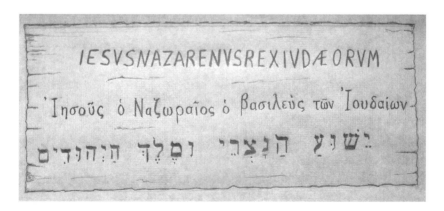

25 Malchus, Slave

Thwack. Thwack. I could see Caiaphas's thin smile curve upward as they whipped him. There were three malefactors in the procession, but the soldiers seemed to be paying all their attention to the third man, who kept stumbling.

"Get off the ground, you fuckin' bugger! No sleepy time for you!" One of the soldiers kicked him in the side and tried to grab him at the shoulder. "Up, up!"

The man bowed his back against the heavy wooden crossbeam and painstakingly staggered to his feet trying to balance the weight from right to left, without falling again. The crossbeam seesawed, then planed for a second as the man took a hesitant step forward.

"Go, go, we haven't got all day!" yelled another soldier as he cracked the whip across the man's left flank. "Ha ha, your friends are already waiting for you! They've got your feast all prepared!" He nodded in the direction of a hill in the distance where a small crowd had gathered. The sun was pounding down and carrion eaters swooped in the sky, cawing. There were three large vertical stakes on the hill, silhouetted against the sky.

The man took a step forward, then took several quick steps to the side as the crossbeam slanted to the right and threw him off course. He looked like a bird with his wings spread, catching every breeze. His hair and face were soaked with sweat, his eyes caked with blood.

A crowd had lined up on either side of the road, shouting.

"C'mon! Teach us a parable, Master!"

"What does the Kingdom of Heaven feel like now, you wretch?"

"Aw shaddup. Can't you see the fellow is half dead?"

"What're you? A sympathizer? This man is a blasphemer!"

"Yeah, he deserves to die!"

"Ha, ha. Let's see how well the birdie flies!" said one fellow as he reached out from the right and pushed the end of the crossbeam, causing the man to stagger to the left, where someone pushed him back to the right, like a child's toy bouncing from wall to wall. He managed to stay on his feet and keep walking. Valiantly, I thought.

"He'll be lucky if he makes it to the top of the hill," said one of the Saduccees, standing next to Caiaphas.

"What does it matter?" responded Caiaphas, his eyes transfixed on the moving figure. "He'll be dead either way."

Caiaphas looked merrier than I had ever seen him. He was clutching and unclutching his fists, his eyes sparkled, and his lips remained frozen in that tightlipped position he always got when things were going his way. He was an ugly man, essentially.

I was dog-tired. I had been up all night with the arrest party, and now at Caiaphas's behest I was attending the crucifixion. As a rule, I did what I was told to do. But I also wanted to see what would become of this man. His name was Jesus.

Thwack. Thwack. The whip came down on Jesus again as he faltered near a group of weeping women and fell to the ground. One woman wiped his forehead, another tried to offer him water but was chased away by the whip which hit his side. Jesus spoke some words to the women. The crowd was yelling.

"Can't they get on with it?" yelled Caiaphas in frustration.

"Get those silly women out of the way!" yelled another in our group, echoing impatience.

"Enough, get going!" a Roman centurion rode up on a horse to hasten the parade along. Thwack, thwack. More whip lashes catching Jesus on the legs.

Jesus rose from the ground to his hands and knees, bowed his back, and used one hand to balance the crossbeam as he stood up. He swayed for about thirty seconds from left to right, took a step forward, then fell flat on this face. Laughter from the crowd. It seems some joker had tripped him, and felt very pleased with himself.

Caiaphas was snarling silently. Women were wailing. And every few seconds the sound of the whip.

Finally one Roman comes up dragging a well-dressed foreign fellow with big hands and enormous calves. "Get down there and help him!" he yelled as he shoved the man toward Jesus. The man hesitated, afraid. He looked as if he had been chosen at random because he was sturdy and a stranger, and had no friends to rally 'round.

"But I have nothing to do with him!" the man yelled back. "He's a criminal!"

"Get the fuck down there and help him carry that thing, or you'll be carrying your own!"

The man started forward with clenched fists but thought better of it when he saw the soldier's hand go to his sword hilt. So he turned and got down to the ground next to Jesus, got one shoulder under the crossbeam and put his other hand under Jesus's armpit, and using nothing but brute strength and persistence lifted them both—and the crossbeam—to a standing position.

In this manner they trudged slowly up the hill.

The nailing part is always brutal. I had seen it before, and I didn't relish seeing it now. As I saw the blood spurt out of Jesus's wrists, and his feet, I remembered my own blood from the night before.

It was dripping from the place where my right ear had been. It was during Jesus's arrest in the garden. I am Caiaphas's chief servant (or slave, depending on how you look at it), and probably the smartest and most talented one he has. I think well on my feet. Despite my size, I have earned the respect of Caiaphas and many of his colleagues. That's why, I suppose, I was part of the arrest party. Just to make sure things went smoothly.

And they did, up until one of Jesus's followers drew a sword. Then my whole world tilted over.

"Lord, shall I strike with a sword?" said a stocky hirsute fellow.

Lucky for me there was moonlight, or torchlight enough, because I saw the flash of steel just a second before the sword came down on me with full force. I had time to dodge to the side before it cleaved my skull. So instead, it cut off my right ear.

I fell to my knees dazed, my right hand covering the gaping hollow in my head. No one seemed to notice that I was down. Nobody came to help me. The blood trickled through my fingers and soaked my garment. I was becoming dizzy with pain but more than anything, with despair.

You see, I am a small dark-skinned man, with nothing much to recommend me except my brains and my music. I am from the upper Nile, a land called Kush. I was sickly as a child, and my full growth rendered me only slightly larger than a young girl. Delicate of body and beautiful of face, my chief utility in any other society would have been as a catamite. But my tribe in Kush did not do things that way. They tried to make a warrior out of me. I cried tears of remorse each night over my daily failure and the unspoken rebuke from our elders. I did not lack courage, I could run like the wind, and I never backed off from a fight. But I could not hold my own in combat with the other young men, and was quickly, bloodily defeated again and again. As if a girl had gone off to fight with baboons. My shame was almost insurmountable, and I don't know what I would have done had not my ears saved me. You see, I had a gift. I could hear sounds that others couldn't. I could hear a lion pressing its soft pads on the forest floor, a wildebeest munching grass on the other side of the watering hole, a snake slithering up a tree trunk. Our village elders eventually recognized the value in this, and instead of forcing me to fight, began to use me as a scout for hunting parties. This was a task I performed well.

But my keen hearing provided another unexpected talent, and that was music. Bird song in the early morning held a special delight for me. I could distinguish one song from another—the tweets, the warbles, the clicking—so that what was a chaotic burst of noise to most, to me was an intricate harmony of separate sounds and rhythms, whose sources I knew the names of, down to each fowl and feather. As a child, I had listened to the musical instruments of my native land, memorized the melodies, and invented others to replicate bird calls. I began to fashion musical instruments on my own and play them in my spare time. Music to me was better than magic. It could charm my beastly playmates, quiet my mother's anger, or make my father love me. It set a mood. It was my way of keeping our village happy.

Music also kept me from disintegrating in the years after my village was raided, my family killed, and I was sold as a slave to Ethiopian tradesmen moving through Kush. I eventually arrived in Alexandria, where I was sold again, then again, each time prey to masters who enjoyed young men as a diversion from their wives and found my silken, boyish physique and lustrous eyes enticing. Eventually I ended up with a Jewish trader who marketed me in Judea. What landed me in the hands of Caiaphas was not (thank the gods) sodomy, but my music. He was entranced by it. Out of boredom, or carelessness, I was playing one of my homemade instruments that day in Jerusalem.

"Is this fellow for sale?" a wizened, richly-clad elderly man asked the slave marketer as he listened to the wistful melody I was playing from my native land.

"Why yes, sire, why not?" answered the merchant.

"I thought he might perhaps be entertainment. I'll take him, and the two next to him. My steward will settle up with you."

And with that, I was marched off the slave platform and toward the great Jewish Temple. That was four years ago. My stature in the eyes of Caiaphas has increased tenfold since that time. He discovered shortly after purchase that I also had a brain. I do my various jobs with excellence, which he demands, and of course am respectful of his authority, obsequious when called for. But above all I play music. It is the one thing that disarms him. He will sit quietly for hours listening to me play. It is why I am favored above all his other slaves.

But since the sword came down in the garden, I am wondering what will become of me. Will I play music again? Will I lose my status? Will I be sold? Will I return to my degrading life of anal copulation with other masters? Will I even live? And the blood pumping out, and the shouting, and the dizziness.

Then I heard his voice, commanding his disciples to "Stop! Enough of this!"

He walked up to me, touched my ear. That was all. I can't describe the feeling that came over me. It wasn't just that the pain ceased. It was that all my fears, my resentments, had left me too. My years of prostration before various masters, gone in a flash. I saw his face and his face was like light itself. His voice was music, more beautiful than I had ever played, intricate, meaningful, intelligent. I'm not sure what happened next. Perhaps I fell asleep. When I came to myself it was mid-morning and I was alone in the garden. The crowd had left, the soldiers had departed. And the man himself was gone, probably in chains.

But my right ear was miraculously back on my head, good as new. It struck me that a peculiar mercy had befallen. I was as surprised by the fact that it had happened to *me* as I was struck by the mercy itself. Because I, the pretty boy catamite, the small dark-skinned slave so easy to overlook, had been looked upon and saved by a trapped man facing his own destruction.

I quickly got to my feet and ran back towards the Temple. I was vaguely conscious that Caiaphas would be wondering why I had not returned with the others. But in the forefront of my mind was the face of that man. Jesus.

When I got to the Temple I learned that he had been on trial for several hours, and was now standing before Pilate. I raced to the Hall of Judgment, but couldn't move through the mob to reach the place up front where Caiaphas was standing. So I loitered at the back, listening and waiting. I knew the proceedings were leading to his death. That was what Caiaphas wanted, and if I knew Caiaphas he would get what he wanted. I spotted a number of our Temple spies and paid agitators among the crowd, and knew they were working their poisons upon an ignorant multitude.

Finally, there was Jesus. A few feet behind Pilate in a purple robe, bloodied, barely standing, his hair soaked with sweat, and a strange crown on his head. Pilate had Jesus moved to the back of the Judgment Hall then came out alone to the street several times to speak with Caiaphas and his brethren. Finally Pilate ordered Jesus in front of the Judgment Seat, sat down in his curule chair, and gave sentence. The crucifixion march had started toward Golgotha. Two other malefactors with crossbeams on their backs marched with him, a little in front.

I maneuvered my way into a position on the periphery of Caiaphas's group and followed the crowd to the top of the hill. I was close enough to watch Caiaphas and hear his comments, but not close enough for him to address me.

Clank, clank. They nailed the spikes into his wrists. Now his feet. I watched his face grimace, the blood spurt, but he did not cry out. It was a wonder he was even alive at this point. The Roman soldiers were laughing and distractedly making jokes while they did the nailing. One was telling the other about the jolly little piece of ass he was planning to devour that evening. For all their detachment, it was as if Jesus were a board they were nailing to another board.

Finally the nailing was finished and they rocked Jesus's cross into its mount, using brawn and a couple of ropes. He hung there between the two other poor slobs who had been nailed up minutes before. He was naked. Soldiers nearby were on the ground tossing lots for what remained of his one good garment, a seamless robe. There were tituli on the lateral crosses stating thievery and banditry, but above Jesus's head was a plaque in Latin, Greek and Hebrew saying "Jesus of Nazareth, The King of the Jews." Probably Pilate's attempt at a joke.

Four women stood near the base of the cross which held him, no men of his company in sight. No wait! There was one man I thought I remembered from the garden, a young fellow. He was standing back among the crowd, as if trying not to be conspicuous. His eyes were fixed on Jesus's face, watching him.

And Jesus said to the older woman at his feet, "Woman, behold thy son."

Then Jesus looked directly at the young man in the crowd and said, "Behold thy mother." I guessed that the elderly woman might have been Jesus's mother, and that he was entrusting her care—no, commanding her care—to this younger man.

The young man nodded with complete understanding, left the edge of the crowd, and went forward to gather the older woman to himself, and to melt with her back into the crowd. They remained there, watching. The other women continued to stand at the base of the cross. They looked exhausted with worry and grief, but remained silent. No soldier chased them away.

The sun, which had been beating down relentlessly at the beginning, had now disappeared. The sky had darkened and looked ominous. A chill wind picked up. More than two hours had passed, and many of the excitement-seekers had left. Only a small crowd remained, some seated on the rocky ground, and all of them were trying to shield themselves against the weather. Many still had their eyes fixed on Jesus's face, as if to catch any sound or breath he made. The Roman soldiers were seated some ways off drinking posca (a cheap, flavored wine mixed with vinegar), and occasionally bursting out in a big guffaw of laughter as they exchanged stories. Once in a while one soldier would look up at the sky worriedly, and hunch his garment tighter around his shoulders.

Then I heard it. I looked around, but nobody else seemed to notice. I heard it again. It burst upon me and got louder: Miraculous sound. A chorus of voices. Angels' song. It was all around us and drumming in my ears, lifting me with its joy, overwhelming, glorious, sublime. I looked across the way: no sign that anybody else heard anything at all! Caiaphas had left, but a few of his henchmen had stayed behind on his orders to watch the end. They looked bored and sullen, resentful of having to sit in the cold.

What was happening? It was as if all of Heaven had broken loose into this world of man, but nobody heard it. Nobody noticed. Only me.

"Alleluia! Alleluia! For the Lord God Omnipotent reigneth," the chorus sang. "And he shall reign forever and ever! The kingdom of this world is become the Kingdom of our Lord, and of His Christ," it sang. "Alleluia! Alleluia!"

The music was almost deafening, but I never wanted it to stop.
At this very moment he said, "I thirst."

The whole crowd looked up. This was the first word they had
heard from Jesus's mouth in several hours. From the crowd's viewpoint, it was the first sound to break the silence.

One soldier popped up from his place on the ground and filled
a sponge with some of the vinegar mixture he and his compatriots
were drinking. He held it up to Jesus.

Jesus seemed to receive the vinegar, but I couldn't tell. Then he
said simply, "It is finished." And bowed his head and gave up the
ghost. The Heavenly chorus burst into a torrent of majestic, triumphant song, louder and even more glorious than before. It was as if
all the angel armies of God were singing in victory! Music fit for a
king—or rather for a King of kings! And it continued without ceas-
ing. Nobody seemed to hear it but me.

I waited and watched during the next hour while a soldier, with
apparent orders, took a sword and pierced the side of Jesus to make
sure he was dead.

Then a well-heeled man whom I recognized as Joseph of
Arimathea, and others with him, took the body of Jesus down from
the cross and carried it in the direction of a garden.

Following in this procession, and making no attempt to conceal
himself, was a member of the Temple hierarchy named Nicodemus!
He was carrying a heavy load of something wrapped in a bundle.
So Nicodemus had been a secret supporter! I wondered how many
others there were.

I followed them at a distance and saw that they stopped in front of
a hollowed-out cave in a huge wall of rock. There was a disc-like stone
on a track, rolled to one side and serving to seal the cave when rolled
in place. They placed Jesus's body on a slab inside the cave. Nicodemus
unpacked his bundle, which turned out to be some kind of dressing for
the body—probably myrrh and aloes. They proceeded to wrap the body
in a winding sheet, with the spices, then wrapped his head in a separate
cloth. When they finished, Nicodemus and Joseph heaved the rolling
stone disc into place, sealing it. Both men were silent with grief, or at
least I heard no words from them. But I was still hearing the music!

When Nicodemus passed me, making his way back to the Temple, I stepped out of the shadows and made bold to speak to him. I was fairly well known in the Temple as being in the company of Caiaphas, the one who played music, so I hoped that he might recognize me.

"Nicodemus, sir, may I speak with you?"

"Why yes, of course," he said warily. "You are servant of Caiaphas, are you not? What are you doing here?"

"Why yes sir, I am. Malchus, by name. You see, I was part of the arrest party and—"

"You were in the garden with him when they took him?" he frowned.

"Yes, sir. Caiaphas sent me and—"

"Who else was there? And how did they find him? Who led the arrest party?"

"It was that man called Judas, I believe, sir. He made negotiations with Caiaphas and his circle beforehand. He accepted money, and—

"Well what do you want to say to me? I'm sorry, I'm rather distraught and don't feel there is much time to . . ." He moved away from me and started walking briskly down the path. I ran after him.

"No sir, I understand! It's just that Jesus healed my ear when they cut it off in the garden! I don't know why he did it, but he did, and he saved my life. And I heard voices and angels' choirs—"

"*You what?*" He stopped his fast pace and turned to look at me. "Slow down, man, you're being incoherent. What do you mean you heard angels' choirs?"

"I heard his voice in the garden, and it was like music itself. When he healed my ear, he was like light itself. And then I fell asleep. When I woke up it was morning and they had disappeared. There was utter silence."

"And afterwards?"

"Afterwards I ran to the city but was too late to see almost anything. Pilate was getting ready to sentence Jesus. Then they led him to Golgotha."

"Hmmm."

"But after that, I heard the *music*—"

"What do you mean, the music?"

"Well, at the very moment Jesus was dying on the cross I heard a whole host of voices from heaven, singing and praising God. The voices would not stop, sir. They are still in my ears now, but fainter."

"What were they saying?"

"The main thing I remember is their saying that 'the kingdom of this world has become the Kingdom of our God, and of His Christ!' And oh yes, that 'He will reign forever!'"

"Hmmm. This is all very hard to take in. Tell me, did anyone else hear these voices you are talking about?"

"No sir, as far as I could tell, no one. Everyone just went on as normally."

"Extraordinary."

"Yes sir, it is. I have always had acute hearing, but nothing like this."

"Tell me more about yourself. Malchus, you say? Where are you from?"

"The land of Kush, sir. But first, sir, if you don't mind, I would like to hear more about Jesus."

Nicodemus eyed me warily and searched my face. Then he relaxed and said, "What would you like to know?"

"Everything, sir."

"But there is no time. Aren't you expected back by Caiaphas?"

"I am not going back to Caiaphas."

"What will you do?"

"I don't know, I don't know," I said. "But more important than that, sir, more important than my life itself, is to learn everything you know about Jesus."

Nicodemus looked at me for a long moment, then smiled and took my arm.

"Come with me," he said.

26 Mariamme

I kept thinking I would wake up from my nightmare, and he would be there, clowning around, making some astounding comment. But now instead I saw this gaping, solemn hole, cold, dry, full of dry dust, and all of life was whirling down into it. I wanted to lie down in a field somewhere with my cheek next to the ground, and become part of the earth. I wanted to give up. I wanted to die.

If only I hadn't rattled on and on about all I had to do, getting things in order, seeing my family. I didn't think to ask him about himself, what he was thinking, what he was worrying about. Did he know what was going to happen? The thought crossed my mind that he knew all along, that this was deliberate, as if he were marching like a soldier towards his final battle. He had talked of his end to some of the disciples, but I thought he was exaggerating. I dismissed it. Instead I prattled on about *my* plans, thinking that would cheer him up. And I wasted so much time away from him. I let him down.

"It's only a short trip," I told them as I departed Bethabara two and one-half weeks before.

"Go," said Jesus. I remember his big, muscular hand patting mine. It was broad and powerful, with splayed thumbs and lots of nicks and calluses. "Stay as long as you need to. Be with your family for awhile. Write to Vitellius." He smiled at me.

And so I went off merrily, and ended up staying longer than anticipated. And I had enjoyed it—all the practical concerns of a secular life. And wonderful letters from Rome: Vitellius was coming back to me! He thought he could be here in six months' time. By then he would be able to retire from the Praetorian Guard with a good pension and some land. But best of all, he wanted to marry me. I had told him all about my following of the prophet from Nazareth and he wanted to know more. He wanted to meet him himself. Vitellius was delighted that I had found a truly good man, a truly good friend, whom I could confide in, and he was flattered that I had told Jesus all about my love Vitellius. Life was so good, so right at that moment. I was ecstatic about my impending marriage. I was overjoyed about Vitellius in general. And I was comfortable at home, happy. I felt no sense of foreboding. Therefore I delayed my return until just before Passover. I knew Jesus would be spending it in Jerusalem.

But as I entered the City with my trusty friends Nainah and Amos, I realized I had been gone too long. I sensed the tension in the air. Jews from all over the world were here celebrating the Holy Day. Roman soldiers were everywhere. Old men were cackling by the fire, torches were burning, dogs were howling, and every shadow cast a sinister image on the street. I had felt uneasy about Jesus's safety before this. Yes he could be fierce when angry. And he was absolutely fearless, but he was too good, too innocent to survive for long against evil men. He needed cynical people like me to watch out for him. Several of his followers—Judas, for sure—felt the same as I and were very protective of him. I sensed that this time, in Jerusalem, Jesus was going to be surrounded and assailed by his enemies. He needed a phalanx of men (and women) around him to make sure no harm befell him. It was late when I arrived, so I resolved to meet up early with him the next day, and become part of that phalanx.

But I heard pounding on my door that very night.

"Mary, Mary, come quickly!" (Some of the women—and often Jesus—would address me as Mary.)

"What is it? What's happened?"

"Jesus has been arrested! In the garden on the other side of the Cedron! He's on trial! The Sanhedrin condemned him and sent him to Pilate," cried Salome, one of the women who also followed Jesus.

"What? When did this happen?" I asked frantically.

"There's no time. Come *now.* I'll tell you about it on the way! We weren't sure where to find you, or even that you had returned—"

"But I sent Amos over to inform the disciples!"

"Yes, that's how I learned where you were staying. Come quickly, *now.*"

I dressed, and we made our way to the Roman Judgment Hall.

Hours later we followed to Golgotha, where he died yesterday in the most agonizing way, yet fearlessly, quietly, humbly. There seemed to be an intense determination in him, a weird persistence in picking up that crossbeam again and again, and carrying it up the hill. As if that were his purpose in life.

But now, I am sick and vacant inside. I can't even speak of it. He is dead. How could God have let this happen? It's as if God Himself is dead.

So we come today bearing spices. It is the first day of the week, the day after the Sabbath, and light has not yet dawned. We are strangely anxious, the other women and I. Anxious to see him again, his corpse? It is hard for me to say. But Joanna, and Mary the mother of James, and Salome and I are walking rapidly through the dark garden jumping at every sound. Then we see the light ahead. Light? What light could there be? Are the Roman soldiers still about?

"Oh no! Help me!" Salome has tripped over something which appears to be a sleeping body. A soldier. There is another one a few feet off. Neither one stirs, even though Salome must have given one of them a good jolt with her foot. So we tiptoe past, clutching each others' arms in fright and draw nearer to the tomb. The light we saw moments earlier seems to be emanating from the tomb itself. *But the tomb is open. The stone is rolled away.* What has happened? The light has a deep glow, purple and gold in the dawning morning and it lingers in the dampness of the air outside the tomb. I loosen the other women's grip on my arm and march forward and look in. The stone slab is empty. A grave cloth and the linen which wrapped his head are folded neatly and sitting on the slab. *His body is not here.*

"What has happened? I can't understand it! Come, come look!"

The others, taking courage, creep in behind me. They see the same thing.

And while we are all four standing there perplexed, two men in shining garments stand inside the tomb. We have no idea where they came from. They are not ordinary men. They are large and majestic. The light seems to be emanating from their persons.

"Get down, get down!" I nudge the others in a whisper. We bow our heads to the earth with our hearts in our throats, and wait.

Beautiful male voices speak out magisterially, and engulf us. "Why do you seek the living among the dead? He is not here, but is risen: remember how he spoke unto you when he was yet in Galilee, saying, 'The Son of man must be delivered into the hands of sinful men, and be crucified, and the third day rise again'?"

We all remember these words, since each one of us had heard the disciples repeat them, and puzzle over them since Galilee. But the words don't register. I myself simply cannot grasp the meaning.

When we look up the two men are gone, but their light lingers in the cave. I take one last glance noting the empty grave clothes, and the empty burial slab, then nudge Joanna next to me. We back out of the cave, and turn and run like race horses down the hill.

"Who were those men, Mary? *What* were they?"

"I'm not sure. But we've got to tell the disciples," I pant as we run toward the city.

We got to the closed room where the disciples were hiding. We ran up the steps and knocked the code. Peter opened the door. "Shhh. Come on in," he whispered.

"Two men, two men in white said that Jesus—" Joanna practically shouted as Peter ushered her in.

"No, it wasn't white, it was shining and there was light all around—"

"They said Jesus was not there!" Salome said excitedly.

"They said *he is risen*," yelled the other Mary.

Every single one of us was panting and gasping from the run back to the city. We had scarcely gotten our breath when we all started blurting it out, in disjointed fashion. What made matters worse was that it was early, very early, and half the disciples were still asleep—or just waking up—so it was hard for them to grasp our urgency, or the gravity of our news.

"Wait, wait!" said James in a kindly way to his mother. "You sound like wild women. Could just one of you, in an orderly fashion, tell us precisely what you are talking about?"

This is when I stepped in. I told what we had seen, and what had been told to us by the two men, in as brisk but detailed manner as I could get out quickly. Despite the extraordinary event I was conveying, I tried to sound as reasonable and rational as possible. The other women did not help, exactly, because they kept adding secondary details which (God help me!) were of course important to them, but resulted in making the discourse more disjointed and emotional than I intended.

The end result was the disciples didn't believe a word of it.

Some went back to sleep, a few made rude remarks about "idle tales" and "silly women."

Peter and John, however, remained silent throughout. Two of the other women huddled to the side of the room, resentful at being dismissed, and now beginning to doubt what they themselves had seen. I went over to Peter and John.

"Well come with me and see for yourselves. I tell you, we saw what we saw. We heard what we heard." I noticed my hands were on my hips when I said this, like a defiant housewife.

John said, "You're right. At least we need to go take a look."

Peter had already moved to the door and was waiting for us. We made our exit. As we ran to the tomb (we started out walking, but then couldn't help ourselves), Peter's eyes took on a faraway stare, as if he were in a trance. John simply looked anxious.

We arrived at the site. The soldiers who had been asleep on the ground had now disappeared. But the stone in front of the tomb was still rolled back. That lent some credence to our "idle tale."

John ran forward and peered into the tomb, but didn't enter. Peter came up quickly behind him, ducked his head and dashed into the tomb coming to a halt when he saw the empty linen burial clothes, and the napkin that had wrapped Jesus's head, but no body. John then went in and saw the same thing. Then they departed. They said nothing at all.

I remain standing outside the tomb again crying, not knowing what to do or what to think. I try to remember what the two shining men told us, but in the face of everyone else's doubt I am beginning to doubt myself. After all, and not very long ago, I was on the verge of a breakdown. I was a dreadful sinner. I had given in to my weaknesses so many times that my words had no credibility. Even the kinder disciples—like Peter and John—had a hard time believing me. I am unstable, given to carnal pleasure, tossed about by my emotions. I am crushed in grief. I have lost my best friend, my brother. And I have had no sleep.

Rather out of despair, and still streaming with tears, I stoop down and look inside the tomb one more time. *And I see them again.* The two shining men! One is seated at the head, and one at the foot of the place where Jesus's body had lain.

"Woman, why are you weeping?"

"Because they have taken away my Lord, and I don't know where they have laid him," I say, still peering into the tomb.

God have mercy on me. I know what the two shining men told us before—that he is alive. But I am speaking as if I have dismissed the possibility.

Then I turn around and see a man standing behind me, just outside the tomb. My eyes fail to register clearly in the dawning morning light and keep me from distinguishing much more than his silhouette.

"Woman, why are you weeping? Whom are you seeking?" says the unidentified man.

I realize now that he is the gardener, so I say through my tears, "Sir, if you have borne him away, tell me where you have laid him, and I will take him away," referring to Jesus's body. I turn back to look inside the tomb and to wipe my tears.

"Mary," the man outside says.

I turn quickly and look more carefully at the gardener. It is Jesus's voice!

"Master!" I yell. I know it is Jesus even though I can't see clearly. No one else speaks that way. No one in the world. I am overcome with wonder, astonished. I step closer towards him. As my eyes focus in the light I see that *it is true*. He is alive!

"Don't touch me," he extends his hands out to keep me at a distance. He continues with a serious look, "for I am not yet ascended to my Father: but go to my brethren and say to them, I ascend to my Father, and your Father, and to my God, and your God."

Then he smiles that wonderful smile of his, full of warmth and mirth, and I obey him. I run as if my life depends upon it and tell the disciples.

Most of them sit silently and noncommittal; some scoff openly; some turn their heads to the wall and go back to sleep. One of them walks over, James, and addresses me in a very patient voice.

"Mariamme, Mariamme. Just think for a minute."

I look at him expectantly.

"If Jesus had really not died—or had come back to life, as you say—why wouldn't he appear to one of the disciples? Peter or John, or even to me, his brother? Why would he first come to *you*?"

I look at James more closely, and see exactly what he is getting at. He is right. What possible explanation is there that *I* would be chosen in this manner?

"Well I realize there are many others who are more worthy . . ."

This elicits a slight smile on James's face, which is quickly suppressed. James is not my biggest supporter.

"And it is surprising, considering my past life . . ."

James gives me a patronizing nod and makes as if to move away. He has made his point.

"But the Lord never followed the rules we thought he would," I say, looking at him squarely. "You know that. He never excluded anybody, he—"

"She's right, James," says John, approaching us quietly. "I've been overhearing your conversation, and I think Mariamme is right. Jesus almost never did what we expected him to. So you can't discard what Mariamme is saying based on your own ideas of what is proper."

John turns to me, "Let's give it some time, shall we Mariamme? Now tell me again exactly what transpired, and what Jesus said to you. And don't doubt what you saw. God willing, we will all see him."

I begin my story again, privately for John. Seeing his respectful attitude, others gather around as well. I can't say they believe me, but at least they are listening.

And as I am speaking, it comes to me that Jesus has planned this all along. His whole life had turned sin upside down. Why would his death not do the same? He never spent time in the days I walked with him singling out the "good" people and reassuring them. He addressed himself to sinners—lepers, blind persons, and people like me. His appearance early this morning first to me, a loose woman with a soiled reputation, had a purpose. In the same way his mercy and kindness to tax collectors, thieves, Roman soldiers had a purpose.

Sometimes I think that the people who will have the hardest time accepting this are the so-called "good" people. I'm thinking of the Pharisees, but also of the disciples who have their own pecking order of righteousness, and tend to think they can "earn" God's good will. On that basis—merit—a lot of people end up shutting themselves out. Jesus never shut anybody out. He knew every last one of us was a sinner. But he turned sin on its head and welcomed us *all* in.

And I believe that the persistence and determination Jesus showed in marching towards his death on that wretched hill will be the same persistence he shows in getting through to us now.

And this is God's Truth. I saw it with my own eyes. The disciples would see it too. God may have ordained death for us all, but he did not ordain eternal death. And I know now that Jesus of Nazareth was and is God.

About the Author

Martha Harris spent her 28-year career as a United States Foreign Service Officer, working at U.S. Embassies in Europe, South Asia, and the Middle East. She speaks Russian, French and Italian, and is an avid student of First Century Palestine. Currently retired, she lives in northern Virginia.

CPSIA information can be obtained at www.ICGtesting.com
Printed in the USA
BVOW07*2056260115

385058BV00001B/2/P